The Long Reach

Michael Leese

ISBN: 9781983105791
Imprint: Independently published

Maria…
The woman who makes it all
possible.

Michael Leese is a national newspaper journalist who worked in Fleet Street for over 25 years, including 17 years at The London Evening Standard. He had always wanted to write a book, especially a crime or science fiction novel, but with work, family life, and lots of other excuses, he never seemed to get around to it. Then in 2007 Michael went freelance and finally had time to sit down and write. Born in Birmingham, his family moved to London where he spent his formative years: he and his wife now live in Dorset close to their adult autistic son. He is a volunteer trustee for the charity Autism Wessex.

1

City Airport, London.

His client, Maxine Dubois, was focusing on her iPad. Her expression, normally impossible to read, was rapt. She'd run the ten-minute clip twice, leaning forward each time she reached a favourite part, the tip of her tongue emerging between her lips as if tasting the air. Dubois went in for the third time. The Courier relaxed a little as he allowed his mind to wander back to the moment he'd first met the pair who had put together this special performance.

He needed something different, and when he discovered their work he found a way to be introduced. At their initial meeting, a year ago, the Courier had known they would be right. Like him, they would only do something if they could do it perfectly.

They were a contrasting pair. The knife specialist was short and pixie-like, with a mischievous smile that lit up her face. The Courier noticed it didn't reach her eyes. The camera user was tall and thin with a faintly quizzical air, as if she had missed a turn and found herself in the wrong place. Many were the victims who had died puzzling over how they had misread the pair so badly.

He'd met them for drinks at a pub in Blackfriars, the pixie soon making him splutter into his beer. Size really matters, she told him: the bigger the better. Laughing at his reaction, she had tapped her forehead. It was the size of what was between the ears that was important. In her opinion this was an area where a lot of men were poorly equipped.

Evidently, he had passed some sort of test; at least on the mental side. As for anything else, even if he had been offered he would have declined. Business could be a pleasure, but you never mixed the two.

Elegant and frosty, the French woman had a mind like a trap and not a trace of sentimentality. Those attributes had helped her create a global business from the failing family concern she had inherited at just 22 years old. Within a decade Dubois had created a conglomerate that spanned shipping and digital media to luxury hotels and high fashion. Not only did she have an unerring ability to pick out a company with potential - she had a gift for identifying talented executives to run the businesses for her. It was a wonderfully successful formula, and she had elevated her role to the point where there was little for her to do, apart from removing the odd senior manager to "encourager les autres".

But Dubois was bored, and heard through a friend of a contact that the Courier was a man who could provide "entertainment". At their first meeting she had immediately thrown down a challenge, affecting boredom and indicating she might leave at any moment. The Courier had seen through that act, understanding that this client was hiding a keen sense of anticipation. Through patient questioning he had learned that, while Dubois had her own ideas, she expected him to provide her with alternatives. As the discussions became more detailed, Dubois had specified that she did not want to have any sort of connection to the victims. That had surprised him since her earlier behaviour led him to think she was driven by a desire for revenge, maybe against a business rival or a former lover.

The revelation led the Courier to what she truly wanted - to take someone who had led an ordinary life, one who would be intensely missed by her circle of loved ones. He was impressed. Not many people thought in such a simple and direct manner.

He had found the victim quicker than he had expected. Anne Hudson was a young woman who volunteered at her local church to help raise money for impoverished families in the UK and abroad. The Courier found her picture on a charity website. She was standing at one end of a five-woman line-up with a shy smile that suggested she hated attention. She had the sort of prettiness that is particular to healthy young women, especially ones that are blooming from pregnancy, without being truly beautiful. It took his team a day to find her.

The picture was taken outside a church in Worcester Park, south London, so that was where they started. A talkative cleaner provided her name and one phone call provided her address. Then it was just a case of doorstepping her home and waiting for her to come out. Which she did, although this time with a baby in a pushchair; the website picture had been months old. They had taken their own pictures and even shot a short clip of video, which had been edited into the package that his client was going through now.

Dubois was still enjoying the video clip, allowing him to study her closely. He was confident she was buying into his plan. What he needed now was for her to agree to the final price. If she wanted what he could provide then she was going to have to pay up.

2

Tower Bridge, London.

Detective Chief Inspector Brian Hooley was wearing his "divorce" outfit: a pair of dark blue jeans, blue cotton shirt and light grey jacket that he had bought the day after his marriage had officially ended. If pushed, he might have admitted to being influenced by the sartorial style of a middle-aged TV presenter who fronted a motoring programme.

His clothes suited his burly six-foot frame, but his tenuous hold on a large bunch of flowers and box of chocolates was doing less for his image. He looked as though he might drop them at any moment as he tried to maintain his hold while looking at his watch. He was 15 minutes early and in a dilemma. Could he turn up before the agreed time?

He decided to wait a little longer but his need for the bathroom was becoming urgent. He thought about sneaking into a nearby restaurant but was put off because it appeared to be full of serving staff waiting to pounce on the first customers of the day. There was no way he could sneak in unobserved.

Although it was a warm day, the wind blowing off the river Thames felt cold, making him shiver. He combined a sigh with a shrug as he reached a decision - he

6

was going to be early. He had been repeatedly warned about being late, even by a few seconds. An attempted joke about sudden death as a cause of lateness had earned him a hard stare.

He hustled over to his destination: an upscale apartment block on the south side of the river. It boasted fabulous views over London's financial district to the east and the London Eye to the west. He caught the eye of the security guard, who grinned in recognition.

Buzzing him inside, he indicated the visitors' book with a nod of his head and watched as the Met detective filled out his name and time of arrival. Writing as slowly as he could had shaved a few more seconds off, so now he was just eight minutes early.

"That's all good, Chief Inspector. Do you want me to buzz up and let him know you're here?"

Hooley returned the smile. "No thanks, Dave; let's make it a surprise."

Since the terrible events of 12 months ago, when a guard had been murdered by a man who had come to kill Jonathan Roper, the area where he sat was now protected by security glass and conversations were through a two-way microphone.

Roper had personally paid for the improvements and also made a substantial payment to the widow, ensuring she could buy a small property near her mother and leaving a little over as well. Although no one blamed him, he insisted and with the money he had inherited from his parents he could afford it.

Hooley pressed the elevator call button. The car was waiting, and the door opened straight away. He stepped inside and went up to the top floor - the third - where Roper owned the three-bedroom penthouse. He glanced at his watch: just five minutes early. Still just managing to hold on to his gifts he pressed the door-bell.

He thought he could hear shouting, but then the door opened, and Roper was there, a strange smile - almost a grimace - on his face. The Detective Chief Inspector was thinking his colleague's thick black hair looked more unruly than usual before he was dragged sideways. In his place appeared a smaller, female version of Roper, who, at five feet two inches in her bare feet, was a foot shorter than the man she had replaced.

This had to be Samantha, or Sam, he assumed. Like Roper she was very pale, her colouring contrasting with her jet-black hair and dark eyes. She had her hands on her hips and was glaring at him with such a fierce expression he took an involuntary step backwards.

"Why are you here now?" she demanded. Her voice was amazingly deep for someone who shared Roper's extremely slim physique, and there was a huskiness to it he would normally associate with a smoker, but he doubted that was true as Roper couldn't abide the smell of cigarettes.

"I'm Brian Hooley. Jonathan invited…"

She cut him off. "I know exactly who you are. I asked you why you are here now."

This doorstep interrogation was scrambling his brain. He froze, his mouth half-open. Time slowed and then Roper reappeared, looked apologetic and slammed the door shut. The DCI pressed his ear against the door. He could make out a fierce argument, and it was Sam's voice that was dominating.

The apartment went silent and he pulled his head back just in time as the door swung open. Roper was back. "Could you knock again in exactly five minutes?"

The door started to swing shut but Hooley managed to jam his shoe in the door. He handed over his gifts and said, "When you finally let me in I will need to go to the loo."

8

The presents were snatched away. Some people might have taken exception to such a bizarre greeting. Hooley took a steadying breath and set the timer on his phone for four minutes and fifty seconds. At least this was happening away from prying eyes.

Not for the first time, he wondered at how life with Roper could quite suddenly take on a surreal quality with activities measured in precise amounts of time that left no margin for human error. He tried to remember the last time arriving somewhere had caused such a furore. A long-buried memory surfaced of the day he had accidentally arrived an hour early at a girlfriend's home, only to bump into the boy leaving. He'd quite forgotten about that and wondered what the girl was doing now. Probably dreaming about the days when boys were throwing themselves at her feet.

But all this over a few minutes? Roper had told him it was important he arrived on time. Now he knew that meant don't be early as well as don't be late. He couldn't help smiling; the lunch they had planned was going to be interesting, especially if Roper's girlfriend was going to remain upset with him.

The alarm made him jump, but he counted to three and pressed the bell. Roper opened the door instantly. The DCI suspected he had been waiting there the whole time. He was beyond being polite. "I'll be with you in a minute," he said, shoving past and heading for the guest bathroom. He'd been to the flat many times, but never when Roper had a girlfriend.

He emerged to find Roper and Sam waiting in the living room. Before he could say hello again she nudged Roper sharply in the ribs and nodded.

"Sorry," said Roper, rubbing at his side - it had been a hard dig - "Sam's flight has been altered and she's leaving earlier than she thought. She's only got fifteen minutes before she has to go so we thought coffee here and then she can head for Heathrow and you and I can go on for lunch."

"Don't you want to go with her and see her off? You should have rung me and cancelled. I'd have totally understood."

Sam spoke. "We've done all that here. Much more comfortable, if you know what I mean." She gave Hooley a surprisingly frank expression and he felt his face warm slightly.

"Er, yes. I think I do." He supposed that anyone who went out with Roper was bound to be a little out there. The man himself was a one-off. Loyal, passionate and capable of making breathtakingly brusque personal comments, totally oblivious to the impact they might have.

Only last week, in the course of work, they had needed to talk to a new forensic scientist. At the end of the interview Roper had said to the woman: "You look a lot older than the picture you've put online."

Shock, rage and embarrassment flashed over her face, to be replaced by misery as she looked as though she was about to burst into tears. Hooley had frog-marched Roper away before he could do any more damage.

Outside in the corridor he had hissed, "How many times do I need to tell you that people get distressed if you criticise their appearance, especially if you have never met them before? That very nice lady you just upset probably likes that photograph and imagines she still looks like that. It's just a small vanity thing and certainly doesn't need you wading in with your size-tens."

"It's size-elevens, actually." Roper had that mulish expression on his face which meant he thought everyone else was being ridiculous and there was no way he was going to climb down. The DCI, worried that the woman would appear at any moment, had grabbed the younger man by the arm and pulled him towards the stairs. "Come on, let's go and get a cup of coffee." The episode exemplified Roper. It wasn't that his observations were wrong, but the way he pointed them out left a lot to be desired.

He came back to the present as he realised Roper was holding up a tempting looking bottle of lager. A drink was a very good idea, and he gave the younger man a quick thumbs up. As he took a swig he risked a quick glance at Samantha. She was still looking at him through narrowed eyes, but he thought she looked less angry.

Holding his hands up in an apologetic gesture he said. "My bad. I realise I should have arrived at the right time. I expect I threw all your preparations out, which must have been very annoying."

In truth he regarded the idea of a few minutes either way as inconsequential, but with Roper he knew that details that could cause the most intense issue. A couple of weeks ago he hadn't been paying attention when it was his turn to get the coffee.

Instead of a latte he'd given his colleague a cappuccino. Roper had reacted as if he was being handed a cup of poison, refusing to accept it. It had taken the rest of the day before they were back on speaking terms.

So he was relieved as Sam broke out a wicked grin.

"There's no need to pretend you really understand. From what Jonathan has told me, you are more relaxed than most neurotypicals. A lot of people would have complained that I was overreacting and not given me the chance to calm down. What they can never get their heads around is that someone like me experiences a physical sensation when someone is late or early. It's not as bad as a nettle sting but a bit more than an itch."

"Sounds like me when someone is slow getting their round in down at the pub." He was pleased with that but noticed from her stony response that she wasn't.

"You've been working in America, Jonathan tells me," he added quickly.

"I have, or in fact I am. I've been working with the NSA for the last six months and it's gone well, so they've offered me a two-year contract based in Washington - and you know what I love most about it, apart from the work itself?"

She didn't wait for him to respond. "You should see the food trucks that arrive for lunch; from every type of burger you can imagine to ceviche, creole and vegan. I love the food trucks. You can eat food from a different part of the world every day."

"I can imagine that Jonathan might like that, especially trying to find his favourite dish. But you two haven't had much time together; how are you coping with that?"

She shrugged. "It's not as hard as people say. We both have busy working lives and then you can always talk on Skype, or whatever. I don't suppose someone like yourself has ever tried anything other than talking, but you would be surprised by all the things you can do on a video call."

He had a horrible feeling she might just be about to go into detail and decided that was too much information. He jumped in quickly. "What I really meant was that you had barely got to know each other before you had to leave. That can be difficult."

"Not really - you just have to be disciplined, like doing some research. I think he's the one for me and I thought that very quickly. I told him we should see how things go and then maybe in another six months, when he comes out, we can talk some more and decide what we are going to do about it. We should have the data we need by then."

Data or no data, he was having trouble with how quickly this conversation had become so personal but didn't want to say anything that might antagonise her; then she said something that made him feel like she was reading his mind. "I totally trust Jonathan and he totally trusts you, so that makes you one of the good guys. In fact, it makes you one of the very few good guys at all."

He was very touched, but before he could reply the phone rang. It was the guard to say Sam's Uber had arrived. She and Jonathan disappeared into the bedroom, emerging with two huge suitcases and two smaller ones for her carry-on luggage. They squeezed into the lift and made their way down, ferrying the bags out to the car where they were stowed away.

"You can see why I needed a ride to the airport. I couldn't decide what to take to Washington, so I think I've packed too much, but best to be on the safe side."

She walked over to Roper and reached up to kiss him goodbye, then clambered into the back of the car which took off straight away. Only as the car vanished from sight did Hooley realise she hadn't said goodbye to him.

He looked at Roper, who was staring at the spot where the car had turned left and disappeared from view.

He patted his arm. "Come on, let's get you something to eat."

3

The Courier was sitting in the expensively upholstered interior of Maxine Dubois' Gulfstream G650. One of the fastest private jets you could buy, it was capable of just under the speed of sound. At around $70 million, only the seriously wealthy could opt to buy one, let alone afford the murderously expensive cost of running it.

He'd been sitting here for half an hour after joining his client at London City airport. He'd been told the plane would be departing again forty-five minutes later so, with just fifteen minutes to go, he hoped she would speak to him soon.

Dubois had chosen dark grey leather to cover the seats and the Courier thought he blended in well since he had chosen one of his many handmade grey pinstripe suits for the meeting. As he waited he looked down and admired the brilliant shine on his shoes that had been applied by the Savoy's service staff overnight. The watch with which he was keeping track of the time with was an antique gold Cartier with a brown leather strap. It was one of his favourites and he always wore it on important days.

It wasn't vanity that made him spend so much effort on his appearance; it was part of the way he sought to blend in and not stand out. Today he wanted to look like any of the bankers who swarmed through City Airport on a daily basis.

When he'd boarded the aircraft, Dubois was sat towards the rear of the cabin with her back to him and her right hand held up in a mockery of greeting. He walked forward and handed over the iPad he'd taken out of a leather carry case.

While she settled to watching the video clip he moved back to the front of the plane and sat where he could keep an eye on events - but especially on Dubois. With less than two minutes to go she was done. Her steward went over to her and bent down so he could hear what she said. Then he took the iPad and returned it to the Courier.

"Madame congratulates you on your choice."

Even though he had been expecting the outcome he had to resist the urge to sigh with relief. He had really wanted this to work and he wanted the money even more. A taste for high-stakes gambling meant he needed fuel for his addiction.

Walking down the steps he turned his mind away from quite how much had been riding on today. Instead he congratulated himself on having the foresight to set up a lucrative business that saw clients hand him eye-watering sums of money, in return for the opportunity to indulge dark fantasies.

For Dubois that meant the chance to get away with murder, literally. She would soon be enjoying a drama of her own devising as she watched from a ringside seat. She wasn't one for actually doing the deed, but she loved being in control.

He'd begun his criminal career as an arms smuggler ferrying weapons into the UK, making decent money - but he wanted more. The drugs business was too difficult to break into, protected as it was by ruthless gangsters, but there was still a niche space for people trafficking.

As London had grown ever larger and richer, he had spotted that demand would rise and since his rivals were hampered by being too large to change quickly he had made even more money.

His new fortune allowed him to indulge a long ignored creative side. Some people referred to what he provided as "snuff movies", but he knew there was more to it than that. Where else could people get to act out their dreams, even if the price was a nightmare for the victims?

4

"I'm sixty per cent sorry that she's gone, and forty per cent pleased."

Hooley chuckled. He doubted there were many others who could describe feelings about their girlfriend in such precise percentages.

"Why such a high number to be pleased? I thought you two were getting along very well."

"We are, but I've never had a girlfriend before and we've had to be together all the time. It's funny because I want to be near her and then I want her to go away.

"It doesn't seem to make sense when I think about it. And to make it really confusing, when I am on my own, at first I feel better but then I start missing her again."

Hooley was able to buy a bit of time as a waiter appeared with Roper's food order, an impressive looking open sandwich piled high with thinly sliced rare roast beef and served with an appetising bowl of chips; the proper English sort, the DCI noted approvingly, not those thin cut French fries.

"I hope you don't think I am being rude by asking questions - I was just wondering how you were able to be so precise about how you feel about it."

"It's simple. Sam was with me for six days and it was the first time anyone has stayed at my flat. In fact, you and Julie Mayweather are the only people who have ever visited. We got on very well, so I awarded ten percent for each day. That made sixty per cent, the bit I feel sad about now, so the rest, the forty per cent, must be me feeling glad."

As a detective Hooley was used to people telling him confusing stories, usually in a forlorn attempt to try and explain how they had come to be in possession of stolen property. So he was comfortable with sifting through apparently conflicting information. This had thrown him.

"Look. I'm really not someone who should be handing out relationship advice but I don't think you are the only person in the world who finds relationships a bit confusing. When emotions get involved, common sense goes out the window - at least, that's what my grandmother used to say."

The way Roper's brow furrowed made him wonder if saying common sense had been 'thrown' out of the window was a tactical error when he was once again saved by an approaching waiter; this one had his toasted cheese sandwich.

Roper polished off the last of his sandwich and neatly placed his knife and fork on the plate. He looked at Hooley.

"How do you know when things are going well?"

"In my experience it's that you're not being shouted at, and that's why I may not be the best person to ask."

*

The DCI's decision to share his office space with Roper had been straightforward. It made life easier for everyone. His younger colleague was too easily distracted when he was surrounded by people, and that was a bad thing because it got in the way of Roper detecting patterns that everyone else missed. He needed a calm environment before he could fall into the near-Zen-like state he needed.

It also kept him apart from the colleagues with whom he could have difficult relationships with. In the past there had been complaints, that he wasn't a team player and had an abrasive manner.

While Hooley felt these issues were exaggerated and used as the basis for unfair complaints it was obvious his partner would never be the most popular man on the squad. No one had ever accused Roper of being the life and soul of the party.

Attitudes towards him had been improving since his brilliant detective work had led to breakthroughs against seemingly impossible odds. Despite this, Hooley knew it was better to keep him close and out of the bear pit.

In a strange way he had grown to enjoy some of Roper's more acerbic comments, especially those about his weight which had finally forced him onto a diet. He was almost twenty-eight pounds lighter even if, as Roper frequently pointed out, he couldn't afford to take it easy as he was still too tubby for his age. But the DCI was never going to be a poster boy for the health lobby and was pleased with what he had achieved. He thought it was many years since he had looked this good and he was glad his stomach had shrunk in size.

It was his turn to get the coffees. He plonked a black Americano in front of Roper and noticed that he was browsing through the 'slush fund': the DCI's personal stash of files about unsolved cases that intrigued him. He turned to these files when his live cases were going slowly.

After moving in, Roper had ferreted out the files and from that moment on he, too, was addicted. He was good at it, closing several cases that had been open for way too long, but it also led to one of the few serious arguments between the pair when Hooley had needed to insist that live cases should take priority.

At the moment they had very little on so the DCI was happy to talk about the past. "Seen anything you like the look of?"

Roper looked up and stared blankly at Hooley before blinking rapidly and seeming to come back from some distant space.

"Sorry, I was in the Rainbow Spectrum. Just read some stuff that didn't make a lot of sense, so I was just trying to see if there are other links around, which I think there are, but it might take a while to get it all together."

Hooley nodded thoughtfully. His colleague only mentioned the Rainbow Spectrum when he was on the brink of some sort of breakthrough. The Spectrum was Roper's own creation and it was a method by which he mentally catalogued different pieces of information, assigning them notional values using the colour of the rainbow. While it was complicated, and the DCI knew he would never fully understand how it worked, it could produce amazing results.

"Well, if it stays as quiet as this, we might need you to come up with something to stop everyone going upside down with boredom."

Roper pulled a face. "I can't promise anything. You know that most of the time these things turn out to be nothing, just lots of different information without any sort of connection."

"Well, don't get my hopes up with your wild enthusiasm."

He glanced at Roper; if he'd been hoping the sarcasm would have an effect he was wasting his time. There was no response at all. He was back in the Spectrum.

5

No one who knew him would accuse The Courier of being a sentimental man, but in a small, secret part of himself, he had nurtured a dream about a happy childhood: one far removed from his own, that had been one long round of drink and drug-fueled abuse.

He could never help wondering how his life might have turned out if he had been brought up in a family that took pride in quiet and normality. Getting up at the same time every day, the same breakfast and the same walk to school. Then, the return home to a loving mother who had prepared his favourite meal. After homework she would allow him to play with friends until it was time for a bath and getting ready for bed.

For some reason just thinking about what had never been made him feel emotional and he liked this rare moment when he loosened the emotional shackles under which he operated. The feeling had crept up on him after he arrived at the three-bedroom semi-detached house his team had taken over for the surveillance operation in Worcester Park.

These were family homes and generations had been brought up in them. They were quite unlike anything in which he had grown up. He was studying a house on the opposite side of the street and at 6.45am they had seen Anne Hudson's husband, Tony, leave the property.

The Courier knew he was off to catch an early train into Waterloo, where a short Tube ride would deposit him close to the office where he was training to be an insurance broker. At his last assessment his boss had lavished praise on him and told him he was set for big things.

That night the man and his wife had celebrated with a bottle of wine. They rarely drank and, when the inevitable happened, they forgot to take precautions and nine months later an eight-pound, four-ounce baby girl arrived which they called Lilly. She might not have been planned but she could not have been more loved - although maybe a bit less so after last night. The infant had been awake from midnight until 3am, according to the night-shift who had been listening in on the recently installed equipment, so the Courier was not expecting to hear from Anne Hudson any time soon.

He was happy to wait. He had allowed for a couple of weeks here as he sought to establish the rhythms of the neighbourhood. The house he had chosen was ideal for his plan. It was a long-established rental property, in a street that had several others, so neighbours were used to comings and goings and paid no attention to new tenants. He kept his eye on the house opposite as he reached for the cup of jasmine tea that one of his team had just made for him. It was cold in the house, so he could see the steam rising from the drink.

The unmistakable sound of a baby starting to cry came over the speakers and he got up to walk to the back bedroom, which had its curtains tightly shut to stop anyone realising that the room was full of monitors displaying multiple feeds from the target house.

As he walked in, there was a loud howl which caused the mother to come from deep sleep to wide awake as she sat up. Another howl saw her jumping straight out of the bed and walking over to the cot where her daughter lay, her face going red with the effort of making so much noise.

She scooped up Lilly and took her back to bed where she made soft noises and then offered her breast to the child, the tone of Lilly's crying telling her that the tiny girl was hungry. She was soon rewarded by seeing her daughter happily feeding. Half an hour later Lilly had drifted off to sleep.

The Courier could see all this through the miniaturised cameras that were installed in every room of the house. The equipment was state-of-the-art and had been expertly customised to fit in with the decor of the house. You'd have needed to know what you were looking for to spot it.

A few moments later he watched the woman carefully place her daughter back in her cot and then quickly strip off her loose-fitting nightie as she went to take a shower. The camera in the bathroom offered a very clear shot of her soaping herself and he noted appreciatively that she was in very good shape, her baby-tummy slowly going down.

Not that he was remotely interested from a sexual point of view, as his own tastes in that area were highly complex and did not include young women. He imagined her furious reaction had she known she was under observation.

He had already come to the view that when the time came she would fight like a lioness, or at least she would if she were given the chance. He guessed that she would have no concerns for her own safety; only that of her daughter. If they underestimated her, they would have problems and that would never do.

Fifteen minutes later, Anne Hudson was sitting at the kitchen table eating toast and Marmite. She had a healthy appetite, helping herself to a third slice. Not that she had any worries about gaining weight. Later today, Lilly would be placed in a three-wheeled sport buggy and would be taken for an hour's run.

Breakfast over, she began the daily chores and was loading a pile of baby clothes into the washing machine when the front doorbell disturbed her. It was a delivery man with a package. He watched her take it back to the kitchen, open it and then beam with pleasure as she saw what it was.

Moments later and the Courier could see it too as she unwittingly put the gold cuff-links and watch on display by holding them up in front of her face creating a perfect angle for one of the cameras in the kitchen. Research had already told him it was the husband's birthday soon, so he was probably looking the present.

He turned away from the screens; at last he was starting to feel that familiar tingle that told him events were coming to a head and soon it would be time to replace planning and watching with action.

Even better, the client had today transferred the first part of the payment. It would cover all his costs, clear his debts and leave him with enough money to get back to the gaming tables. His passion was craps, a game that required minimal skills and maximum luck and freed him from his normal routines of paying attention to every detail, no matter how small or apparently insignificant.

He loved everything about it: the way the dice felt in his hand as he gently shook them, blowing on them for luck before launching them down the table and the muffled noise they made as they tumbled across the green baize of the gaming table.

6

Julie Mayweather had a well-hidden sense of humour. She especially loved practical jokes, and had instantly spotted the potential for one now. She'd been standing in Hooley and Roper's office for almost a minute. They were both so engrossed in their research they hadn't noticed her.

She was there in her role as Head of the Special Investigations Unit but at this moment she had a plan to attract their attention. Resisting the urge to grin, she brought her hands together in a loud clap.

She hadn't seen Hooley jump so much since that time he had been demonstrating the use of a taser and accidentally shot himself in the foot. Meanwhile, Roper had leapt to his feet and was looking around wildly.

Satisfied her work was done, she turned quickly and left, calling out: "Can you two make it to my office in half an hour?"

She had recently been appointed as one of two Deputy Commissioners at Scotland Yard, a well-earned promotion that pushed her into the highest echelons - meaning she had needed to review her role running the Special Investigations Unit.

There had been some talk of Brian Hooley being promoted behind her, but he'd fiercely resisted the idea, arguing they made a good team as it was. In the end, after a little arm-twisting, he had agreed to take up more slack if she remained to provide the strategic direction which dovetailed so well with his old-school know-how.

As she disappeared, Hooley couldn't help but smile. He knew he'd been had but it was his own fault for not being aware of what was going on. The trouble with spending time with Roper was that his immersive techniques of researching cases proved highly contagious.

Roper, still looking startled, ran off, shouting that he was going for coffee. "Just got time for a drink before we go in. Do you want one?"

"No thanks. I've had about five pints of it so far today. I won't be sleeping for the rest of the week if I have any more and it can't be helping my blood pressure."

Given that current health advice was for moderate caffeine consumption he imagined that Roper would agree with him, but not for the first time he was taken by surprise.

"That's just nonsense. People go on about the harmful effects of caffeine but it all depends on how you, the individual, reacts to it. It's only just after lunch now so one more won't affect you at all."

Hooley knew better than to be sucked into a conversation.

"That's a very good point you make, and reassuring for someone like me who likes their coffee - but I still feel as though I am at my limit, so the answer's still no. Thanks all the same."

Twenty-five minutes later an agitated Roper reappeared. Things had not gone well.

"There was a huge queue and I thought I might have to come back before it was time to go."

Hooley silently filed that under "Roperisms": moments when his partner used language so precisely it stopped making sense.

"At least you made it, so let's go."

They hadn't sat down before the briefing was underway. "We've been paid the ultimate compliment of being asked for by Special Branch and the Counter

Terrorism Command. It's not often those two will both ask for assistance."

She had a touch of the theatrical about her and paused for several beats before moving to the big reveal.

"Ever heard of Georgi Yebedev?"

Roper's hand shot into the air. There was nothing fake about it; he was quite unable to hide his enthusiasm. This had earned him the nickname "Keeno", as in "super keen."

"He's a former Russian citizen, now based in London. He's worth in excess of £10 billion but no-one is quite sure of the total and there are questions about how he got it. What is known is that he was one of the group of Russian businessmen and Kremlin cronies who appeared in the early 1990s and grabbed a lot of the state assets following the collapse of the Soviet Union.

"He turned up in Britain more than 20 years ago and has since married the daughter of an English Earl. They have three sons, all of whom are currently at Gordonstoun School, where Prince Charles went. The eldest boy is said to be highly intelligent and will be going to Cambridge to study mathematics.

"There was an interesting development over the choice of school. It has a policy that every pupil must carry out basic communal tasks, like cleaning the lavatories. Mr. Yebedev demanded that he be allowed to send a cleaner to do the work. When that was turned down he asked his sons to try and bribe the other boys to do it.

"Somehow the matter became public, and it was later reported that the headteacher had left Mr. Yebedev in no doubt, that unless his boys did what everyone else had to do, he was welcome to take them elsewhere."

The information was delivered at a clipped pace without hesitation. Mayweather never failed to be impressed at the variety of information Roper had at his finger-tips. Little wonder he was also known as "search engine".

It seemed there was more.

"There was a big profile of him in the London Evening Standard a couple of months ago. It was raining that day so I got the bus and read it on the way home. It's very interesting to read how many rich Russians are over here, especially in London."

Hooley leaned across and tapped him on the arm. "It will be a sad day when that elephant-like brain of yours becomes as flaky as mine and you start forgetting things."

"I very much doubt that will happen," said Roper, his face showing he was not in the mood for light-hearted comments. "I have always looked after myself properly and done everything possible to enhance my neuro-function, something about which I'm afraid you have been very remiss."

Hooley couldn't help biting on the comment. "That's a bit harsh. I've been doing the cross word every day, like you suggested, and taking those fish oils." As he spoke he looked at his boss, but she was maintaining a determinedly straight face, a slightly raised eyebrow the only sign she was listening.

But as Roper went to say more, Mayweather intervened. She knew the DCI was one of the most phlegmatic men she had ever worked with, but even he had limits.

"Let's keep to topic, shall we?" she said. "Your summary is spot on, Jonathan. He may have been born in Russia, but he is now part of the fabric here, known for his generosity and his love of all things English. He's very much regarded as one of the good guys."

"I take it something has happened to challenge that view?" said Hooley, leaning forward in his chair and pulling his emotions back under control.

"There might have been. The information being passed to us is from other intelligence agencies, so I have no way of telling how complete it is, but previous experience suggests we should assume that plenty of details have been left out. MI5 are in on this but if they know anything else they aren't telling me. It comes from a joint US and Israeli intelligence operation that was monitoring some unusual cash flows through offshore banks."

"I wonder if it's something to do with that new software they've developed?"

"I'm sorry, Jonathan?" said Mayweather.

"A couple of weeks ago, on the dark web, there was chatter about some new code that could crack open bank security systems and track money movements back to their origins."

Mayweather looked at Hooley, who shrugged. Not only was this news to him, it took him way out of his comfort zone as well.

"Is this something we should even be talking about?"

Roper looked puzzled. "So long as we keep it to ourselves I don't see that it's a problem, and it might be relevant to what you're talking about. I do know that it is also being discussed at GCHQ."

Mayweather tapped her index finger on her notepad. Hooley knew that meant she was thinking furiously.

"Let's leave that to one side for now. Maybe you're right about the software, but it doesn't matter at the moment. Keep it at the back of your mind and we can discuss it later."

She looked at him, hoping to see signs that he had accepted what she said, and settled for the fact he wasn't arguing with her.

"What we are being asked to look into are some unusual transactions linked to money controlled by Yebedev. He keeps large sums offshore. But over the last year some of his money, and we are talking hundreds of millions of dollars, have been moved to accounts controlled by an Israeli-based entrepreneur who has long been suspected of money laundering.

"The Israeli, Aaron Sopher, spends quite a lot of time here in London but until now there has been nothing to link him to Yebedev. There's more, but MI5 want to brief you. You're expected over at Vauxhall this afternoon; you need to ask for a Bill Nuffield.

"I've been asked not to tell you the details so that you can approach the briefing with an open mind, but I don't think it's an exaggeration to say this is probably the most significant threat we have ever faced. That's why I need my two best people on it."

7

Thames House is the imposing Grade-II-listed home of M15, the domestic intelligence service, and sits proudly on the North bank of the Thames, close to Lambeth Bridge and its sister organisation MI6, the foreign service, housed in a modern building on the opposite side of the river. Friends and rivals, they keep a beady an eye on each other.

Roper had insisted on walking there, setting a brisk pace it left the DCI breathing heavily. As he cooled off he pointed over to MI6.

"I watched that being blown up a couple of weeks ago."

Roper came to a sudden halt, his expression leaving no doubt that he thought the DCI had lost it.

"Ever seen a James Bond movie?"

Roper continued to stare.

"I know you're not a fan of popular culture, but millions of people have seen the scene in Skyfall where that building gets blown up."

He was left talking to himself as Roper moved away. A few minutes later and he was watching Roper squirm from a vigorous pat-down. The younger man hated being touched at the best of times and having a complete stranger lay hands on him was clearly an ordeal as a deep frown appeared on his face.

Hooley thought the whole thing was overdone. Only a short while ago Roper had been given a top security clearance for his work at GCHQ, the British listening post just outside Cheltenham in Gloucestershire, but that clearly counted for nothing now he was back at the Met.

He was tempted to start an argument which would force this Bill Nuffield to come and collect them, but Roper was coping so he contented himself with staring at the guard in his best passive-aggressive manner.

Finally they were inside the building and shown to a waiting area. No one appeared and Hooley was just wondering if he should start making a fuss after all, when a young man, dressed rather like Roper in a skinny-fit black suit, arrived.

He brought them to a room equipped with a few dozen stacking chairs placed in neat rows. They were lined up in front of a large whiteboard. A lectern was facing them on the right-hand side. There were no windows.

A man standing at the lectern looked up. When he spoke, it emerged he was American. "Bill Nuffield. I'm on a sort of exchange programme from the NSA, attached to the Deputy Director General's staff. I'm your point man on this."

He was a tall, rangy man, in his forties, and Hooley's eyes were drawn to a flattened, S-bend nose that had been broken more than once. He either enjoyed contact sports or got in a lot of fights. He had piercing blue eyes and a close cropped, military-style haircut.

Roper had been staring at him and said. "Lake Michigan."

A brief smile appeared on Nuffield's face. "And you must be Mr. Roper. I take it you're identifying where I come from in the good ol' US of A."

He looked at Roper closely, seeming to check details against some internal list.

"I've heard a lot about you from the people here at M15. People say you were smart and different. I can tell that. A lot of Americans would have been pushed to know I come from the Lake Michigan area."

Roper said nothing, adopting one of his more sphinx-like expressions. A lot of people assumed he did this because he was thinking deeply, but Hooley knew it was more likely that the younger man was unsure of himself.

The DCI pushed on. "I understand you are the man who is going to brief us on this Georgi Yebedev character and explain what it is that makes him a person of interest for Scotland Yard."

Instead of replying Nuffield walked over to the corner of the room, where a small table contained a couple of insulated jugs and a selection of cups and saucers. He checked both of the containers and turned back to Roper and Hooley. "Tea or coffee? I've got sugar and milk, and not that awful long-life stuff.

"Most of the people who work in this building went to public school. They all love that stuff. I have a theory it must be something to do with going to those famous public schools of yours."

Hooley suppressed a smile. He knew the man was making an effort to charm. He shared Nuffield's opinion about the background of the many young men who occupied this building.

"I suspect that's going to be two white coffees." He looked at Roper who nodded in confirmation.

Drinks in hand, they settled into their seats as Nuffield went back to the lectern. He shrugged apologetically.

He tapped something on a laptop and the image of a man filled the screen. He looked young, maybe late thirties, although Hooley wouldn't have been surprised if he was a decade older. He had the appearance of someone who worked out. His dark hair was cut short, with no signs of grey, and he had a round face and wide mouth that gave him a kindly appearance, enhanced by his faint smile.

"Aaron Sopher. And don't be fooled by his welcoming expression. We, as in Homeland Security, only recently picked up on what an important player he is on the international scene. Money laundering, people trafficking, espionage, drugs… you name it. He's got fingers in many, many pies."

He looked at the two men. "I can see you both have questions already so let's see if I can guess. The big one is: why don't we just pick him up? The truth is that we should have, while we had the chance, but now he's dropped out of sight.

"Let me take you back a little way. It was Mossad that first tipped us off about him, nine months ago. Up to then he had evaded our attention, which means he is either very, very good, or very, very lucky. The fear is that it's both, and now he's up to something which is raising his importance.

"Once we had him tagged we decided to put him under surveillance, and I mean a large-scale operation split between Tel Aviv, London, Washington and Los Angeles. We were hoping that we would start to pick up other operators and maybe get some sense of the true scale of what he was up to.

"It was all going fine until two weeks ago when he vanished. We don't know if we spooked him or it was part of a bigger plan all along."

"How long was it before you realised he'd gone?"

"A very good question, Mr. Roper. I'm afraid to admit that it took us thirty-six hours before we realised he was in the wind. Since then there has been a massive review of the surveillance operation.

"We have gone through everything and it is throwing out a ton of information. There is one bit that we would like you to look at for us."

He prodded his computer again and a fresh face appeared on screen. This was a much bigger man, broad-shouldered and bull-necked. He was in his late fifties and his large head was closely shaven.

"Georgi Yebedev, I presume," said Hooley. "What a bruiser. I wouldn't want to run into him in one of those cells they have in the Kremlin."

Nuffield laughed. "You're not the only one to make the KGB connection, or I should say FSB, since the Russians would have us believe the KGB no longer exists. What about you, Jonathan?"

"Stalin. He looks like Stalin."

Nuffield nodded. "It's the eyes. When you look at pictures of them side by side they look very similar. If Yebedev had hair like Stalin's you might think they were brothers. He also comes from the same region, so that probably explains it."

Hooley leaned forward. "This is all very interesting, and I mean that, but why are you involving us? What haven't you told us yet?"

Before he could reply Roper jumped in. "It's something bad and something very recent."

"What makes you say that?"

"Because so far most of the surveillance pictures you've shown us were taken a while ago. I can tell from the plants that these were taken in the autumn, and it's early summer now, so there has to be more.

"I think it's very recent because you haven't had a chance to fully assess it yet, and it's bad because what you have seen is enough to reach out to us already. You don't want to waste a moment; that's why you've made a direct appeal."

Nuffield made the mistake of trying to break the tension with a light-hearted comment.

"I'm sorry, Mr. Roper, but if I was to confirm your guess I wouldn't be allowed to let you leave the building again."

Roper was already fairly wound up by being at MI5.

"What do you mean by not leaving the building? You can't hold us here, and the involvement of an American security official in obstructing two British police officers - in Britain, I might remind you - would be very badly received indeed."

Hooley couldn't help smiling as he watched Nuffield's mouth drop open. Clearly no one had briefed him that, as well as being a brilliant analyst, Roper didn't do jokes and could go from zero to angry in the time it takes most people to blink.

To his credit, Nuffield staged a remarkable recovery.

"Hey, let's slow down here. That was my bad. I was told you Brits have an amazing sense of humour but I guess I need to work on my timing, or something. Please, forget the last few seconds and let me start again."

Fortunately, Roper calmed fast and made no more comment.

"What I was trying to do is explain how difficult this is. I can't tell you everything, but neither am I going to insult your intelligence by pretending we have a full understanding of what is going on.

"Let me give a tiny bit of background. The operation that uncovered Mr. Yebedev was sanctioned at the highest level and there was considerable debate as to whether to bring you guys in at all. In the end I like to think common sense prevailed – that, and your reputation for getting results.

"There's a mass of raw data being thrown out and it covers lots of individuals, most of whom we don't have the resources to cover, but Yebedev has suddenly become a person of interest to the UK government after years of being clean. We - that is, MI5 - are now certain that he has reactivated ties to the Russian President's inner circle."

Nuffield came out from behind the lectern and picked up a chair, placing it, so he could sit facing the two detectives.

"Now here's the first of the things that I am going to tell you that I shall deny ever saying if you repeat this to anyone outside this room. I'm also given to believe that your boss, Julie Mayweather, has already been briefed, but I haven't spoken to her myself.

"This concerns the CIA, which always believed there was more to Mr. Yebedev than he would like us to believe. As such, we have, from time to time, put him under surveillance. The CIA never made any attempt to share this information with any other intelligence agency."

He locked his gaze with Roper's. "I know what you're about to say. If we were spying on him while he was in the UK we were probably breaking the law. But sometimes you gotta do what you gotta do, and I am trying to level with you now.

"I know it's not an excuse, but you guys do it to us. In fact, as I understand it, there is some sort of SIS operation taking place in Los Angeles at the moment. I am sure that when the time is right we will be informed."

Roper eased back in his seat and Hooley was again impressed by the way Nuffield had dealt with what might have been an issue for Roper. The younger man hated any suggestion that people were lying to him, so being straight about what had happened was the only answer.

"The next thing I am about to tell you is also strictly because you need to know. When Aaron Sopher first emerged, it shocked Mossad. They don't get caught out, not on their own patch.

"Anyway, it really got them going. They threw some of their best assets at it and got back some disturbing information. As you know, successful jihadist groups need lots and lots of money, and there are many ways of raising it.

"One of the ways is through human trafficking and, in parts of the Middle East and Africa, the IS leadership has created the perfect environment. All the local conflict has millions of people on the move so grabbing a few is like picking cherries from a tree.

"And that is quite a good way of describing it. The militants have their choice of the healthiest and youngest victims, so they have been able to demand top dollar for the people they send through the smuggling networks.

"To make it even sweeter, the IS leadership started taking over the smuggling networks for themselves. They've been very successful and have thousands and thousands of people on the move. They are being taken all over the world, to wherever there is a market for buying slaves.

"There are slaves being kept in appalling conditions in all the major cities of the world. Here in the UK, China, Japan, Saudi Arabia, Europe, Russia, Australia - if there's money sloshing about there's a market.

"What's got Mossad jumping about is that it seems Sopher has had no qualms about exploiting this situation as well and is even willing to work with jihadi groups. Just when they thought it couldn't get any worse, they discovered the link between Sopher and Yebedev."

He got up to get a glass of water and started talking again as he walked back to his seat.

"It opens up all sort of horrendous possibilities, not least the thought of new smuggling routes through Russian territory. But the one thing that is keeping a lot of us awake at night is another piece of information that has emerged.

"We have it on very good authority that two months ago Mr. Yebedev had a meeting with a Russian scientist, Maria Vasilev, in Moscow. She is an expert on miniaturising nuclear weapons."

"You're talking about a dirty bomb. You're worried that someone is bringing a dirty bomb to London." Roper had jumped to his feet.

8

The two men winced as they watched the live feed. The hallway camera was perfectly placed to capture the moment that Tony Hudson slipped on the staircase and landed with all his weight going through his left ankle, bending it an angle it wasn't designed for. The sound was good enough to pick up a double crunch indicating at least two bones had snapped.

It was a spare nappy that had done for him, left on the third step. He hadn't been paying attention as he made his way downstairs for a cup of tea before setting off for work. Now he was lying on his side, panting heavily, and trying his best not to cry out since in his pain-addled state he was thinking that he might be able to walk once he'd caught his breath.

He had made so much noise falling down that his wife was already awake and racing out of the bedroom to find out what was happening, her heart hammering as she feared her husband had run into burglars. Seeing him crumpled at the foot of the stairs, she almost fell herself as she rushed down.

Twenty minutes later and paramedics were carefully loading him into the back of the ambulance for the short trip to the A&E department of the nearest hospital, Epsom General, where they would begin piecing him back together.

It was a tearful parting as the husband had insisted his daughter get the priority treatment and that his wife should stay at home rather than come to the hospital. He had told her he would be fine as soon as he got there since they could provide him with proper painkillers. The A&E department was no place for a newborn. He said his medical insurance would allow him to get a private room and then she could bring their daughter in for a visit. His wife had covered his ankle while they waited, so neither had to look at it, but they both knew he was going to need an operation.

Ten minutes after the ambulance departed two cars pulled up. The first to arrive, by just a few seconds, was a silver Fiat 500 that parked up and the woman's mother, looking anxious, jumped out and hurried up to her daughter's house. She was greeted with an emotional hug before stepping inside and closing the door behind her.

Almost simultaneously a second car, a dark blue Ford Mondeo, dropped the Courier outside the rental house. He watched the scene over the road through the corner of his eye, guessing the older woman was the mother and wondering if she would be moving in for a few days to help her daughter out.

The accident was both an opportunity and a set-back, at least as far as the Courier was concerned. He could seize the moment and, once Anne Hudson was on her own, grab her straight away. Or he would have to postpone, possibly by a couple of weeks, while the husband recovered at home.

The Courier let himself into the surveillance house and was gratified that no one came to greet him. That meant they were concentrating on doing their jobs, and he wanted to know exactly what was being said in the house opposite.

He walked upstairs and into the back bedroom where most of the equipment was set up. His two men were watching a live feed and wearing headphones as they listened in. One of the operatives raised a thumb to acknowledge his presence, but that was all. He went back downstairs to make a cup of tea and wait for one of them to break off.

Forty minutes later, the older of the two men was talking him through what they had overheard.

"The mother obviously knows a bit about these things and says if it's a bad break he will need metal plates and be in hospital for about a week. Her mother and father live in a large house close to the hospital and they are suggesting daughter and baby come to stay."

"Did they decide what they're going to do?"

"Not for definite. Our woman is still in a state of shock but I'd put money on her ending up at her mother's, at least for a while. They've sent her father up to the hospital to be with the husband and he's going to ring in when he has some news."

The Courier closed his eyes, a signal that he wanted to be left alone while he thought. It looked like the first option was being taken away which meant he would have to put everything else on hold for a couple of weeks to see how things panned out.

He was under no great time pressure as he was always careful to allow a generous margin, which in this case amounted to almost six months before he had to pull everything together. He quietly congratulated himself on planning for some unforeseen event like this.

However, he had not given up all hope that it might work out in the short term. If Anne Hudson decided she wanted to be at home, and if her mother didn't move in, there would be a perfect opportunity to make the snatch. He admitted there were too many "ifs" in that plan but he would prepare for it anyway.

The second operative appeared with fresh news.

"They're having quite the discussion. The daughter is arguing that the baby is sleeping well and she doesn't want to risk that by changing her environment. She is also telling her mother that she doesn't need to come and stay. That got her mother going on about what happened if she fell down the stairs in the night, but the daughter is having none of it.

"She told her, 'I'll be really careful about keeping the stairs clear but, let's face it, we've had all the bad luck we are going to get this week. What could happen that would be worse?'"

9

Hooley felt a chill down his spine as Nuffield's reaction showed that was exactly what they feared. He'd grown up during the height of the Cold War when people were convinced that a nuclear war was inevitable.

Then the worries had seemed to fade away, only to return with the rise of extremism, but now it seemed London was back on the target list. He had one straw to clutch at.

"I was under the impression that suitcase bombs were one of those fantasy things that sound great in theory but are impossible in reality. I'm sure that the last time I read anything sensible about them you would have needed a suitcase the size of a London taxi cab."

"Unfortunately, the technology has leapt forwards in recent years. We have reason to believe that the Russians really are ahead of the field in this area so, while reducing a nuclear bomb to the size of a suitcase remains difficult, it may not be impossible.

"The only consolation is that our scientists argue that such a device would be far too heavy to lug around. Imagine a suitcase that weighs in at north of two hundred pounds; even a weightlifter would struggle to stroll through Hyde Park with that. But there is a theory that you could break the weapon down into three component parts which would make it possible to carry."

"You're not making me feel any better about all this," complained Hooley. He could recall countless occasions when the Met had been placed on a bomb alert for London, but not once had he been told to prepare for a nuclear explosion. "What sort of damage would such a bomb do?"

"It's very hard to say. But at the very least, you might be talking about a blast area a hundred metres across or more, and then the resulting fallout affecting a much wider area, depending on the weather conditions. It would be one of those times when you would pray for London rain."

Roper chipped in. "If they could walk it in the terrorists could place it exactly where they wanted. Can you imagine something going off in Covent Garden at lunchtime?"

Hooley was looking for lifelines to cling to.

"Am I right in thinking you don't think anything is here at the moment? You'd have the Army out if that was the case, and declare a national emergency; you wouldn't be wasting time talking to the pair of us."

Nuffield rubbed his hands together in a sort of washing gesture. Hooley thought a psychiatrist might be interested in that.

"That's right. But we would like to know what a wealthy, London-based, Russian oligarch is doing talking to an obscure but brilliant scientist in Moscow, and to a major criminal man like Sopher.

"MI5 suggested Mr. Roper would be the perfect man to get involved as it was likely to take a great deal of analysis and that is something he is famous for. In fact, if I have understood it correctly, his Rainbow Spectrum may be the ideal tool for dealing with what is likely to be a lot of apparently unrelated information. At the same time it was suggested I join MI5, on secondment, and help to brief you guys. I understand you come as a pair, so the feeling is that you would be the best team to work on this."

Hooley glanced over at Roper, who was frowning deeply, and he guessed it was because Nuffield had referred to the Rainbow Spectrum. He hated people he didn't know having any knowledge of his unique mental filing system.

He knew the best way to take his mind off it. "When will you have any information for us?"

"I'm having some background material put together as we speak, and the main file is being redacted right now. There's going to be a lot of blanked pages I'm afraid, but hopefully there will be something in there you can use.

"Plus, you have my promise that I am doing my best to get information released to you - but we are talking about the highest classification of material, so it won't be much, and it won't be soon."

With that, he headed out, promising to be back in fifteen minutes with whatever was available. Roper took the chance to help himself to more coffee, knocking back three cups in quick succession.

"If I did that the caffeine jolt would make feel all jittery."

"I don't have control issues, so it's quite easy."

Hooley waited. He knew there would be more eventually. He didn't have long to wait.

"I think a lot of the things are in the mind. Look at you in the pub the other night. You had no problem knocking back four pints of strong lager even though you only had a packet of crisps to eat."

"I picked up some food on the way home," he said defensively.

"Yes, and I bet it was fish and chips again. Well, that's no good for you, as I have told you many times before."

"Yes, you have told me, many, many times. But as I keep telling you, life is too short to keep avoiding fish and chips."

"Your life will certainly be a lot shorter if you carry on."

Roper looked as though he was ready to pursue the discussion but at that moment Nuffield reappeared, carrying a slim, black leather attaché case. He held it up.

"Everything I've got for you is in here." He opened the case and produced a short, typewritten note that appeared to have some sort of stamp on it. "You will need this to get the documents out of the building. Without it security would arrest you on the spot."

"That reminds me," said Hooley. "They're a pretty grim lot here. They gave Jonathan a real going over when we arrived. What was all that about?"

"I shouldn't really be telling you this, but we had someone trying to hack into our systems earlier on today. They got past the firewall which caused a panic, and security were ordered to pay attention to anyone who looked like a hacker."

"But just because I'm not a youngster doesn't mean I couldn't have been the one you were looking for."

Nuffield grinned. "I don't know if anyone has ever told you this, but you really do look like a cop. I can imagine you playing a part in some TV show and having a catchphrase, with a British twist, for when you were arresting the bad guys. Something like: 'My old granny can punch harder than you.'"

10

In the face of intense lobbying by her mother, Anne Hudson reluctantly agreed that she would move in with her parents, at least until her husband was back home. She knew it was sensible to have the help while her husband recovered but she'd been enjoying life in her own home and knew her mum would insist on getting closely involved.

As she started packing up, she reminded herself she was lucky that an over-helpful mum was her issue. The baby girl slept through all the preparations, which didn't take long as Grandma had bought duplicates of everything that might be needed for overnight babysitting duties, including a cot.

She couldn't help smiling as her mother made a very poor job of pretending that she wasn't excited at her son-in-law's accident opening an opportunity for her to get her hands on her granddaughter. Five hours after her husband left in an ambulance, the two women set off for Epsom in a small convoy.

The Courier was quite relaxed as he watched them leave. He had already ruled out any thought of grabbing the woman today, so her heading off to stay with her parents made no difference except in one crucial way: he would be losing key surveillance data.

While he probably couldn't do much about the parents' home, the hospital was a different matter, just so long as they were right that the husband was going to end up on a private wing rather than an open ward. He called up one of his team and explained what he was going to need, asking the man to meet him over at Epsom later that afternoon.

*

The Courier was on the third floor of the town centre car park when a white van drove past and pulled into a parking bay. He got out and walked to the rear of the vehicle where he climbed into the back, leaving the door slightly open.

Sitting inside was another of the Courier's team. On his way to this meeting he'd called in at the hospital where he'd stolen a security badge and was now creating a new pass with a grainy photo that might, or might not, have been the Courier.

Half an hour later, the Courier was on the private wing and looking for the father, Tony Hudson. He found him in a room at the far end of the corridor and knocked once on the half-open door before walking in.

Flashing his bogus credentials, he announced himself as "Martin, from patient services," and asked permission to carry out a swift inspection to make sure everything was as it should be. Hudson had only just been given a dose of strong painkillers so was in no state to work out what was going on.

Had he been more alert he would have been impressed that Martin was doing such a good job, taking time to check the underside of the bed, the visitor chairs and the bathroom. By the time he left, apologising for the disturbance, the Courier had left four tiny listening devices that he was confident would pick up any word spoken in the room. It was overkill but he was cautious man.

Congratulating himself on a job well done, he walked out and nearly collided with a woman carrying a clipboard. He checked her badge and saw it identified her as "patient services", so he mumbled an apology as he quickly pivoted and left the ward. Hudson, now firmly in the grip of the opioids, did not register that he seemed to be receiving special attention.

Outside the Courier found a spot that allowed him to check the signal strength, which he tested by listening in. Unsurprisingly he spent a lot of time listening to silence, apart from a nurse who looked in to make sure the patient was doing well. As he waited he sent a signal that activated a tiny recorder. Whatever was said would now be captured.

It was the eighth day of surveillance before he finally got what he was looking for. It turned out that Hudson's operation was being judged a success and he was now being put through a daily routine of adjusting to his crutches before being allowed home.

When his wife came to visit with the baby that afternoon he was able to tell her he was being allowed out the following morning. To keep her parents happy, they had agreed to spend the first couple of days at their house, but Hudson made his wife promise it would last no longer than three days.

Listening to the key passages of audio, the Courier was in two minds. Part of him wanted to carry on being as cautious as normal. That would suggest he waited until the husband was well enough to get back to work, which might be fairly soon or, at worst, just a few weeks.

But these unexpected delays were making him restless and he felt only action could scratch the itch. He was also growing ever more eager to get back on the gaming tables, so he decided not to wait any longer than necessary - once the family had settled back into the routine of everyday life, they would go in. With the father out of action, it was only the woman to worry about. He liked those odds.

11

"I suppose that when you compare Roper and I, it's not that hard to work out which of us writes his own computer code and which of us struggles with sending text messages."

"You and me both," said Nuffield. "Someone once persuaded me to use my thumbs to text; all it did was sprain my knuckles. Anyway, back to business. If you are going to walk back to the office, then I'm afraid that standard procedure means I have to get a couple of armed guards to accompany you and the file I have just prepared. It might be easier if you went by car."

Roper had been closely studying the documents and now rejoined the conversation.

"There's nothing in here that would give anything away and the redacted material is exactly that; no one could work out what any of it meant. I don't see why that requires armed guards - there's nothing worth looking at. I can't imagine why..." He stopped suddenly. "I get it. You don't even want people to know there is a file on this Yebedev."

Nuffield shrugged as though he was suggesting 'what can you do?' but Hooley noticed that the seeming apology never got as far as his eyes, which had assumed a steely look.

"I get this is a bit of overkill, but I'm afraid it's the rules and I have to follow them, and so do you two gentlemen. But perhaps I should explain what role we are hoping you are going to play. We want a low-key operation that tracks what Yebedev is up to and who he is meeting.

"Julie Mayweather has already agreed that you can both be seconded to this job and, if you need any resources, either contact her or myself. I'll send you my contact details while you're heading back to Victoria. Just so you know, our main focus, as in MI5, will remain on Mr. Sopher and where he has disappeared to.

"It looks like he's become a financial enabler for some seriously bad people, so we want to get the drop on him ASAP. It may be that our paths cross, so if you could bear that in mind, and stay at arm's length if Sopher shows up on your radar, that would be helpful."

Hooley felt that icy sensation running down his back again. He'd been hoping for something interesting, and now look what they had been given. His mother had always warned him 'be careful what you wish for' and he was thinking he should have borne that in mind.

The enormity of what they were talking about had even slowed Roper down. Normally when they started a new assignment he bounced around like the bunny in the battery advert; now his expression showed a sort of grim determination and Hooley knew there was no chance he could be pushed off this particular hunt.

"Well we'd better get started and, unless my colleague surprises me, we'll be walking back, so armed guards it is."

As they arrived back at their own building he noted security had been stepped up since they'd left with a couple of policemen guarding the entrance. They walked in to their office and Hooley had an overwhelming urge to scratch at a point just between his shoulder blades. He contorted himself as he reached behind to hit the perfect spot and send relief flooding through his body.

"If you were a senior member of the Royal family you would have to get used to it."

He turned to stare at Roper. "I'm sorry, what did you say?"

"That if you were Prince Harry, there would be no use getting all wound up because you had an armed bodyguard. You kept looking at where they had their guns holstered under their jackets. It was obvious you were worried about it; even I could tell."

Hooley shrugged. "I belong to that generation of coppers who don't like guns and I never will like them. I know we live in different times now but that's how I feel."

He sat down and immediately started tapping away at his keyboard, about to start digging into whatever background material he could lay his hands on. This was one of those occasions when he envied Roper his single-minded approach.

For the DCI it was proving a bit more complicated than just another case. He'd liked Nuffield, but the man was also a member of the clandestine services and the one thing you could be sure about was that you were never told everything they knew.

12

A restless night at home, sleep punctured by vivid dreams of being threatened, left Hooley in poor shape for a productive day. His mind kept wandering the moment he tried to do anything. In the old days he could have taken himself out for the day, claiming to be meeting informants or following up on clues. But now he was the boss and that option was closed off to him.

The idea of a quick pint was lovingly contemplated and then dismissed before he finally accepted there was only one avenue that was realistically open to him.

"Fancy a coffee and a doughnut?"

If he'd wired Roper directly into the building's electrical pathways he could not have produced a faster response.

"Get me three doughnuts, the sugar frosted ones only, nothing with chocolate on it, and an Americano with cold milk on the side."

Order delivered, he snapped back into studying the documents he had on screen. Roper was definitely more of a thinker than an action man. Not that he lacked courage, but he did prefer reading to guns.

Hooley walked out, shaking his head. Where some people might have found the abrupt set of commands borderline rude, he knew the younger man considered he had been "maximising his economy" by issuing a set of precise demands that didn't use wasteful words like "please" or "thank you."

He was halfway through the door when his colleague called out. "Don't sneak a doughnut in while you walk back. I saw the jam on the corner of your mouth the last time you went. For you it's just wasted calories that will make you fatter and kill you earlier. I've got a list of all the damage sugar can do - you should read it."

Hooley gritted his teeth, his irritation compounded by the feeling he'd just been caught with his hand in the cookie jar. Working with the most eagle-eyed investigator in London did present a number of challenges.

On the way back from collecting the order he enjoyed a pleasant sense of defiance as he stopped to eat a contraband doughnut, although he very carefully wiped his mouth when he had finished.

As he walked back in Roper gave him a suspicious look.

"You took your time. Did you sneak a doughnut in before coming back?"

Hooley feigned a nonchalance he didn't feel.

"It was busy; you know how they can get down there." He rummaged in a bag he was holding and produced a small piece of chocolate brownie. "I did get this for myself though. It's the smallest thing they do."

He quickly handed over Roper's share and sat down at his own desk quietly congratulating himself on fending off the accusation. He ate the brownie slowly, savouring each mouthful as though he had won first prize in a lottery.

His sense of triumph was short-lived. "You did eat something on the way back. You'd never have been able to eat that brownie so slowly unless you'd already had something to take the edge off your appetite."

A good detective has many skills. Knowing when you're beaten is prime among them. It was time to surrender, otherwise this could go on all day.

"OK, you got me. I confess, but I really felt the need for something sweet. Ever since you got me to cut down on the beer I get these strange cravings from time to time. Anyway, the odd doughnut is not going to do me too much harm, and I did enjoy it."

Roper looked less than convinced but let the matter drop, something the DCI had hoped would happen, reasoning that, at this early stage, the younger man would be intent on reading everything he could about Yebedev. He needed to be quick about it as all the surveillance photos taken by the MI5 team would start arriving from tomorrow morning.

After a couple of false starts the DCI finally got stuck in. If he spent the rest of the day in research, he would treat himself to a couple of pints at his local pub. All good deeds deserved to be rewarded, he thought.

As the day wore on he found the work more interesting than he had expected; but then people worth several billion pounds do have a sort of fascination, and everything was spiced with the mystery about how exactly Yebedev had managed to earn such riches.

According to the MI5 research, he had risen without trace. One minute he was a relatively minor manager working in the state-run energy sector, the next he controlled vast assets. It was obvious that he owed his wealth to his contacts, but who were they?

He was also surprised to learn there was some doubt about whether Yebedev was the ultimate controller of the assets or was acting as a sort of guardian on behalf of a third party.

Along with a great many wealthy Russians, he had a home in London, but unlike many he seemed to spend most of his time actually in the UK while his fellow oligarchs enjoyed life flitting around the world or spending time on luxury yachts.

It appeared that the only time he regularly left the country was for summer holidays in the South of France. He owned a fabulous villa close to one belonging to Sir Elton John, and the odd trip back to Moscow where he maintained a palatial flat in one of the most prestigious and heavily-guarded buildings in the city.

Wealthy people like London for a number of reasons. Great schools, restaurants, stable democracy, easy property laws - but above all were the services devoted to making sure rich people stayed rich. It was the mix of lawyers and financiers that did it.

As noted earlier, what really marked out Yebedev was the way he threw himself into life in London, participating in a wide range of high-profile social events as well as being a generous giver to various charities that took his eye, although none that advocated more financial transparency amongst the very rich.

Many Russians tended to be clannish, partly because of language issues, but it was also a question of trust. They preferred to keep relations with the British on a professional level, treating them as servants - trusted servants, to be sure, but rarely true friends.

A smaller number kept their distance because they regarded themselves as a cut above, their only contact with the locals being to hire them, as butlers, guards or nannies and other domestics. These jobs were sought after because they were well paid, although the employees soon learned they would earn every bit of their money.

In this sense Yebedev followed the rule of thumb. He even had three butlers, which Hooley thought was ridiculous: a senior butler with two junior butlers as his assistants. While the top man stayed close to his boss the under-butlers would be sent on ahead if the family was moving between homes in London and the country, or to the south of France.

But, while Yebedev lived a life of unimaginable luxury, there was nothing, until now, to prove he was involved in anything remotely criminal. He even paid some tax in the UK which, while nothing like representative of his fortune, was still a six-figure sum. He let it be known that since he spent most of his time in England he should at least make a financial contribution.

The briefing document finished with a list of charities to which he had made donations and it did seem that he was very generous, although the cynical side of Hooley couldn't help noticing that Yebedev made sure people were aware of what he donated.

Reaching the end, the DCI thought it was surprisingly light on real detail and was similar to one of those lengthy features that are carried by certain types of magazine: the pictures of glamorous wife, lovely children, fabulous homes and expensive cars all being used to hide the paucity of information.

He turned his attention to the redacted document, which he gave up in disgust after just ten minutes. As far as he was concerned, the amount of stuff that was crossed out with thick black stripes turned it into gibberish. He looked over at Roper. If there was anything to be had out of it then he was the only man for the job.

Glancing at his watch, he saw more time had elapsed than he had expected. It was time to head off.

"I'm going to call it a day. What about you - are you sticking around much longer?"

The younger man looked up and scratched his head.

"I think I will finish now. I couldn't see anything worthwhile in the folders we've been given so I've set up a search on the dark web to see if that produces anything, but I can leave that to run."

As well as his Met terminal, Roper had an 'air-gapped' laptop that meant he could access material that might have compromised the security of the police system.

"I also want to do a general Internet search, but I can do that tomorrow as well. I could do with getting home for a spot of time in my flapping room; I've been noticing that I am a bit out of sorts so that should sort me out."

Roper had developed a unique form of meditation where he could transform his mood through repetitively flapping of sheets of paper, which he found deeply calming. Many years ago, he had been embarrassed to discuss it but Hooley had instinctively understood how important it was and encouraged him to talk about it.

As he learned more, Hooley was deeply impressed with the impact it had on his friend and colleague, seeing first-hand how it helped him relax and focus when events were threatening to overwhelm him.

Roper could easily let his desire to get to the truth of things overwhelm him and it had led once to his suspension from Scotland Yard. If it hadn't been for Hooley's intervention it could have seen him kicked out of the force. Unbeknown to Roper, he had even tried it himself but soon gave up. It might work for Roper, but not for him.

His mind turned to more tangible things as he started to anticipate his first sip of beer. The pleasant fantasy was spoiled as another thought followed hard on its heels. For some reason their trip to MI5 and the subsequent assignment of armed guards had got under his skin.

He was also realising that his obsessing about armed guards was to try and stop himself thinking about what was really bothering him: a nuclear bomb going off in central London. He had a horrible feeling that, when it was found, he and Roper wouldn't be far away. He wondered how effective those protective suits were.

13

He didn't know it, but when Tony Hudson appeared in the front doorway of his mother-in-law's lovely detached house on the outskirts of Epsom, there was muffled cheering from the dark blue Nissan parked a short distance away.

Inside was one of the Courier's best surveillance operators. He had the patience for the work and didn't allow his mind to drift off even when nothing had happened for days. What made Hudson's appearance important was that he was followed out by his wife and mother-in-law, between them carrying the luggage and the baby, meaning they would be heading back to Worcester Park.

Hudson, balancing unsteadily on his crutches, made it to the family car and slid on to the back seat where he could stretch out his plaster-covered leg, while Lilly was secured in her baby seat and the cases went into the boot.

The last four days had been a real struggle for the observation teams since there was nowhere to hide and observe the property. They'd had to keep rotating different vehicles in the hope that local residents wouldn't notice, but the longer they kept at it the more chance there was that a nosy neighbour would spot something.

With everything packed away mother and daughter embraced and broke apart, with the older woman looking like she might cry. Then Anne Hudson got behind the wheel and drove off.

By the time she arrived at Worcester Park the Courier and the rest of his team were waiting. They were planning to take action in four days' time. That date could be moved around, depending on circumstances, but at least they had a target and that helped maintain concentration and morale. It was surprising how quickly even the most professional of teams could become anxious and fretful if they got it into their heads that things were going against them.

As the family moved back into their own home the cameras and listening devices worked smoothly. Always a step ahead, the Courier was thinking about the process of removing the equipment. In an empty property the job was easy enough but this one would have the husband in, which meant he might need subduing.

Even for professionals that was harder than it sounded. People fought back and, after being injected with tranquillisers might suffer an allergic reaction. He didn't want the added complication of the man being dead, as that could lead to a murder investigation.

If the woman vanished, and they left behind no clues, it would confuse any investigation and give them more time to get clean away. That was the key to his success: sweating the details so that, when the job was done, the only thing left behind was an unsolvable puzzle.

He went to make himself a cup of tea. He had the unusual feeling that things were unravelling in some way he couldn't quite identify. He expected it was caused by the unanticipated injury to the husband but he needed to make sure he wasn't missing something obvious.

He was just finishing his tea when one of his team appeared, looking like she had something important to say. He nodded to show she could talk.

"We just listened in on a conversation he had with his office. He's going to work from home for a couple of weeks, but he needs to go in next week for a meeting so they're sending a car for him."

"That sounds promising. What day and time will he be going in?"

"It's scheduled for Wednesday - and he'll be picked up at 10am and should be back by 4pm, at the latest."

"Excellent. That fits nicely with our timetable and they should have fallen back into their normal routine, or as close to it as possible. Spread the word and make sure we are ready to move at noon on Wednesday.

"Can you make sure someone goes to double check the holding cell we have prepared? Can you tell everyone to carefully go through what is expected of them? If there is anything bothering them, no matter how small, come and tell me.

"I want this treated like we are all back at the start line again. Make sure that the day team is ready for a final briefing at lunchtime tomorrow, and I want the same for the night team at 10pm."

The woman was ex-Army, and he suppressed a smile when he noted her right arm quiver as she stopped herself from saluting. At least he was still capable of giving orders, and that had to be a good thing.

14

It had been such a long time ago that he had been able to fool himself it never happened. He'd been in England for fifteen years, quietly inserting himself into London society. His generous contributions to charity and the arts made him a sought-after figure.

He even had a business plan for his donations. He didn't just hand out money to any good cause: he was careful to find out what the really influential people were interested in and had invested in making sure he had the information to always back the causes closest to their hearts.

So, when he heard that one influential society hostess was becoming interested in a revolutionary radiation therapy for treating a rare type of children's cancer, he had quietly stepped in and helped set up a well-funded charitable trust.

He had long ago realised that selective giving was the key to winning acceptance. He knew, and didn't mind, that he would never be part of the inner circle; not even marrying a beautiful and fabulously connected English woman could do that. But he had paved the way for his children to be warmly embraced into the very heart of society, while he was a key player in the next ring out.

So when the call came, Georgi Yebedev had dropped the phone in shock and had to scramble to pick it up. Panic-stricken, he had missed some of what had been said and apologising asked the caller to start again. The voice on the other end might have been gentle in tone but there was steel underneath and he was left in no doubt that his family would be killed if he didn't do precisely what was asked.

He didn't know the people behind the threats but he knew of them - every sensible Russian did - and he knew what they were capable of, so he immediately let it be known that he was ready to receive his instructions.

It was then he was told his first lie. All that was wanted of him was a small task that might take up a few hours of his time as he made sure the secluded guest house on his Oxfordshire estate was available for a few weeks. Do this small thing and never hear from us again.

Three weeks went by and his "guest, or guests" departed, the house cleaned until it shone. He was sure this was to erase any trace of who had been there. He was even told it had been noted how willingly he had acted to repay his debt. It was unfortunate that sometimes people forgot where they came from and that led to unpleasantness which everyone wanted to avoid.

Much as he wanted to believe the whispers, he knew better; the price he had paid was trifling compared to what he had been given. He feared that, now this had started, there would be no escape for him until he had nothing else to give.

The pressure of waiting changed him from a loving, carefree husband and father to someone who took offence easily and literally jumped every time his phone rang or message service beeped. Strangely it almost came as a relief when the call he feared finally came.

This was a new voice, strong and full of power. He was to go to Moscow where he would meet a woman, a hero of the Soviet Union and brilliant scientist. She would provide him with all the answers he could ever need.

A couple of weeks later he was on a flight approaching Moscow. As it descended, his mood hardened.

He might not want to be here but he had to shove his doubts out of his mind. He'd had a good life from the money he had taken and now he needed to get this right so that his family could survive. He was no longer scared for himself.

The scientist had come to meet him at the airport, keen to get started as soon as possible. A short woman, she had a shock of thick blonde hair that looked as though it was styled with the help of a pudding basin, and her clothes were of a design that may once have graced the pages of Soviet era catalogues in the 1950s. But it was her shoes that really stood out: they looked like they could withstand bricks being dropped on them.

As he shook hands with Maria Vasilev, he put these thoughts from his mind. He was a long way from home and the elegant Jimmy Choos in which his wife would occasionally totter about, before surrendering to the pain caused by eight-inch heels.

At first, Vasilev was good company, full of energy and a seemingly inexhaustible source of gossip about the people with whom she worked with. While Yebedev knew none of them, her stories were vivid enough to make him feel like he did.

She was also familiar with several excellent restaurants that had taken classical Russian cooking and elevated it to haute cuisine, so much so that he had surprised himself by asking for a second bowl of a spiced cabbage soup.

This period lasted most of the first week and Yebedev kept his counsel. He knew they were marking time and, on day six, the situation changed. She took him to another restaurant, where the other diners seemed to be drinking heavily but the conversation rarely rose above a murmur.

A waiter came over with a bottle of ordinary vodka and two glasses. It wasn't anything like the fancy brands they had been drinking; this was a basic, popular Russian variety and he suspected it had been chosen to send a clear signal. The party was over.

This was confirmed when Vasilev poured out two glasses and knocked hers back before immediately refilling. She picked up the glass and held it towards him.

"A toast, to the good old days." The second glass disappeared, and he quickly drank his first one.

"You may not be aware, but this used to be a sort of house restaurant for the senior people at the KGB. The food was never very good, but the vodka never ran out and it was understood that whatever was discussed in here stayed in here."

There were no more toasts and the waiting staff stayed away as the scientist talked through exactly what was expected of him. As she talked he was astonished to discover it was a plan that had been decades in the making.

His first task was to provide a secure address in London to which objects could be delivered. Some would be coming from Russia, others from all over the world. Most of the components had been sent to their holding destinations during the 1970s and the people looking after them had recently been alerted they would be on the move again soon. The plan was simple and should ensure no one picked up on the true source of the material.

Yebedev would also need to rent flats for a team of people putting the parts back together. It was expected that this would altogether take six to eight weeks. To his relief he was told he did not need to arrange for the delivery of the plutonium; that would be dealt with separately.

He couldn't help wondering about the damage and vowed to keep his family away from London for as long as he could. It was far too late for him to get out now but, in his heart of hearts, he knew he should have listened to the voice that had warned him: the more people gave you, the more they expected in return.

15

It was the uniformed police officer monitoring the new metal detector who had reminded him. After Hooley had finally cleared the machine at the third attempt, several coins and a penknife had triggered the alarms, the man had said. "A lot of people have started arriving a few minutes early because this thing slows everyone down. Anyway, have a nice day, Sir."

It triggered his memory of being told off for arriving at Roper's apartment too early. Then he realised the younger man hadn't once mentioned his girlfriend since that day. He decided to make sure everything was OK.

He walked into their office and said. "I keep forgetting to ask: how was Samantha's journey to Washington? I take it she arrived OK and you've been chatting to her since."

"We're not talking, so I don't know. The last time we spoke was when you saw me saying goodbye."

This wasn't the answer he expected and it took him a few minutes to translate the words in his head. When they did finally make sense he stared at Roper, hoping he would say more, but the way he was studying his screen suggested that was it unless Hooley could prod more out of him. He decided to leave it for the time being.

It was only 6am. They had decided on a prompt start to maximise the time they could spend reading into what was an unfamiliar subject matter. They worked in what the DCI liked to think of as their customary companionable silence, although Julie Mayweather had once remarked that "it would be easier to get blood out of a stone than get you two to speak when you're doing research".

Although Hooley had scoffed at the suggestion, he did realise they could go all day without talking - so he did make the occasional effort to break things up a bit. He'd been mulling over going on the coffee run and decided to use it as an opportunity to get back to Samantha.

"It can be very difficult when you are working a long way away from each other; it puts a strain on any relationship, so it's probably completely normal if you have had an argument, especially when feelings are running a bit higher after you have to separate."

"We haven't had an argument; we're just not talking."

He could have left it there but now he was intrigued.

"But if you haven't had a row, why aren't you talking? In my experience that sort of silent treatment only happens when you've got real problems. Towards the end of my marriage we both realised the best way to avoid arguments was if we didn't speak to each other at all. I know that's not on the marriage guidance recommended list, but it worked for us."

"The reason we're not talking is perfectly sensible because we are so far apart. Sam and I have worked out that, office to office, we are 3,691 miles apart, so we both need to get on with our lives and jobs.

"Neither of us likes talking for the sake of it and realised that the best thing to do was to not bother each other with pointless conversations. She gets some time off in six weeks, so we will be talking then, when we have something to say, and not before.

"It means we will actually have a conversation to look forward to. It's just common sense when you think about it. We realised that a lot of people ring each other up every day and have nothing important to say and we didn't want that to happen to us."

"Fair enough that you don't want to talk all the time, but haven't you gone a bit far the other way? I mean what about calling each other once a week, say Saturday? As ancient as I am, I can remember a time when I loved talking to my wife."

A look of horror appeared on Roper's face. "You're not talking about phone sex, are you? I think that sounds very unhygienic."

"What? No! Where did that come from?" He felt his face going red. "We hadn't invented phone sex in those days and, anyway, she'd have killed me if I'd tried to suggest it... and I'm not saying that I ever did," he added hurriedly.

"Look. I get it that you two don't want to live in each other's pockets, but six weeks seems an awfully long time and everyone gets in touch after a journey to say they arrived safely. I mean what if something had happened?"

Roper's expression went from irritated to pained, tinged with sympathy.

"That's where so many people make mistakes. If there had been something serious with the journey, then I would have known. It's not as if there could be some sort of crash or incident and for it not to be all over the news. So why ring to tell me she got there safely? She either did or she didn't, and talking about it won't change that.

"And we didn't just pick six weeks without thinking about it. We both deal with intelligence material and, even though hers is very top secret, the same rules apply, especially when you are trying to analyse it and do whatever research needs doing.

"Giving ourselves six weeks means that we should have got on top of whatever you are looking at. If you haven't worked it out by then you are probably never going to, but at least we won't have wasted valuable time by annoying each other.

"So that means we are giving ourselves the best chance to get on top of our jobs without being distracted by someone ringing up to ask how we are. Sam is like me: she hates people asking how she is. No one ever wants to know the real answer; they just want you to say, "I'm fine, thank you." But if you tell people the truth, that maybe you don't feel well, or something, they don't want to know. So what's the point?"

The DCI was genuinely flummoxed. As much as part of him wanted to tell Roper he was wrong, another part of him could see where he was coming from. It did make sense, in a weird kind of way. He supposed that Roper was actually putting forward quite a convincing explanation for keeping a little mystery in your relationships.

He wondered if he and his wife might have benefitted from such an approach. Who was he kidding? She always liked to know what he was up to. Even now, after their divorce, she made a point of checking on his progress, either through their children, or on those unavoidable occasions when they needed to communicate about some shared issues, when she attached a personal question to an email. Was he eating well? Getting enough sleep?

He suspected there were times she hoped to get news that he was suffering a painful, if non-life-threatening, medical condition. But she also just liked to be in the know, and would have been quite unable to cope with Sam and Jonathan's silent approach. That was the thing about taking logic to the extreme: sometimes it could make the brightest people seem a bit daft.

16

Roper was leaning back in his seat, his feet on the desk and eyes firmly closed. He'd been like that, unmoving, for the last half-an-hour. Hooley winced as he thought about trying the same thing. His back would probably implode.

Finally there was movement. Roper swung his feet back to the ground and looked slowly around the office. He was giving every indication that he wasn't quite sure where he was.

"Welcome back," said Hooley. "Am I right in thinking you're been checking out your Rainbow Spectrum?"

"How could you possibly know that?" Roper looked annoyed.

"Trust me. I've worked with you long enough to know the signs. Feet on the desk, eyes shut, unmoving. I don't need to be a detective on that one."

Roper still looked disgruntled but Hooley shrugged. It was what it was. "Don't get side-tracked by me guessing what you were doing. More importantly, have you made any progress? I could tell you a lot about Yebedev but nothing that links him to any crime."

"You were right. I have been using the Spectrum, and for a while I was worried that something was going wrong."

While he had never fully understood how Roper used the Spectrum, Hooley had come to think of it as a method that never failed. Now he knew why his colleague had become oddly defensive when he had raised it.

"Are you still having problems? Maybe it's just something that you need to give time to."

"I've worked it out," said Roper and, as he spoke, the DCI noticed that he was visibly relaxing, with the deep frown slowly disappearing.

"I was looking at it the wrong way. You know I see things in colours so I can assign the same colours to different bits of information. That's what lets me see links that aren't obvious. It's not something I can always control - it just sort of happens.

"I've been digging around in some Russian archives using some translation software to help me read them. I found lots of little bits that fit into different colour codes but I couldn't get everything to link up and point in just one direction.

"Then I added in what we got from MI5 but, again, it just gave me little bits. There's nothing solid out there, other than he seems well-liked on the social circuit and gives quite a bit to charity. We already knew that.

"I was getting a little frustrated but drew up a profile of him anyway, based on what I had. Then I ran it through my Rainbow Spectrum to see what emerged. There was nothing, and I was about to give up when I realised that actually told us quite a lot."

Hooley grinned. "Classic. I'm looking forward to hearing how nothing is a lot."

"Don't you see? There is nothing about his life in Russia before he gets rich. Then nothing emerges about any ongoing links to Russia, or other Russians afterwards. Don't you think that is a bit odd?"

"You're saying it is as though he suddenly appeared," said the DCI, who was starting to think he knew where this was headed.

"I think he might be the ultimate sleeper agent. His cover is buried so deep that even he may not be aware that is what he is. He might have gone his whole life without being activated but now I am certain that is what has happened."

"And are you thinking that is bad news?"

Roper gave him an approving nod. Hooley smiled. He could put up with a bit of patronising in return for demonstrating he had a few little grey cells of his own.

"It's very worrying. While I was at GCHQ I had some pretty intensive training on espionage tactics. Using sleepers is a bit old school, and rarely used, because normally people like to get quick results.

"But if you have a sleeper asset and then activate it, you clearly have a purpose in mind. We know that Yebedev met a Russian nuclear expert so I didn't need to put that into the Spectrum to know what it meant. There is a plan and it almost certainly involves a nuclear weapon.

"Just to be sure, I ran everything through the Spectrum anyway and got something strange."

Hooley looked quizzical.

"The answer came up in a colour I've never seen before. It was a sort of muddy red, as though two colours had been mixed together but you could still see both. Normally you just get the one colour."

"Sounds like a John Le Carre novel," said Hooley. Listening to Roper, he was starting to realise that, wherever this case was heading, it was going to be beyond a bit of straightforward policing. What Roper said next confirmed this view.

"One of the things I learned at GCHQ is to always try and talk to the people who put the original reports together. You can get a lot more background information and insights - the sort of stuff that often gets left out.

"I'm thinking that the Russian scientist behind our suspected suitcase bomb emerged in the 1980s, so we should be able to find people who were directly involved and can fill in some of the missing details."

"Good idea. Let's go and find one of our Cold War warriors."

17

Bill Nuffield sounded genuinely pleased to hear from Hooley, and, after listening to the request, said he was confident he would find someone who would be willing to talk to them.

"Let me ask around and find out who might be happy to talk to you. Old spies can be a little paranoid - I guess it goes with the territory - so a lot will say no because they will think you are trying to set them up in some way.

"The Soviet Republic may have collapsed in 1991 but for a lot of people, who are still around, the Cold War never ended. They argue that the FSB is an awful lot like the KGB it was supposed to replace, and that it would be a mistake to underestimate them. The old KGB saw the writing on the wall very early on and was ready for change."

A low chuckle came down the line. "I suppose I'm starting to sound like a 'Cold War warrior' myself. What I'm trying to explain is that people on our side would be suspicious of being approached by people they don't know.

"I'll probably need to work through intermediaries but that's no problem. I think most people will accept my bona fides and some of them may well be aware of you guys anyway. As soon as I get something I will be back to you."

*

It took a week, but Nuffield proved true to his word - although it was Julie Mayweather who confirmed the meeting when she appeared in their office.

"I've had the Commissioner's office on. They'd been asked to confirm you two are who you say they are. Which, as far as I know, you both are. So, a Sir Robert Rose will be coming here, tomorrow at 2pm."

She was dressed in what she referred to her civilian outfit: a dark grey trouser suit of a classic design that complimented her slim physique without being too showy.

Realising that the DCI was about to protest, she said, "Sorry Brian, there was no negotiation. If you need to talk to this man, then you will have to cancel anything else. It's 2pm tomorrow or not at all. Apparently, he's off on a trek through the South American jungles so won't be around for a month or more."

"He's one of the names I've been checking out," said Roper. "He was one of two deputy Director-Generals in the 1980s. He had a reputation for being extremely competent and was regarded as one of the most successful people they had, as well as being well liked by the staff."

Mayweather folded her arms. "Not a day goes by that you don't surprise me in some way. I'm not complaining, but how come you've been looking into him? I have to admit that I don't recall his name."

"I've been doing a bit of background on who might be willing to talk to us. I guessed they wouldn't put us in touch with a real-life agent, and it seemed pretty obvious that it would need someone senior enough to handle our questions and understand what could and couldn't be discussed without getting special clearance.

"Once I worked that out it was fairly easy to find the names of people who would fit that profile. Sir Robert was top of that list, so I looked into him. If we ended up with someone who was very anti-KGB, we'd have had to take that into account against what they told us."

"Do you mean that type of person would be more likely to believe there was a suitcase bomb, for instance?" asked Hooley.

"That's exactly what I'm thinking. They might see us as meddling in stuff we don't understand so they would make it hard for us to get to the truth. But someone like Sir Robert has always been seen as very calm and very organised. He would be much more likely to stay neutral and give us good information."

Mayweather went to leave, then stopped in the doorway and gave Roper a thoughtful look.

"I'm glad you're on our side, Jonathan. I wouldn't like to think how it would turn out if you ever joined up with the bad guys."

18

They were going in at night, with everything hinging on the most unpredictable element: a crying baby. Since the couple had returned from her mother's house, the infant had taken to waking at all hours of the night and taking time to settle down. Anne Hudson had established a pattern of taking her daughter downstairs and getting comfortable on the sofa. More often than not, both would also fall asleep.

Once that happened, two teams would move in. One would grab the sleeping Hudson; the other would race upstairs to subdue her husband. He might not have been able to put up any resistance, but he could shout.

There was no certainty about when the baby would start crying. Sometimes it started before midnight or sometimes any time up to 4am. Last night she hadn't made a sound, sleeping peacefully until just after 6am.

The Courier glanced at his watch again - just after 2am. He stopped himself from sighing as he didn't want his jitters to infect the operation. Twenty minutes later he jumped as the sound of the little girl starting to cry filled the speakers.

The watchers were always impressed by the speed with which mum responded. She was up and heading downstairs before her husband had shown any signs of realising that something was amiss.

For the next half an hour they watched intently as Anne Hudson soothed her baby, offered her milk and cuddled her close. She went quite still. They waited five minutes to be sure both were asleep.

The snatch squad was dressed in black and merged into the shadows. The closest street lights had been sabotaged days earlier, and the team had pinpointed local CCTV. One camera had been sabotaged by having thick grease smeared on the lens.

The lock proved no barrier and the door was opened with minimal delay and the gang slipped into the house. Barely visible in the gloom, they moved in on the sleeping pair. The leader gave a chopping gesture with his hand: the gesture to move.

Men on either side pinned her arms and legs, a powerful hand was clamped over her mouth and the fourth person picked up the baby and held her with surprising gentleness. The incapacitated mother was injected with fast-acting tranquilliser and bodily lifted into the air.

The baby, miraculously still asleep, was carefully placed back on the settee, surrounded by cushions to keep her stable. Anne Hudson took moments to go under and she was already being carried out by two of the men. Another two raced up the stairs.

The pair with Hudson waited inside until they heard a van draw up. Moving fast, they transferred her into the back of the vehicle. They didn't expect her to wake up but were taking no chances. She was expertly gagged and zip-locks secured her arms and legs.

Back inside the house a third team of two was grabbing the surveillance equipment. In less than five minutes they had everything apart from the cameras and microphones in the couple's bedroom.

The wife had left the door open when she went downstairs. Tony Hudson was snoring loudly, knocked out cold by the liquid morphine he swallowed at bedtime. Ten minutes after breaking in, the job was done and two vehicles carrying the gang and their victim were on their way.

Most of the snatch team piled into the first van and the team leader was picked up in a second van driven by the Courier. As both vehicles moved off, there was no-one to hear the baby take a breath to indicate she was about to start howling.

They headed for the A3: the normally busy stretch of road linking London and the south coast. Even at this hour there would a steady flow of traffic. Driving carefully, the Courier kept a few hundred yards back. Up ahead the first van braked as traffic lights went red.

Waiting patiently, they moved off again when the signal changed. The first vehicle was halfway through the junction when a car, moving at high speed, appeared from the right and smashed straight into it. The force of the impact moved the van 20 feet, the car embedded in its side.

The harsh noise of the impact was replaced by a strange silence. Then the Courier became aware of lights coming on in buildings all around the junction. The massive crash had clearly woken people up and they were looking out of their windows.

He needed to act fast if there was to be a chance that anything could be salvaged from this disaster. Shouting at the men in his vehicle to get ready, he ran to the scene. He was greeted with carnage. The men in the back were lying in positions that would have been impossible for anyone alive, and the woman was crunched awkwardly in one corner, bleeding heavily from head wounds; it looked like she had a broken arm.

The operation was over. In this state Hudson would be rejected by the client. His only option was to clean up and get out of here as fast as possible.

He grabbed the still unconscious woman by her feet and pulled her towards him, then taking her head in his hands he gave it a savage twist, breaking her neck instantly. The action gave him a momentary sense of satisfaction.

Walking to the front of the van he saw the driver was alive but trapped in the wreckage. Getting him out was not an option. The man didn't flinch as he had his neck expertly broken. He knew his family would be well taken care of.

He waved the surviving gang members back into his vehicle and drove away to distant sound of police and ambulance sirens. He was careful to stay within the speed limit.

19

Brian Hooley was looking forward to meeting Sir Robert Rose. Roper had given him a dossier on the retired spy chief which made it clear he had been a hugely influential figure in his day. Not just in the UK, but also working with the CIA back in the days when it was the most powerful US intelligence organisation.

The man had enjoyed a ringside seat for some of the most extraordinary moments since World War II. The DCI had an image in his mind's eye of Sir Robert in the type of handmade suit worn by Prince Charles.

Instead he was introduced to a very fit man in his mid-70s. He came across as mildly eccentric in a good way. He radiated good humour and this was reinforced by his choice of clothing: an electric blue jacket teamed with oversized black trousers and a pair of very expensive shoes that were firmly in the category of "having seen better days".

Sir Robert quickly took control. Retirement had done nothing to dilute his natural air of command.

"You two are getting quite a reputation," he said, settling into one of the chairs in Mayweather's office which had been borrowed for the interview.

"As you know, my side can be a bit sniffy about policemen, but there is more than a grudging respect for you two; you seem to make quite a team, and the threats we face have blurred the lines between the ways we all operate. I give you a terror leader; you show me a master criminal.

"Everyone is fascinated by Mr. Roper's Rainbow Spectrum. It sounds like the codename for some sort of undercover operation that we used to run back in the 1960s. I can quite imagine Michael Caine playing the lead role in a film."

The retired spy chief tugged at the sleeves of his shirt and carried on. "I gather you are interested in what I can recall about Maria Vasilev?" He sipped at the coffee the DCI had poured for him, then looked at the cup with raised eyebrows.

Hooley correctly interpreted his reaction. "I'm afraid that Jonathan and I have developed a shared passion for strong coffee. I forget that it's not to everyone's taste. Would you prefer something else, or can I make a weaker version?"

Sir Robert dismissed his concerns with a smile and wave of his hand. "Not to worry; it's at the top end of my tolerance, admittedly, but it will keep me sharp for the next hour or so - and I suspect I am going to need that with you two.

"Oddly enough, Vasilev is one of those who has stuck in my memory. At the time you imagine you will recall everything, but it's surprising how many people and events slip the memory. She appeared in the 1980s as one of many young Soviet prodigies.

"She was assigned to their nuclear weapons programme and before long there were rumours that she was making some sort of progress. We didn't know what that progress was, but it was clear that her bosses were getting excited.

"I don't think it's any secret that by that stage we had quite an insight into their operations; a lot of Russians could see the writing on the wall and were making decisions to improve their own situations by making a little money from us.

"Without going into too many details, we were able to build up a reliable picture of her. Vasilev was certainly no idealist. But she was driven by a sense of pride in her work, not some misplaced desire to defeat the West. We confirmed that Vasilev was working on a miniaturisation programme."

He slowed down, and Roper took the chance to ask a question. "Do you think technology has improved enough to make that more likely?"

The retired spy chief looked thoughtful and took his time answering.

"There have been some big advances, but there are still problems." He spread his hands in an apologetic gesture. "Allow me to digress a little. You will of course recall Winston Churchill's famous saying that Russia was 'a riddle, wrapped in a mystery inside an enigma'.

"While that was a wonderful observation it has given rise to the idea that all Russians are fiendishly brilliant, which is a bit misleading. The old Soviet Union operated in the same way that any bureaucracy does. In a way their job is to manage the allocation of limited resources to all the competing demands.

"Even the old KGB couldn't just keep pursuing some pet project without proving there was a chance of getting a result. I imagine that is still the same - although I am retired, after all."

Roper was looking very bright-eyed. "With your experience, and what you said about the pressure to get results, do you think she would have given up the project?"

"Perhaps but also recall that I mentioned events. Maybe Vasilev had given up on the idea a few years ago, but something has brought it back to the front of her mind. The one thing I can tell you with total certainty is that such ideas are very seductive. It is rare for them to die away altogether; more a question of going into hibernation."

"So you think there is a very real threat: Not just weapons as deterrents, but people looking for opportunities to use them against an enemy?" Roper had leaned forward as he spoke.

Sir Robert took a moment as he gathered his thoughts.

"You have to remember that life was a bit more straightforward in my day. We always knew who our enemies were and could plan accordingly. I think today's generation have forgotten that there are people out there who wish harm on us and our way of life.

"I'm not talking about terrorists. They will always exist. What I am talking about is state-sponsored aggression. So, yes, I do think there is a real threat."

That answer seemed to satisfy Roper, and they spent another hour with Sir Robert. By the end of the interview Hooley was pretty certain that the former secret service man was holding something back, but he couldn't quite place what. He supposed there must be a million secrets in that world.

The meeting could have gone on longer but the DCI was happy to end it after two hours. Roper was showing all the signs of becoming too fixated, starting to ask dogmatic questions that earned him quizzical looks.

Hooley knew that Roper could blur the lines from focused work practice to a personal crusade. He was anxious to keep the balance right because getting it wrong was what had led to him being suspended on misconduct charges.

As they showed Sir Robert out, the DCI walked back to his desk wondering what would happen if everyone brought Roper's directness to the party. He wasn't sure the world was quite ready for that day just yet.

20

Roper was holding his jacket, his eyes screwed up as he dabbed sticky tape at bits of fluff only he could see. The DCI left him to it. Roper had a surprisingly complex relationship with his clothing and when he was being this careful it indicated he was thinking hard.

But, much as the DCI remained fascinated by the extraordinary way in which Roper's mind worked, he knew it was perfectly possible that his colleague might not say anything for the rest of the day.

Ordinarily that was never an issue, but this time he was eager to hear what Roper had made of their meeting so took the unusual step of interrupting him.

"Sir Robert wasn't quite as I expected. I anticipated meeting an old Cold War warrior with a bristling moustache."

To his surprise, Roper looked cross. "If you had listened properly to what I said about him there would have been no surprise. To my mind he was exactly what I was expecting. As I told you, he was the man who kept the organisation running smoothly; he wasn't one of the old-school types at all."

Roper could try the patience of a saint, and Hooley thought there was little wonder his dentist had recently told him that he had started grinding his teeth.

He said: "What I meant was that back in his day the threat of nuclear war was taken very seriously; something I know a little bit about, since I was around then. I recall that even some quite sensible people were talking about taking out the Soviets before they took us out."

Roper didn't respond, so Hooley tried a different approach. He said, "What did you make of what he told us?"

"I think he was very rational and didn't seem to be pushing any sort of agenda. I particularly liked his explanation as to why he thought Vasilev probably wasn't building a suitcase bomb, although he was right to warn about developments in technology."

He broke off, then added: "In a way, he reminded me of how you help me to understand the world better. That same approach of letting you work it out for yourself."

The DCI was taken aback by this unexpected comment. "That sounded suspiciously like a compliment. Tell you what, I'm going to go mad and celebrate by getting the coffees in. I take it you'd like yours accompanied by the usual bag of doughnuts?"

That brought a smile to the younger man's face. "That would be great. At the moment all I can really do is load up on as much information as possible. We don't really know anything yet, so I expect I am going to be tapping into the Rainbow Spectrum quite a lot. A good sugar hit is just the thing."

21

Two phone calls had reduced the Courier to a cold fury. Dubois had instantly dismissed his suggestion that he provide her with an alternative victim for her fantasy trip. Instead, she had demanded the return of the money within the next 48 hours.

To really rub it in, Dubois had carefully told him that she did not reward failure and because of what had happened she never wanted to hear from him again. Her voice had been as cool as usual but he detected a note of malicious pleasure. She clearly belonged to the school that said the only time to kick someone was when they were down.

The second call had proved every bit as infuriating. The gambling club he used had informed him that the money he had paid them so far was being treated as a joining fee that only got him through the door. To get access to the table he needed to prove he had the cash equivalent available of five million pounds.

So now he was down the fee that would have come in at ten million pounds. Factor in tens of thousands more on costs, including the gambling cash, and he had largely wiped out his cash reserves. What he had left was earmarked for the families of his dead operatives. He briefly considered withholding this cash but knew he couldn't. The guarantee of financial security was what allowed him to keep such an accomplished team - and ensured their silence.

Very reluctantly he set up the instructions that would see the client repaid. He only had one option. He had never quite relinquished his previous role as a smuggler but largely subcontracted his operation to a trusted aide who paid him a steady fee in return. Now he needed cash fast, which meant he needed to let it be known that the Courier was back in business. There were plenty of people out there who would willingly pay for his specialist delivery services.

His mind made up, he calmed down enough to be more rational. While he was still angry over the crash that had ruined the project, he had to admit it was sheer bad luck and could have been a lot worse.

To say the crash was attracting attention was an understatement, with the biggest source of curiosity being the discovery of Anne Hudson's body and nobody being able to explain how she had got there.

On social media the husband was being smeared by people who claimed he must have been involved, despite there being no evidence to support the idea. From watching the TV news reports it turned out the driver of the car had been as high as a kite on a potent mix of alcohol and drugs.

The Courier read the latest newspaper reports carefully and was reassured that the police investigation was going nowhere; at least their careful precautions had proved up to the task, and he sincerely hoped it stayed that way.

He started to put some serious thought into how he was going to mark his return to his old business. With a growing demand for slaves, especially fit young women and children, plus people who wished to move highly valuable artefacts without attracting the attention of the authorities, it was a business where you could make a lot of money.

He started letting a few people know he was back on the scene and, within a few hours, the first tentative replies had returned. Today he was meeting with one of his best contacts, a former Serbian army major who had a reputation for being tough, discreet and brilliantly connected.

He also served as a sort of unofficial contact point for wealthy east Europeans and enjoyed especially good relations with many of the wealthiest Russians - in the past, they had been very good for business.

So long as you delivered the goods at the time and place agreed, they were happy to pay up for services rendered. With luck he would have clawed his way back within the next few years.

As dull as he found the work, the money would allow him to give serious thought to that retirement plan. What he was doing wasn't without risk. New players were coming into the business all the time and, while most worked at the bottom of the market, it was only a matter of time before the top end started feeling crowded. Indeed, he knew he was already causing ripples of discontent since his return was not being greeted with joy unbounded.

Nonetheless, he was one of the best around. If you had a project that was making others blink, then the Courier was the man. His fees were huge, but they came with an assurance that any task would be completed.

Sitting in the living room of his small flat near Sloane Square he decided to treat himself to a dinner out at a nearby Drones restaurant. He hadn't intended to go back to his old line of work but now that he had made the decision he would celebrate it.

Because of the new players who had emerged since he had last been directly involved he would have to tread carefully, and it would be sensible to spend a little of his cash on obtaining good intelligence about the nature of the opposition he would be up against. He knew that some of them were every bit as ruthless as he was.

22

It had been two weeks since the failed attempt to grab Anne Hudson and the officer in charge of the investigation, Detective Inspector Stan Newlove, was running out of ideas and any leads. As he paced around his office, his thoughts turned to his old mate Brian Hooley and his 'oddball' sidekick Roper.

He was reminded of them when he received an unexpected phone call from Deputy Commissioner Julie Mayweather. She was after his input on another matter and suggested he come to the Victoria office to talk to her.

Newlove wasn't a fanciful man, but he knew when the stars were aligning. It had been five years since he's last seen Hooley, or even been in the same building as him. Then, just after the DCI had been on his mind, a rare opportunity had presented itself: he could team up with his old mate while talking to Mayweather.

He fired off an email summing up the situation and was delighted to hear back saying he should drop by Hooley's office after his meeting and he could have all the time he needed to talk things through.

On the day, his discussion with Mayweather only took half an hour and she ended it by offering to walk him round to Hooley's office.

"Brian told me you were making full use of your time over here: something I approve of. I gather you're working on that odd case about the woman with a broken neck. As it happens that's exactly what I'd normally get

Brian and Jonathan to take a look at. It sounds right up their street - a mystery with no clues."

Newlove gave her a rueful smile, but before he could speak she cut him off with a wave of her hand.

"Don't worry. What I meant was that it sounds the kind of thing they love, but they are going to have to be careful about getting too involved as they are on a pretty major investigation at the moment and that is the priority."

"Thank you, ma'am. I will bear that in mind. To be honest, I think I just need someone to talk to and check I'm not missing some vital detail."

The DCI was talking on the phone as his old buddy walked in, his chair turned so his back was to the door. Newlove glanced at Roper but he appeared to have eyes only for his computer. Just then Hooley swung back and smiled, pantomiming that he was nearly at the end of his call.

Quickly bringing the conversation to an end he jumped up and extended his hand.

"Great to see you, Stan. How are you? It's been a while since we last spoke; everything all right at home?"

"All good, thanks mate, and I was sorry to hear about you and your missus. I sometimes wonder why Yvonne puts up with me and all the hours this job takes out of you." He looked at Jonathan. "I take it this is the famous Mr. Roper?"

"Yup, that's him. Hang on a minute; I'll prod him so you can say hello - although I warn you now that he does have his own special approach to meeting people."

Despite being talked about, Roper was lost in whatever document he was looking at, so Hooley resorted to his trusted method of grabbing his attention - he threw a scrunched-up piece of paper at his head.

Roper looked up, blinking rapidly, saw Newlove and asked the DCI: "Who's that?"

Hooley gave his friend a conspiratorial wink and said, "This is DI Stan Newlove, another long-serving Metropolitan Police detective."

The younger man seemed unimpressed and was turning back to his computer when Newlove called out: "I'm in charge of the investigation into the case of the young mother who was grabbed from her home. It's a bloody strange case and we can't make any sense of it. I was hoping you might find time to have a quick look and give me your opinion."

Roper looked surprisingly keen. "I've been following that one. I had been wondering if the woman was taken because her husband was involved in something, or maybe they'd borrowed money from the wrong people?"

"We've looked into all that and there's nothing to suggest they were anything but an ordinary middle-class family. All their financials are straightforward, the husband has a decent job, they're not involved in drugs or have any other criminal connections. We've even been looking at the neighbours but everyone seems to be straight as a die and the husband claims there are no issues with anyone, not even a dispute about parking spaces.

"I've even been trying to establish if it might be a case of mistaken identity - the wrong woman was snatched - but that's getting us nowhere. This is rapidly becoming one of the most confusing cases I have been involved with.

"It has all the hallmarks of a professional job. Somebody went to a great deal of bother in knocking out all the local CCTV and there is evidence that there may have been some sort of equipment placed in the house."

"Surveillance equipment?" asked Roper, who hadn't taken his eyes off Newlove.

The DI nodded. "That's as good a guess as any. It was one of my best forensics people who spotted it. It looks as though something was placed in the sitting room and also slight evidence in the bathroom, kitchen and overlooking the stairs."

"You don't suppose it's got anything to do with MI5, or some other spy outfit?" asked Hooley. His recent dealings with the organisation had improved his opinion of them but he was very well aware of their abilities.

"Yeah, we have tried that as well. But, trust me, you don't get a lot of sense when you ask spooks if they have been up to something they don't want anyone to know about. I've got a few more lines of inquiry out but I'm not hopeful.

"And if one more person cracks that joke about 'if I told you I'd have to kill you', I may not be responsible for my actions." He stopped talking and thumped his right fist into his left hand a couple of times. Hooley could guess what was coming.

Surprisingly it was Roper who beat everyone to it. "You want us to have a look at it for you, but you're embarrassed at passing this on so soon after taking control of the case because it will make you look incompetent."

Newlove went very pink and started spluttering. "I wouldn't put it in those words."

"Neither would I, but I did warn you that Jonathan is out on his own when it comes to making direct statements," said Hooley. "You should have seen your face though. I thought your jaw was going to hit the ground."

He patted his friend on the shoulder. "Look, what Jonathan meant to say was that we would be delighted to have a look at it for you. I've never heard of anything like this either. It does seem very professional yet with no obvious motive. We are working a case at the moment, but that is going so slowly I would be delighted to have something else to worry about."

Newlove looked relieved and opened up a briefcase he had been carrying.

"I've got a case overview in here, plus I asked my team to prepare a list of headings which can give you some idea of what else is available. As you can imagine we've generated a lot of material, but this is more by way of an overview."

He handed over the material and went to shake Hooley by the hand, but the DCI had other ideas.

"If you can stay around for another hour or so I can get out for a quick drink; may have to be non-alcoholic, but it would be good to catch up. I can find you somewhere you can work if you're up for it."

The DI looked delighted. "I'd like that very much indeed - and I had allowed the rest of the day for this visit, so no problem. Give me a desk and I'll keep myself busy until you're ready."

23

It was close to two hours before Hooley was able to get back to Newlove and, as he left to collect his friend, he asked Roper if he could get him anything whilst he was out.

"No, thanks. I'm too hungry to wait for you so I'll go in a minute. There is one thing though. Could you ask the Detective Inspector about the attempted break-in a few days after the wife was found murdered? I can't see any reference to it."

"Yeah, sure, although I hadn't realised there had been a break-in - must have missed that."

He took his friend to a small pub off the beaten track; it was busy without being overrun, and they found a space at the bar which ran along almost two thirds of the pub before making a dog leg to the right.

They shared a bottle of sparkling water and Newlove remarked wistfully on the good old days.

"I know what you mean. This would have been the start of a lengthy session with no return until tomorrow morning, at the earliest. Mind you, I think my liver is probably quite grateful that things are a lot calmer nowadays."

After half an hour Hooley was starting to apologise to his friend about the need to get back to work, which Newlove took in good spirit.

"I never expected to get any time in the pub, so this has been a bonus, and I am really grateful you guys are going to take a look at my case."

Hooley tapped his forehead. "I almost forgot: Jonathan has a question. He wants to know what happened about the break-in."

The DI had been about to swill the last of his drink and now stopped with the glass half-way to his mouth.

"Does he mean the one that happened after the wife was snatched?" Seeing Hooley nod he carried on. "How on earth did he know about that? I thought we'd done a good job of keeping that under wraps and I made sure that never got anywhere near the media."

He looked so perplexed that Hooley had to laugh.

"It's a funny thing about Roper: although he is a bit of a loner – actually, make that a lot of a loner - he does seem to have his own special array of contacts. There aren't many of them, at least I don't think so, but they all seem to be plugged in."

The DI gave a rueful shake of the head. "Well, you can tell him the truth is we're not sure what happened. A neighbour was adamant that he saw someone, dressed in what he described as a ninja outfit including face mask, lurking in the front garden.

"Our boys had left contact numbers after talking to everyone, so he rang, and we got a patrol car there within 10 minutes, but there was no sign of any break-in or an attempted break-in. It was double-checked in the morning and still nothing, so it's a bit of a puzzle.

"The neighbour was adamant about what he saw so we've left it open, but it is, like the rest of this case, a mystery. Even when we get a line of inquiry it just goes nowhere. I've never worked a case quite like it."

Hooley was back in the office and was telling Roper that there was nothing on the break-in.

"Stan was quite surprised that you knew anything about it at all. He said they had kept it quiet, mostly because they couldn't make anything of it, and added that only a handful of people knew about what the neighbour had reported."

As he spoke he watched Roper very closely and was unsurprised to see an enigmatic expression creep across his face. While he would never tell a direct lie, he was remarkably good at evading questions. Any suggestion he was connected to a private network of information was greeted with surprise.

"I hadn't realised there was so much secrecy over it," he said. "I thought I must have read it in the news, but I was obviously wrong. It does seem to be very interesting though. To have someone going back to the house reinforces the idea that a lot of planning went into the woman being taken."

"How have you arrived at that conclusion, then? Stan's been on the case for a while; he didn't mention anything like that over lunch and he's one of the most thorough and open-minded detectives you will meet."

"Well, it was the suggestion that they think surveillance equipment was in the house that got me thinking; and we also have the witness who saw someone trying to break in. I've thought of various reasons why that might be and the most obvious is that they left something behind.

"It can't have been something obvious, because the police have been all over that house, so maybe it was something very unusual. Do you recall that case we worked on where someone was using AI-controlled surveillance equipment?

"What if it was something like that - tiny, difficult to see and very specialised? It's the sort of thing that can get left behind when people clear out."

"OK. That's an interesting theory, but does it take us anywhere?"

"Well I did think that if they had surveillance gear in there they needed somewhere to monitor it from, which means there is one thing you should ask the Detective Inspector; I've looked at that road on Google Street View and it's not the sort of place where you could park a van for very long, not without it being noticed. So maybe there are some rental properties very close?"

Hooley wasted no time in calling Newlove and filled him in on Roper's analysis. His news was greeted with a low whistle of appreciation.

"Funnily enough we have got a list of rental properties in that area. I wasn't thinking exactly along the lines Roper suggested but I wondered if they had a base. There is a house almost opposite that is rented out to an offshore company. It was taken a few months ago and has another eight months on the contract.

"We've been trying to get hold of the company, but no success, and we've been in the property and found nothing. It is on my list of things to get around to, but I think it has just gone straight to the top.

"We'll go through that place with a fine-toothed comb. The officers who first checked it out reported that the place was very clean and tidy, so someone has gone to a bit of effort - which makes me think there may be something to Jonathan's idea.

"I'll let you know how we get on but it's going to take a while. I'll need a full scenes of crime team going through that place and I'm going to have to argue to get the budget for it and then the time needed.

"But Jonathan's theory that there might have been a team of people in the house monitoring cameras and sound devices should give me exactly the ammunition I need when I go to the boss. He's desperate for a result on this so hopefully he'll sign off for what we need.

"I tell you what, there will be more than a glass of fizzy water in this if this gives us a result. You can tell Jonathan that his fan club just grew by one."

24

"Would it be helpful if I explained to you how a self-sustained fission chain reaction happens? It's fascinating and quite amazing how they worked all this out in the beginning."

"No, no, no…" Hooley could think of nothing he wanted less, and to get his point across he stuck his fingers in his ears. He and Roper had been batting this back and forth for most of the morning.

Roper was obsessing about the need to talk the DCI through the technical details. Hooley was equally determined to avoid getting drawn into a prolonged conversation about a subject that he had little interest in beyond the obvious: nuclear bomb… very bad.

"All I need to know is: how plausible is the threat from one of these devices? You and MI5 have raised this, so what's a poor old copper like me supposed to make of it? It sounds terrifying, but is it ever going to happen?"

He looked over at Roper and noticed his complexion - or complete lack of it. He was extremely pale-skinned normally but when he was working flat out he seemed to go a whiter shade of pale.

He made the ill-advised decision to crack a joke.

"If it started snowing and you went outside you'd look like the Invisible Man: just your suit and hair showing."

Roper treated this attempt at comedy with the contempt it deserved.

"I suppose you want what you like to call the 'idiot's guide' to all this?" He sighed heavily before carrying on. "Well the truth is that a suitcase bomb is more possible than I had thought. The last time I read about it was at school and then the argument was that it was just a fantasy and would need a technological revolution to come true.

"But if you think in terms of small, portable nuclear devices, then you are starting to talk about real possibilities. Some of the biggest changes have come in the electronics you need to get one of these to work - they've got a lot smaller, lighter and more reliable.

"Then the components needed have reduced in size and weight, so that all helps too. Maybe you might need a few suitcases to spread the load, but you could make it happen. In fact, the technology to do so has been around for a lot longer than I had realised."

Roper paused and gave him an appraising look. "You do know more than you let on. Are you sure you don't want all the technical details?"

"No."

"Fine. Well, we also need to remember that someone trying to make a small bomb is probably more concerned with generating radiation since the explosive capacity will be relatively low. That's why people talk about 'dirty bombs.'"

"This is not doing a lot for my peace of mind."

"There is some good news. Whatever method is used to create a device that can be detonated, it is going to need weapons-grade plutonium and that's not the easiest thing to get. Even at the height of the Cold War, both sides were careful about who got their hands on that.

"Even today, with the technology far more widely available, it is still hard to find and those people who do have it tend to want to hold on to their stocks because it is so rare. There is one big unknown about all of this." He stopped talking and looked directly at Hooley. The DCI thought it was never a good sign when he did that.

"You're going to tell me something I'm really not going to like, aren't you? Well, there's no point in sitting on it."

"The old KGB were said to have established buried weapons caches all over Western Europe. Most of those were traditional weapons and ammunition that would have been used to arm revolutionary groups, so very dangerous, but quite small scale.

"But it was also claimed that some of the stockpiles had nuclear potential. No one is quite sure what that means. It could be that we are talking about lots of different bits of equipment stored in lots of different places. Or it could be that they left entire weapons systems in place, ready to be used in action the moment they were unearthed."

"Well you're certainly managing to give me the shivers. How likely do you think it is to be true?"

"I don't think anyone really knows, maybe not even the Russians themselves. I found some reports about a Russian defector who was claiming that the Soviets had "lost" some of their nuclear stockpiles. No one could decide whether to believe him, and in the end it was officially claimed that he was just bluffing to try and cause a bit of panic.

"It may be that there are nuclear stockpiles hidden away and someone must have the locations. But at the height of the Cold War both sides were operating on a strict need-to-know basis, so it may be only a small handful of people are now left who know the truth."

"So how does this impact on what we know about the meeting between Maria Vasilev and Georgi Yebedev?"

"Again, that's hard to try and deconstruct. If there are stockpiles, and she helped put the contents together, I doubt if she would have been involved in choosing the locations. From what I know the KGB kept the scientists well away from that end of things.

"But maybe she has been looking for information and recently found it. That could explain why there was a meeting. Maybe some of this stuff is here in the UK and is just waiting to be dug up and used here in London; it would cause panic.

"With the wind in the right direction you might be looking at millions of people being affected."

Hooley's mouth had gone dry. "I don't like to think about that. I can't begin to imagine a bomb exploding, let alone the disruption it would cause. There would be mayhem."

25

"We can't be certain about any of this." As he spoke, Hooley knew he was trying to make the situation sound less frightening than it was. The trouble was that they might not have had any hard evidence, but Roper was convinced - and that was the next best thing.

The pair were briefing Julie Mayweather after she called them in for an update. This was the second time he had gone through what they knew, or suspected, and he wasn't finding it any easier. A gloomy silence filled the room, in sharp contrast to the times when the three had animated discussions about the wildest theories.

Mayweather and Hooley were sitting down while Roper, full of nervous energy, was slowly pacing around. The DCI was staring off into the middle distance, a frown on his face, and his boss thought it highly likely this concern was mirrored in her own expression.

She watched Roper as he moved around. He looked very pale and his skin seemed more tightly stretched over his face than normal. She felt a need to reassure him.

"You're quite right, Jonathan. You are quite right to raise this in the way you have. Just because we may not like what you are saying doesn't mean we shouldn't be listening to it. We need to examine every possibility so that we can be thinking about the right response.

"One thing I do have to ask. Assuming the worst, do you have any sense of what timeline we are operating to? Is this stuff already here, or is it on the way? We clearly need to start thinking about how this might be smuggled in."

Roper sat forward, his eyes bright as he ran through his thoughts.

"My best guess is that they still need to bring it in and that is going to take a lot of planning. But I'm not sure about an alert. That might create panic and tip them off that we know."

Hooley nodded. "My instinct would be to play it close for a while. You're going to have to tell key people but we should try to keep it as limited as realistically possible. The government can raise the threat level warning without having to be specific."

"What if one of these nuclear stockpiles is here in the UK already?" Mayweather wanted to know.

"I think that is the least likely option," said Roper. "There are very few - a handful is the best guess, and it is highly likely that the majority are in the area covered by the old Soviet Union.

"There may be one or two in Europe at most, but the records indicate that they never tried to get into Britain. They didn't need to take the risk. There are plenty of seriously isolated spots in Western Europe where something like that could be easily concealed and picked up again without risking witnesses."

Mayweather had another question.

"How are they going to get the weapons-grade plutonium here?"

"It won't be easy, but it won't be impossible either; it just needs very careful planning. You don't need a huge amount in terms of weight, just a few ounces. With proper shielding it still won't be that large. Just bulky and heavy."

Mayweather looked at Hooley. "Reminds me of our first case."

"It does. Those were a worrying few days."

Roper looked quizzical so she explained. "Brian and I first put the Special Investigations Unit together because of a case involving a Russian called Alexander Litvinenko. He was poisoned in central London - and it was always suspected the Russian state was behind it."

"Yes, I have been reading about that recently because I wondered if there were links to our case. He was contaminated with polonium-210."

"We didn't know any of that at first, so we were visiting all the places where Mr. Litvinenko had been and picking up traces of radiation without realising it. Brian was among those who needed to be checked out.

"I was very concerned about him, and the rest of the team. We had a big test carried out here in these offices because of contamination. We had to keep it very quiet because it would have caused a lot of distress. As it was they discovered traces all over London, as I recall. There's something about being poisoned by something you can't see which is especially frightening.

"In a way it is very similar to what happened in Salisbury, where the Russian spy and his daughter nearly died. No-one realised at first that they had been poisoned with a nerve agent."

Hooley rubbed his hands together.

"When we realised the full implications of the Litvinenko case it caused quite a bit of panic. There was even talk about setting up those mobile decontamination units. The decision had to go right to the Prime Minister. In the end he was saved from having to do anything because the experts said you would have needed to come into direct contact with the polonium."

Roper said. "Was it ever established how it got to London?"

Mayweather shrugged. "There were a lot of theories. It came here under Russian diplomatic immunity or was smuggled in from a container ship - as you know, there are many smuggling routes. Some even said they brought it in on a domestic airline flight from Moscow to London.

"In those days I don't think the technology at our border controls was good enough to pick it up, although I think things are a lot better now."

"This is fascinating, and I need to see your original files," said Roper. "Now that I know you were both around, I will be able to ask you questions."

Hooley made a "hah" sound.

"You can ask any questions you like, but I may not have all the answers you are going to need. Some things about that case will stay with me for the rest of my life. A lot of it I've just forgotten."

He lapsed into silence until realising he was coming under an especially searching stare from Mayweather.

"I suppose I might as well tell you. My wife wouldn't let me in the house for two days. I had to bring her a signed medical certificate that said I was totally clear of radiation before she would allow me through the front door. I had to stay at a local bed and breakfast.

"The scientists involved all decided I was bonkers because I kept badgering them for this certificate but eventually they gave in. Even then she was still suspicious. I had to post the certificate through the letter box and then wait at the end of the drive.

"When she decided I was OK to come back in she made me go into the garage first and take all my clothes off. Then she made me wait until it was dark before burning everything in the back garden. Even one of my favourite jackets. I was heartbroken about it. I'd had it since I got made detective - it had real sentimental value for me."

Mayweather was laughing so hard she had to dab at her eyes.

"You managed to keep that one secret, Brian. If the team had found out you would never have heard the end of it."

"Trust me, I put a lot of effort into making sure that was kept very quiet. I told the scientists that everything we did was covered by the Official Secrets Act; at least that stopped them blathering."

Roper was looking puzzled. "I don't know why you think this is a laughing matter. I think Mrs. Hooley was being very sensible."

The look the DCI gave him reminded Roper that he really wasn't very good at reading body language.

26

Mayweather glanced at her watch. Her father had given it to her to mark her becoming a Met police officer. It was a cherished memento and had been there through the key moments of her career. Looking at it now was an uncomfortable reminder that a countdown clock was ticking.

"I need to go and see the Commissioner. He's one of the people who definitely needs to know the direction we are going, and you can be certain that he, in turn, will take it straight to the top. That means Downing Street will be involved."

Hooley may have briefly lightened the atmosphere, but now that was replaced with a brisk determination to take care of business.

"While I'm with him, is there anything you want to flag up? Do you need more people? This is going to be one of those times when there's not going to be a problem getting you the resources you need."

Hooley rolled his shoulders to try and alleviate the ache in his back. This case was a pain in the neck - literally.

"There was one thing you might be able to chase up for us. Bill Nuffield made it plain that we are not seeing everything that MI5 has. I think events have moved on and they should review that decision.

"He told us he was working hard to get what he could and I think he's on our side, so maybe a push from the Commissioner will help. I get the feeling the spooks can get a tad obsessed about clearance levels. Jonathan and I do need to know.

"If he's right in his assessment – and, how many times has he proven himself? - then the fewer the obstacles we face from our own side the better. I'm not saying this is the case, but if there is a bit of top-dogging going on then it needs to be nipped in the bud."

"I think that last point is well made, Brian. I don't want us to get into a situation where we turn around in a few weeks and wish we had done more to ensure things ran smoothly."

She glanced over at Roper. "I also agree with Brian about your ability to predict what might happen. Are you using your Rainbow Spectrum on this? The Commissioner is bound to ask."

"It's very strange but I keep hearing that all sorts of people are aware of the Rainbow Spectrum. Why is everyone so interested in it?"

"Because you have invented a unique approach to problem-solving. It's left a lot of serious people seriously impressed. To go back to my earlier question: what would you like me to tell the Commissioner? Are you using it?"

"The honest answer is yes and no. 'Yes,' because I am starting to store a lot of information in that part of my mind but also 'no', because nothing is quite making sense yet. But you can say it is starting to come together."

"I might find a way to put a more positive spin on that, Jonathan, but thank you for your honesty." She stood up and as she reached for her jacket, Hooley cut in with a laugh. "You could tell him about my 'lager protocol' if you like."

"Ah, I think I know this one, Brian. It's the idea that there's nothing that can't be put into the right perspective with the help of a nice cold pint of lager. While there may be some truth in that I think I may stick to the Rainbow Spectrum for now."

She made to leave; then a thought struck her.

"Regarding that polonium case. You and I were introduced to a quite brilliant scientist who was brought in to beef up security. His name was Paul, something. Was it Paul Ross?"

"Paul Moss, that was his name," said Hooley who had surprised himself with his recall. "Must be going on ten years since we spoke to him."

"It probably is, but I bet he's going to be a very good person for Jonathan to start with as he looks to see how something might be brought into the country. Who knows, maybe they have sniffer dogs for that now."

"Dogs would be no use because radiation doesn't have a smell - at least, nothing anyone has found up to now - but I do know there has been a lot of top secret developments in recent years. If your guy knows about them then he could be really helpful."

"I'll track him down," said Hooley. "He should remember me so that will help speed things up although, from what Jonathan just said, it sounds like another reason to get our security clearances beefed up."

The two detectives left Mayweather and headed back to their office. Roper was just about to get back into his own research when Hooley called out.

"Rather than just work on until I can't read anymore - and I know you have never reached that point - let's set a deadline of 7.30pm to call it a day then we can head off to my local Indian for dinner."

Roper's response was animated. "That would be great. We haven't done that for ages and I have been building up to trying a new dish."

Hooley couldn't hide his surprise.

"I was under the impression that you eating anything other than lamb rogan josh would bring you out in spots."

"This time I'm going to have a chicken vindaloo."

"Are you sure? That's one of the hottest things they make; I've never dared try it, but I did see some bloke going very red in the face last Saturday night. He was eating it for a bet and I got the impression the kitchen made sure he remembered the experience. He was a bit loud when he came in but soon quietened down after that."

"I want to try out a theory I've been working on. I've been practicing eating chillis at home and I have managed to raise my resistance to them. I can manage to eat a Scotch Bonnet now which is at least 100,000 Scoville Units."

"Well, I don't know about your Scovilles, but I do know that a Scotch Bonnet is lethal. If you can manage one of those, then I guess you will be fine. But may I ask what's bringing about this desire to try something different?"

"I've been reading about chilli pepper and found out it has a lot of good properties. The ingredient that causes the sensation of heat is capsaicin - that can help with reducing blood sugar, boost circulation, which may help with dementia, and provide help against strokes.

"When you eat it, it also makes the body produce endorphins which helps you feel calmer and more in control. I don't like to use the expression 'superfood' but chilli is very good for you and, even better, you can train yourself to eat the hottest available."

"I'll take your word for all that but I'm afraid you're on our own when it comes to that. I once tried something called the Nagga chilli while I was on holiday on the Isle of Wight. We visited this place where they were offering samples.

"At first I didn't feel anything; then it was like all the air was sucked out of my lungs and the burning pain began. I couldn't speak and it felt like I couldn't breathe. My wife was furious because people were giving me funny looks. I wondered what was going to kill me first: her or the chilli."

27

The Chief Constable, Sir Thomas Warner, asked Mayweather to meet him at Whitehall. He was needed at a COBRA meeting, the Whitehall venue used by senior government officials to discuss national issues of safety and security.

That Sir Thomas was there today was a coincidence, as his PA explained, but Mayweather couldn't help thinking it was a worrying omen.

The young man passing on the message was blissfully unaware of her worries as he chatted away. "He's getting there early so he can talk to you. He says that COBRA is one of the few places where he can be sure he won't be disturbed. Between ourselves I think he rather enjoys the opportunity to disappear from view, even if it's just for a little while."

He was one of the new breed of officer recruits, with a first-class degree from an Oxbridge college and on the promotion fast track. After twelve months as a patrol officer in East London he had been seconded to the commissioner's team.

Mayweather arrived thirty minutes early and decided to take a few minutes in St James's Park. It was a warm spring day and she suddenly needed the reassurance of being near people who were untroubled by the potential nightmare she was thinking about.

Feeling refreshed, she arrived to discover Sir Thomas had cleared a forty-minute window for their session. Mayweather was quickly shown inside to find he was already there, pouring himself a coffee as she walked through the door.

She declined his offer of a drink. They weren't close, but they enjoyed an excellent working relationship and she admired the intelligence he brought to his work.

"Sorry about the last-minute change of location, but I really needed to talk to you away from Scotland Yard and this served the purpose. We've got it to ourselves for a little while, so I won't waste time because this is important.

"If you don't mind, let me go first. As you may know, the Mayor of London and I don't see eye-to-eye on a number of issues. In fact, our relationship has been deteriorating. He thinks we aren't doing enough to catch criminals. I keep pointing out that I don't have enough policemen to do everything that he wants. But then we had that problem with the Mayor's relative."

A few months back one of his cousins had her home broken into in a wealthy part of west London. The neighbourhood police had told her it was too minor to attend and issued her with a crime number.

"This is the woman with a blog post and a column in the Evening Standard who said that ordinary Londoners, like herself, were being ignored by the police. The trouble is that her 'ordinary' is a home valued at twelve million pounds."

"Exactly, and the fallout is still going on with some unpleasant comments on social media. A couple of nights back it took a nasty turn. A mob turned up and threw stones through her window, injuring one of her friends. She's gone into hiding and the Mayor has gone mad.

"He has demanded my resignation. Long story short, he has the power to do what he wants, so rather than fight, I'm negotiating. We have agreed a framework where

I leave in eighteen months having hand-picked a successor - and I would like that person to be you."

Mayweather was stunned but she knew this was no time for false modesty and was determined to be as honest as the Commissioner had just been.

"I won't pretend that it hadn't crossed my mind, especially since I was promoted to Deputy Commissioner - after that the only steps are either up or out. But I certainly wasn't expecting to be having that conversation today."

"Neither was I until this morning, but I had a breakfast meeting with the Mayor and laid out my plans. I told him he could accept, or I would fight his attempt to remove me and, while I couldn't win, the resulting fallout would do him no favours at all. He may have a colourful reputation but he is a practical man, so we thrashed out a lot of the details on the spot."

Glancing at her watch she saw they had used up half their meeting time.

"I'm assuming I can think this over?"

"Of course. But you need to decide by the end of the week. Not a lot of time, I know, but there we go. Now, I suspect what you are about to tell me is going to change the mood."

He was right, and it was a very sombre Sir Thomas who spoke when she had finished.

"Definitely not a great time for you to be thinking about taking over the top job, but if you do accept I won't be going anywhere for a little while so we can keep you focused on this."

He paused while he collected himself.

"There is no doubt you are right to trust Mr. Roper's instincts on this. His track record is too good to ignore. I've only met him the once but I have to say he is a fascinating man: fiercely intelligent and passionate about police work. He and Hooley make quite the pair.

"I will also make sure MI5 is brought to heel over withholding key information. Whatever resources you need, just ask. I'll let my PA know you now have top priority on all requests. One last thing: have you thought about just having this Yebedev arrested?"

"We did, sir, long and hard. But, as Jonathan said, we don't have anything on him apart from a photograph. If we arrested him on that his lawyer would have him free within the hour, and probably launch a claim for wrongful arrest.

"We believe the best thing to do is to keep him under observation. It's not going to be easy because he is either at home, on his yacht or spending time in some of the most expensive hotels and clubs in London. But it feels like our only choice."

28

Paul Moss was a great bear of a man, with unkempt hair and a luxurious black moustache that made him look like a South American bandit. All that was missing was a gun and a string vest straining over his generous stomach.

That stomach was now helping to compress most of the air out of the DCI as he was wrapped in an enormous hug. Roper found the display so alarming that he had backed into a corner of the large room which, in a few hours, would be filled with people come to hear Moss talk. He couldn't keep the horror off his face as he watched Hooley struggling to free himself from the embrace.

Somewhat reluctantly, Moss briefly let go before grabbing the detective's shoulders in two meaty hands. Hooley staggered slightly under the downward pressure, only retaining his balance because he was being supported while Moss closely studied his face. He was so close the DCI could smell the coffee the man had drunk recently.

"It's been too long, Brian. Until I saw you just now I hadn't realised quite how much I missed you. You're one of the few senior policemen I've come across with a decent sense of humour. The young ones now are so serious, but then I suppose we live in a serious world, more's the pity."

He glanced over at the cowering Roper and grinned in a sly way.

"I see it's true what they say about him. Can't stand being touched and needs to be given plenty of space. But then anyone who can come up with something like the

Rainbow Spectrum is unlikely to be one of the normal bores."

He pointed his right hand at Roper and curled his fingers in a come-hither gesture.

"Don't worry, I only squeeze people who really want me to do it. Your DCI denies it, but I know how much he likes it really, especially now he has been forced from the loving embrace of his wife."

The DCI started spluttering. He'd totally forgotten what a genius Moss was for collecting gossip so his remark about his marital status had taken him by surprise. Behind him an equally amazed Roper was wondering how this scruffy-looking giant could know about the Rainbow Spectrum. He ventured a little closer but was still some twenty feet away and was trying to maintain that distance.

"You'll need to come closer than that. We can't be shouting at each other while discussing top secret matters. Who knows who might be listening outside the doors?"

They were in a basement conference room of a central London hotel. In a few hours it would be full of people here to listen to Moss talk about the latest terrorist threats. What neither detective realised was that this conference was connected to the COBRA meeting that the Commissioner attended after his meeting with Mayweather.

Moss was now giving Roper a very direct look.

"I've had someone from the Commissioner's office telling me I have to give you two everything you need about a matter that couldn't be explained over the phone but would be when we met.

"So here we all are, at our meeting; the very least you could do is come over here and meet me properly rather than trying to vanish into a dark corner. By the way, your black suit helps you blend into the shadows but that bright white shirt of yours really works against it."

The words were washing over Roper like a wave and, in other circumstances he would have left as quickly as possible - but there was something about Moss that not only kept him there but actually drew him in; he even found his feet slowly walking him forwards.

Finally, he was just four feet away and Moss was holding up a hand again, this to suggest he stop where he was.

"Any closer and people would say we were friends," said the giant, giving him a theatrical wink.

Roper was so nonplussed by the performance that he blurted out: "What would be the best ways of bringing weapons-grade plutonium into the UK?"

"I take it you mean some outside group would be doing this and would be doing their best to avoid detection?"

A quick nod from Roper. He had become instantly focused and didn't want to waste time.

"And I'm thinking that since you're with the great Brian Hooley, you want to know how things have changed since the Litvinenko poisoning case?"

This time it was Roper who provided the affirmative with the briefest flicker.

"Well, you wouldn't try sneaking it through Heathrow again - things have got a lot more sophisticated since then - but there are still enough ways of doing it to make the hair fall out of those tasked with stopping it.

"I can give you a bit of a heads-up, but I am not going to give you all the details. I know you have the highest clearance but, in these matters, we try to keep it compartmentalised. So, a lot of people know a small bit and a much smaller number of people know a big bit and then there's me, who knows an awful lot."

Hooley glanced at Roper to see how this was being received and was relieved to see the younger man didn't look as though he was going to argue.

"From what you've just said, would it be reasonable to suggest that main ports of entry to this country are probably well-protected?"

"Yeah, that's right. Look: I'm not going to be giving away too many state secrets when I say that technology has really jumped in the last few years and it is possible to install radiation scanners at airports. Not something you could have done at the time your boss and I first met."

"Before we go any further, are you two here because you think there is a genuine threat? You're not asking me for some game-playing exercise - you think something might actually happen?"

Now it was the turn of the two detectives to shrug their shoulders.

"Well, I'll be. No wonder I was woken in the middle of the night. Well I guess the best way I can help you is by pointing out the problem areas - and be prepared to get even more worried."

By the time he finished talking, Hooley thought he had a distressingly long list of possible ways of smuggling plutonium into the country. Moss tried to cheer him up with a teeth-rattling slap on the back. While it failed to do that, it did have the bonus of taking his mind off his troubles - at least until his body stopped vibrating.

"Look, guys, I don't want to know who you're up against here. But the only time I would be getting really worried was if it involved brilliant Russian scientists with a history that stretched back to the KGB and the old Cold War days."

The way the pair reacted to this statement made even the ebullient Moss go pale.

"Oh dear. I was only joking but now it looks like the joke's on me. I'm thinking that may be exactly what you are up against. Now I can see why you've been a little anxious since you got here."

29

Georgi Yebedev was alone in his Sloane Square mansion. It was constructed from three neighbouring homes he had knocked through over a five-year period. From the moment he had arrived in London this was where he had wanted to live.

He was sitting in his second-floor study, a space that other people would have called an apartment in its own right, given that it was a suite of rooms which allowed him specific areas for work and play. He had even recreated a London pub with original fittings, including a beautiful polished oak bar and brass railings.

Satellite allowed him to access live ice hockey matches from Russia, a real passion of his, and of course football from the English Premiership. While he wasn't close to the Russian owner of Chelsea the two men enjoyed a cordial relationship and liked to compete over who had the biggest yacht. Yebedev was about to take possession of a newly constructed vessel that would give him bragging rights by 10 metres.

The door that led into his personal zone had red and green "traffic lights" in a panel. Today the red light was blazing telling his staff to keep out. Only his head butler could come in, and even then only if there was a crisis.

The children were away at school and his wife had gone to the South of France, taking a friend with her, after complaining that spring was late coming this year, meaning London was damp and grey. She'd even pined for the crisp, clean coldness of Moscow, still emerging from the grip of winter.

He was mulling over his instructions to organise the importation of the various bomb components to the UK and to do it without gaining attention from members of the Russian mafia, many of whom seemed to operate in London with apparent impunity.

Vasilev had been very clear on this last point. Her information was that the British were aware of the outright gangsters in their midst, and preferred to keep them under observation. That way they had some idea of what was going on.

She had advised Yebedev that he too was on the radar - his extreme wealth was enough of a draw to merit that - but his behaviour over the last 20 years made it unlikely he was under close watch.

"Their best people are looking at our best people," she had told him, before choking on the tea she had swallowed laughing at her own joke. He had cautiously patted her on her back and she made a quick recovery.

"The point is that you are not a criminal, so you will be way down their list of priorities, so long as you are careful."

She'd rummaged around in her bag and produced a hardback book which she passed to him. He saw it was a spy novel by John Le Carre, titled Call for the Dead.

"It's the first in the series and people who know say you should read that and get some ideas for what you need to do to avoid detection. I doubt you'll need to go as far as dead drops in Green Park, but it will tell you about basic anti-surveillance techniques."

He shrugged and didn't bother to mention that he was a huge fan of Le Carre. Part of him couldn't wait to walk down the street using shop windows to check if he was being followed, but a much bigger part felt sick at the obvious danger he was placing himself in.

"When you rent the accommodation and the space to build the laboratory, you must be careful to do it through third parties and ideally offshore companies, but be careful not to leave any traces that could be followed back to you."

She stopped and took a cautious sip of her tea, suddenly looking tired.

"I don't like having to spell this out to you, but you need to understand there is no going back to where you were. You have been selected and we are not waiting for you to make up your mind and tell us that you agree to do this.

"If anything goes wrong, you will be held to account and you and your family will pay the price. We have a long reach so there is nowhere you can go where you will be safe. If you start having second thoughts, just think about your children."

He couldn't stop the feelings of anger that bubbled up as he listened to these threats against his family. He was strong enough that he could have reached across and throttled this woman where she sat, but with all his physical strength he was powerless. She was just the messenger. He clenched and unclenched his fists to relieve the stress.

Vasilev paled and moved away from him as she sensed the sudden danger she was in.

"It gives me no pleasure to pass this on." She wanted him to know that she was just following orders. "But I have also been told that this is the only task that will ever be asked of you.

"Complete this mission and you will never hear from us again, and your family will be quite safe to live their lives."

His journey back to London had seemed to drag on but by the time he arrived home he was beginning to regain his equilibrium. He needed to think because whichever way he looked he had a problem that needed to be factored in.

It was all very well ordering him to stay away from fellow Russians but how else was he going to find the people he needed? He could hardly enter "smuggling gangs" into Google. He was going to have to find someone who could navigate their way around that world, while ensuring they kept their mouth firmly shut.

He sank back onto his antique leather settee; this space was styled after the London club to which he had tried and failed to gain membership. It still rankled that the British looked down their noses at this nouveaux-riche Russian. He supposed it was because most of them envied the resources he could draw upon. If he owned a large ancestral home, he could easily afford to maintain its upkeep without having to put up with paying visitors.

He forced himself to calm down. If he and his family were going to come out of this alive he needed to make some hard-headed decisions. The task was straightforward even if the means of achieving it were going to be complex.

The longer he thought, the more one solution remained in view. It was going to cost him a lot of money, but he could easily afford to be generous to the right person, and what price could you put on keeping your own family alive?

30

There are rarely any certainties in life, but Julie Mayweather knew she could be sure of one thing: if she told Brian Hooley something in confidence, then it would remain that way. Never once, during the near-thirty years they had worked together, had he ever let her down.

He was listening attentively now as she ran through her conversation with the Commissioner and his offer to ensure she took over the top job at Scotland Yard.

Just a decade ago, they might have been enjoying a single malt; now it was a cup of instant coffee from the canteen. Hooley wasn't entirely convinced it was a change for the better, but he knew senior officers couldn't really afford to have it known they were drinking in the office.

It was late, getting on for 8.30pm, and she had been talking quietly for the best part of ten minutes but now she was drawing to a close.

"I'm sure it won't be as straightforward as Sir Thomas says, but with him and the Mayor behind me there has to be very strong possibility that this will go ahead.

"While I feel quite certain that I do want the job, I wanted to hear myself talking out loud about it and there was only ever one person who I was going to be doing that with. What do you think - anything sound a bit off to you?"

"Not a single thing. In my opinion, you should have got the job last time and it was only the old boys' club that stopped you. But the world's moved on now and I think we can all stand the 'shock' - he mimed quote marks around the word - over having a woman in charge.

"I've never mentioned this before but there was real disappointment around here when you lost out, so your team is going to be delighted if you do succeed."

"I bet they're all hoping you'll get the top job if I'm moved on. You're not without your own fan club, you know."

Hooley was silent for a while as he gazed down at his hands that were crossed in his lap. She knew he was thinking deeply and was content to leave him to start talking once he had marshalled his thoughts fully.

"Funny you should mention that, but I've been thinking there should be a change for a while now. You and I have been running this team for a long time and I think it's time for fresh minds to take over.

"The nature of crime is changing again - the web, terrorism and global conflict - and we need to bring in a new generation of leaders. I'm not talking about me taking over; I mean we should be finding replacements for the two of us.

"The timeframe of you becoming Commissioner allows us an opportunity to identify the right people and get them in place. By the time we are ready to stand aside they will be up to speed and sorting things out the way they want it."

"What about you? What are you going to be doing in all this?"

"Well, I do have something in mind, and I have been waiting for you to get offered the top job before I came out with anything."

"Are you trying to tell me you knew this was going to happen?" Her expression was a mixture of amusement and curiosity. She'd long thought her deputy was one of the best-connected policemen in the Yard.

"I wouldn't say I knew in a very precise way, but it wasn't the hardest thing to speculate about. You're just too good and you have one added bonus."

He looked at her expectantly.

"Go on, tell me."

"You don't have any ghosts rattling around in your closet, and you might not believe how many of your contemporaries have reasons to be very nervous about anyone checking too deeply into their background."

"Ha! I can confirm that I am clean as a whistle but as for my rivals, I suspect you're being mischievous."

The DCI laughed and held his hands up in mock apology.

"It's certainly true that I had been thinking you might move on, and that's why I've got one eye to the future; and, as I said, I do have an idea."

She nodded to show he should go ahead.

"My big concern is making sure that Jonathan is OK, and I want to keep him close to me. He's an awkward sod but at the same time one of the best people I know and there's no way you and I could leave him here. He has too much history with some of the guys and he won't last if we're not there to watch his back.

"So that got me thinking. If you are the Commissioner you get the chance to do what you like, within reason, so why not set up a new, smaller team? I can be running things, for now, and it leaves Jonathan to provide the sort of input that only he can, and we hand-pick some other talented mavericks to work alongside us.

"I'm betting that if we put the word out we will find all sorts of people hidden away and not getting to do the work they are capable of because they don't get the recognition they deserve, or the opportunities to prove what they can do.

"If we had a few more with Roper's skill at research and keeping up to date with the real world imagine the possibilities. I bet we could even start predicting crimes." He paused. "OK, I may have got that last bit from a film, but you know what I mean.

"Just take one example. We really need a couple of computer bods. Roper's not bad but even I know he's not in the super league. Then we can shape the team to work hard and help to bring down some of the criminals who at the moment are getting away with murder because they can hide behind firewalls."

He stopped talking and then burst out laughing.

"I've just thought of a name for us. We can call ourselves the Odd Jobs - or maybe, even better, the Odd Bods."

31

Pressure does strange things to people. In Yebedev's case, it made him forget that he had the answer to his problems right in front of him. It had taken hours of near panic before he remembered.

The man he needed had connections in a complex smuggling operation that saw a huge amount of stolen art and antiquities being shipped to Russians living in the UK. Yebedev had never used the service himself but he had an idea about how to make contact.

The trade was run by ruthless operators, since you don't get to ship ancient treasures out of Middle-East war zones unless you know what you are doing, and the costs involved were astronomical.

The man he needed was former KGB agent Arkady Sokolov. If you needed to source something particular, then he was the man you turned to. He wasn't cheap, but he was discreet.

Sokolov had styled himself as a 'citizen of the world', flitting between Russia, the USA and capital cities all over Western Europe. But he had also developed a passion for the so-called London season and could always be found at events like the Henley and Wimbledon.

Yebedev knew this for certain because he was himself a huge rowing fan and, for the last ten years, had been quietly spending large sums of money on it. Every year he sponsored a private box, entrance to which had become highly sought after once people discovered they could eat as much of the finest Beluga caviar as they could manage, only leaving room for the rare vintage champagnes. People did like to eat and drink on someone else's tab.

To reach Sokolov, he was going to have to be subtle. Trying a direct approach would be a waste of time since the former agent only dealt with people he knew and whose backgrounds had been thoroughly checked.

There was a way to speed the process up. He was going to have to pay a large amount of money to a very discreet public relations company that was run by a former British government minister and aristocrat, Sir Valentine Topper, a baronet.

While Sir Valentine had impeccable connections and position within society, he had inherited severe financial problems caused by the ever-spiraling costs of maintaining a crumbling mansion and several thousand acres of the most worthless type of land, good only for sheep grazing. He had suffered the indignity of becoming the first Topper to actually need a job, although this was somewhat mitigated by his being selected as the candidate for MP for his very safe constituency.

It was while he was hosting a summer drinks session on the Terrace of the House of Commons, aimed at promoting Anglo-Russian relations, that Sir Valentine had first met Sokolov - and they had hit it off straight away. They made an unlikely pairing. Sokolov was a small, broad shouldered man who wore cheap off-the-peg suits, had thinning hair and used a translator, even though he had perfect English.

Sir Valentine, on the other hand, was the product of an excellent breeding process. He was tall, handsome like a film star, and had an imposing presence, peering down his slightly oversized nose when he spoke to anyone. His suits came from the best tailors on Jermyn Street and fitted him like a glove.

Within minutes of being introduced, Sokolov had done away with his translator as the two men spoke, ignoring the others around them until their aides reminded them that they both had duties that needed to be performed.

They had arranged to meet for lunch the next day. Sokolov said it would be his treat and insisted on the Ritz. It was to prove the start of a highly successful business relationship that gave the Russian access to all manner of contacts and, for Sir Valentine, it provided the funds to afford the lifestyle into which he had been born.

Of course, if reaching Sir Valentine was easy any fool could have done it. But, once again, Yebedev showed he had lost none of the networking skills that had first earned him attention in Russia and he had been able to use the services of a globally-known public relations company to make the introduction. The reference they provided won him the coveted meeting.

A few days later found Yebedev sitting across from Sir Valentine in the private dining room of a private members club in Belgravia. The Russian had chosen a three-thousand-pound bottle of Australian Cabernet Sauvignon; he wanted Sir Valentine to know that money was not an issue. The enthusiastic way that the former cabinet minister savoured it suggested that he had judged things about right. Sir Valentine was a wealthy man, but that sort of money for a bottle of wine was too much even for someone like him.

The dining room was perfect. It was big enough for eight, so it did not feel like they were eating in a huge empty room but had the space to spread out. The waiting staff were incredibly efficient and, once they had cleared away the main course, the two were left with a second bottle of wine and a large pot of coffee.

Yebedev got straight to the point.

"I have a number of extremely valuable items in Russia that I would like brought to this country and I don't want anyone to know about it. The objects vary in size and importance and I am willing to pay whatever the cost.

"If the initial shipments go well, I would like to discuss even more delicate items to bring here, but there would be no obligation to accept this until I give full disclosure on what is required and it is decided if this would be feasible."

Sir Valentine blinked slowly as he listened. He had heard many such proposals over the years and now prided himself on his ability to detect if someone was genuine or not. He'd already had background done on this man and it was positive to the extreme.

He noted Yebedev's body language was open and he showed none of the signs that Sokolov had taught him to watch out for. Accomplished liars are good at avoiding the telltale signs that can give you away. They won't be caught glancing to the right, or blinking rapidly, but subtle things like wrinkles appearing around the eye or spots of colour briefly popping up on the cheek can catch out the best.

"I am sure there is nothing my colleagues can't help you with. Before I go on, am I right in assuming all the items are in Russia itself?"

"Some are, some aren't. Some are hidden away, others are hidden in plain sight."

Sir Valentine thought this was a very Russian answer. He went on. "That shouldn't be a problem, although each item will be discussed in detail and we never claim that we can move everything.

"If you wish me to take this conversation further then you will need to pay one million pounds sterling into a bank account for which I will give you the details. The money must be there in three working days, is non-refundable and does not count against further costs.

"In addition, once we have established the exact nature of items and provided the cost of moving them, the money must be paid in advance and we accept no liability for anything going wrong; all work is carried out at your risk."

Yebedev made to reply but was silenced by Sir Valentine holding up his hand.

"There is one more thing. Once the total costs have been established there will be a two hundred per cent surcharge of all the costs involved, including the one-million-pound cost. This will be payable in advance."

A very small part of the Russian wanted to tell this insufferable Englishman what he could do with his million-pound bonuses and payments in advance. A much bigger bit of him held out his hand and said: "It will be a pleasure to do business with you."

32

One of the rules that Hooley tried to stick to was 'never assume'. It was classic old-school stuff and a useful reminder to keep an open mind during any investigation, but it was beginning to dawn on him that he had just made a classic mistake with Roper. He had assumed his younger colleague would be enthusiastic about his plan.

The first part had gone well. He'd suggested they visit one of Roper's favourite cafes. That part of the plan had gone well. It was French-run, offering table service and a collection of seriously good cakes and pastries. He had waited until mid-afternoon before suggesting they head there for a break and a chance to discuss his idea.

Luck seemed to be on his side; a table came clear as they walked in. It was at back of the cafe and offered a degree of privacy. Had they arrived during the normal lunch period customers would have been queuing out of the door, but at just after 3pm they were able to walk in and sit down.

Or at least Hooley had. Roper had stopped by the counter to carefully study the cake selection and finally joined him at the table to announce that the daily special - an elaborate work of glistening chocolate perfection - was the one to go for. Even sitting a few feet away, the DCI could see this was a special treat and instantly abandoned his latest diet.

They were served by a pretty young waitress with dark hair pulled back in a ponytail and wearing a crisp white blouse and black trousers, with a French style white apron wrapped tightly around her middle. Hooley thought she seemed interested in Roper, but if he had noticed he was doing a very good job of disguising it and she tossed her head as she walked away having taken their order.

Before he could say anything, Roper jumped in.

"Do you realise that you always choose this place when you have just put yourself on a diet, then every time you say the cakes are too good to turn down and you order one?"

He hadn't realised that, but recognised there was a sliver of truth in what had just been said.

"I wish you hadn't told me that. I suspect you may be right, as you usually are, but I hadn't realised that was what I was doing, so now I will have to stop coming here."

"Only when you go on a diet. The rest of the time is OK."

Hooley was about to say more but decided he was going to make himself look ridiculous so, looking around to double-check there was no-one close enough to eavesdrop, he launched into his idea.

When he finished talking Roper didn't respond, which was quite usual when he was presented with a new idea. Hooley knew the young detective sometimes needed time to adapt to a new approach, but this silence went on.

Even the reappearance of the waitress, who banged Roper's plate of cake down with a real sense of relish, did nothing to disturb him. Embarrassed, Hooley tried to smile apologetically but she treated him with the disdain he deserved.

Sighing, he pulled his own slice towards him and cut into it with a fork before placing it in his mouth. It was every bit as delicious as it looked, and he sat in silent heaven as he slowly made his way through it. He had hoped this would encourage Roper to get stuck in, but he remained in silent contemplation, his hands on his knees and his gaze off in the middle distance.

The DCI was just attempting to hoover up the crumbs on his pate when Roper finally spoke. To his relief he didn't seem angry, it was just that the plan had triggered some intense thinking on his part.

"I don't always get on with people who are like me."

The words hung in the air for a moment as Hooley carefully absorbed them and then he had to restrict the urge to laugh as he took them on board, his amusement triggered by a sense of relief that he had an answer.

"I know exactly what you mean, and there have been occasions when I have been accused of not playing well with other people. We are going to be really careful to make sure that we all get on - maybe not as best friends, but with plenty of respect for what we can do."

Judging by the deep frown that appeared, Roper was still going to need some persuading.

"Look. We have 18 months to get this right and we don't need to find loads of people - half a dozen will be enough to get us going. To be honest the idea may not work out that well, but I'd really like to give it a try and I was wondering if you might have someone in mind.

"What I don't want is to get going and then discover that we are having to go elsewhere for help. I want this to be a really tight unit with everyone able to contribute, and to do it in an environment that they can thrive in.

"I know you won't mind me saying this, but I told Julie Mayweather how pleased I was at the enormous strides you have taken and that's why so many people are talking about you. But you wouldn't be able to work your magic in a traditional squad, and we need to remember that."

While he'd been talking he was pleased to see the frown disappear; Roper looked like he was buying into the plan. He decided to keep pushing ahead and bring Roper alongside.

"Is there anyone you are aware of who might be interested?"

Roper went to say no and then slapped himself on the forehead.

"I got so worried for a moment that it stopped me thinking properly. Peter and Chrissie might be just the people we are looking for. They're really clever data analysts at GCHQ who I got to know while I was working there. You said you thought we needed people like that and I totally agree. Data mining is always the key and they are happy to go through mountains of work."

"You don't think we would have an issue talking to them - I mean, GCHQ would be OK about it, would they?"

"I can't see any problems; people move around all the time and moving to Scotland Yard would be no bad thing."

"Fine. In that case why don't you talk to them? No rush, because we don't need to see anyone straight away, but find out if they would be interested and stress that at this stage this is only a chat; we can't be sure this is going to happen.

"Also, can I remind you that the information about the boss possibly moving to the job is for our ears only at the moment? She wanted you to know in advance to give you a chance to deal with it - are you happy about her moving up?"

There was no hesitation.

"She should be in charge."

"I'm pleased. Before we spoke there were two things worrying me: how you would react to that, and you are fine. The other is what about the name: Odd Bods?"

"I really like that. It sounds just right and it's a lot nicer than some of things I used to get called at school."

33

It was a numbers game, and it worked. The Courier knew that if he sent enough kids through the system, some of them would get through, and the one thing he didn't have a shortage of was children who could be sent into the UK.

The flow of refugees from war zones meant it was inevitable that refugee families were getting separated in the chaos, making easy pickings for the smuggling gangs targeting the young.

At first the kids scooped up by the Courier and his team thought they had been really lucky. They were fed, given somewhere warm and dry to sleep and even had basic medical needs taken care of.

Far from being kind his team was looking to separate out the best prospects, with strong healthy children two to four years old providing the highest and most reliable income.

Those who didn't measure up were either abandoned on the spot because they were so ill or sent through border controls in an exercise designed to flood the immigration system with children who needed a lot of care and attention.

Among this "border fodder" were the older kids, since he knew demand started tailing off fast once children reached the age of ten and trying to find anyone who would pay good money for teenage boys was tough, although older girls held a better value.

The Courier operated on the principle that anything up to ninety per cent of those he picked up would fall into the low financial value and could be used as pawns. One van-load of children would briefly swamp the system, creating the window to transport his most valuable cargo.

It didn't work every time but those who did make it were the ones he could charge serious money for. Once over there, he had another neat trick up his sleeve. When he had more kids than orders he would allow the excess kids to be found in the UK, maybe wandering around a motorway service station.

These children would be taken into local authority care and placed with foster parents or in children's homes. Safe and secure, these children could be left "safely stashed" until a buyer had been found, whereupon they would vanish without trace.

Operating this way meant his team had to be alert and organised, but while it could be painstaking at times, his guarantee of quality meant he could charge the highest prices. Like any business predicated on supply and demand, the cost could vary enormously. He once recalled having to sell off a nine-year-old for less than fifty pounds.

He was able to mitigate against these price variations by being able to meet very precise criteria of age, sex, appearance - even down to height or eye colour. Tick all those boxes and it was a top payday. What happened next never entered his mind.

He had been pleased with how fast his operation had ramped back up and the money was flowing in steadily. For all that, he still faced significant issues. After all his costs the money, while very decent, wasn't so good he would recoup all his losses soon.

He was also facing problems that hadn't been so acute a few years ago. National governments were getting better at co-ordinating their responses, so finding unsupervised refugees was getting harder, but that wasn't the most concerning change.

His bigger issue was that there were so many more people working in the field and they were not just ruthless - some of them seemed to be quite unhinged. The worst were the jihadi groups, who had realised that starting wars was a good way to make the money which allowed them to wage new wars. Where these groups controlled territory and populations, they realised it was far more lucrative to pressurise people into leaving using smuggling gangs the terror groups controlled.

All those involved in human trafficking have ruthless as a default setting, but these people brought a fanaticism no one wanted to encounter. It meant he was having to work with mercenary groups to ensure his people had the protection they needed.

It was yet another cost but he could sense the odds were slowly mounting against him. In the past he had been sure his intelligence, coupled with a forensic attention to detail, would keep him safe. Not anymore. The longer he stayed doing this the more certain it was that he was going to be hurt by it, probably terminally. There were only so many times you could play chicken on the motorway before you got squished.

He rarely drank alcohol or took drugs, but sometimes they helped him to escape. He was back in London, in a rented flat close to Baker Street tube station, while he thought about his next steps.

He'd cracked open a bottle of expensive cognac and poured himself a generous measure. After a couple of sips he felt the soothing sensation of the alcohol and laid back on the sofa. The huge flat-screen TV was on, but he was barely aware of what it was showing; instead he was enjoying the play of light on the amber liquid in the glass he was holding in his right hand. He estimated the measure he'd poured himself cost about five hundred pounds but the soothing effect it was having made it a price worth paying.

He sat up, decision made. He wasn't someone who needed to run through endless discussions and thought processes to make up his mind. He'd stripped it back to the numbers. His earnings from trafficking were coming under pressure, and that would only get worse.

The really major money was in drugs, but anyone trying to break into that market probably had a death wish. His new plan meant he would need to suffer a short-term cash flow problem before the money started to flow. He calculated that he was close to making a sufficient profit that would give him the cushion he needed. Just a few more weeks would do it.

34

Hooley ended the call and stared thoughtfully at his phone before putting it back down on his desk.

"That was Bill Nuffield. MI5 is planning to give us some more background information and we will get it later today. I know we don't really know him that well but I got the impression he was still holding something back.

"I suppose that's second nature to those guys and, to be fair, there have been plenty of times when I have withheld information until I was quite sure I could trust the people I was dealing with."

Roper was stretching in his seat, raising his arms level with his shoulders, which Hooley thought made him look a scarecrow.

"I expect you're right," he said. "I don't have the full facts but I am willing to make an informed guess. I think they must have a source they trust who is telling them something really bad is imminent."

"Really? Care to share your analysis on this?"

Roper stood up. "I will, but let me go and get lunch. I'm starving. Smoked salmon and an Americano alright for you?"

"Er, yes, thanks," said Hooley, who realised that for some reason he was standing up.

The DCI had managed to contain his interest while watching Roper make his way through the usual double sandwich order. He wasn't feeling that hungry so had tucked his food away for later.

Roper tidied up and reached for his coffee, which Hooley took as a cue.

"Are you going to expand on your theory?"

Roper stared at the bottom of his cup as if trying to see patterns in the coffee dregs. He obviously didn't find anything, as the cup was tossed into the waste basket.

"I don't have any information that you don't, but I do know that intelligence organisations sometimes have information that they can't discuss, or even admit they know about."

Hooley's eyes narrowed. He'd anticipated the answer might not be easy.

"You can be sure that MI5 will have been really careful about how they ask around. They wouldn't want to risk alerting the wrong people that they were aware something was going on.

"I have been trying to think about the most likely way they will have gone and I keep coming back to the idea of a deep cover source. But talking to those people takes time; you can't just ring up because you would give their cover away.

"And, just because we are dealing with MI5, it might be MI6 that has control over the source and would be unlikely to share any details. The Cold War might be officially over but espionage is still alive and well.

"Of course the biggest problem is that we don't know what it is that they don't know."

Hooley made an effort to get his head round that but sensibly gave up.

"I think you may have outdone yourself with that one."

Roper tried again. "It makes perfect sense that they may have something that they can't tell us about without giving away another secret. I wonder if they think this is a rogue team of Russian agents.

"It could be that their source has confirmed it is not any sort of officially sanctioned operation - and that might be the worst case of all."

35

For the second visit to Century House they were waved through minimal security where they were met by one of Nuffield's team, a man who was nodded at respectfully by the guards.

They were taken to what their guide called a secure briefing room. On a desk were two sets of print-outs marked 'Top Secret'. A stern-looking woman was standing guard. It was explained that they could have twenty minutes with the documents. This time they had to sign a contract to confirm they would not make a record of the information provided.

Hooley's first impression was disappointment; the first few sheets contained very little that a diligent internet search couldn't produce. But then he turned the page and read something that set his heart pounding in his chest.

It seemed almost certain that the Russians could not account for an unknown quantity of weapons-grade plutonium. The radioactive material was part of a stash of weaponry that the KGB had ordered to be buried in a heavily forested area of Romania during the 1970s.

The site had been quietly forgotten about for the next forty years, until some documents had surfaced from the Kremlin archives which provided accurate location data. The Russians assembled a recovery team which set off to retrieve the plutonium.

It was especially prized as, not only did it have an intrinsic value on the black market, the material had slipped through the net so there was no trace of it and it could be kept out of the hands of UN weapons inspectors.

But, when the Russians reached the location, it was clear the site had been ransacked many, many years ago. While no one had any idea how much had been taken, the feeling was that, at the very least, it must have been enough to create a bomb.

Hooley had read the documents twice before turning to look at Roper, and saw that his worries were clearly being matched by his fellow detective. The thing about the younger man was that, while he could get anxious about relatively minor things, he was generally calm about the big picture unless there were real grounds for panicking.

He was about to ask him what was going through his mind when Nuffield's man came back and swapped the documents for a tray of coffee. He placed them in a thick black file and handed it to the woman, who immediately left.

"Bill sends his regards and his apologies because he won't be able to see you today, although he promises he will fix that very shortly. He's asked me to tell you that he shares the concerns that you now have and is attempting to get some more context on this, although his exact words are "don't hold your breath".

"He thought you might like a few minutes to discuss what you've read, which is why I've bought the coffee for you, and then I will be back to escort you out. I'm afraid I can't discuss any of this with you since I don't have the clearance you two have been given."

With that, he spun on his heels and disappeared through the door.

Hooley decided to busy himself with something familiar as he poured out two drinks, blowing on his to cool it down before taking a sip. He grimaced; the drink was far too bitter for his taste. He thought it matched his mood.

"There are times in this job when I wish I didn't know the things that I do, and this is turning into one of those. This latest seems to be making it all the more likely that making a small bomb is going to be easy to organise, if it hasn't happened already.

"What amazes me is how they seem to have lost track of something that is so dangerous. I don't even like to think about what else might have gone missing or people have just forgotten about."

Roper didn't respond at first. He confirmed Hooley's suspicions when he said. "I've just been in my Rainbow Spectrum and I think I must be right. This is a rogue operation - and has its origins in the Cold War.

"I've been reading that KGB officers were creating cases of money and weapons, then deliberately sabotaging the paperwork. In some cases, they even murdered the people who had delivered the items to be sure of complete secrecy.

"After that, it was just a case of keeping their heads down for a little while and then returning to collect stuff that, to all intents and purposes, had never existed in the first place.

"What my Spectrum is telling me is that the file we have just read has to be an account of an official Russian inspection. In other words they may be as worried about this as we are."

"Does it really make that much difference whether this has got official sanction or not? Either way we have got people threatening to make a nuclear bomb." Hooley closed his eyes and shuddered. "Just saying that makes me feel ill."

"I think it does matter. As I was taught at GCHQ: if the other side are doing something, and we find out, at least we can talk to them and maybe head off a serious incident.

If we don't know who is behind this then there is no one we can talk to, which means we can't negotiate with them.

36

The Courier had always understood that it was a good idea to keep his top people close. When he had cut back his smuggling operation, he had hand-picked the best to move over to the new project.

Over the last few months there had been many occasions when his foresight had proved invaluable. His return to people trafficking had proved especially problematical and, without the input of those he had retained from the old days, he would have failed.

But even though he had achieved a degree of success there was no longer any doubting his belief that he needed to get out sooner rather than later - or risk running headlong into a serious problem with one of his many rivals.

If he needed any further confirmation that his time away had generated issues, it was highlighted by the collapse of his network of key contacts. He had once had border officials on speed-dial. Not anymore. Many of those he knew were either retired or had switched allegiance to one of the new gangs.

He had tried bribing his way back into their favour but the officials were far more afraid of their new paymasters than they were of him. As a final attempt he had called in major favours to gain meetings with two key immigration officials, one in northern France and the second his contact for southern England.

Between them the two men could control the flow of illegals across the English Channel. The French official had looked terrified when he had finally agreed to meet. In response to being shown a suitcase full of high denomination notes he had gone totally white.

"You don't understand; our time is gone. If I try to stop working for these people, they will kill every member of my family and every member of my wife's family. They have no inhibitions.

"I have never pretended to be a good man - I always wanted the money - but at least with you I could tell myself that the refugees were treated with a basic level of respect and provided with food and water.

"You can forget that with these new people. They couldn't care less what happens, all they want is money. In some cases they have no intention of transporting the refugees but murder them the moment they hand over the money."

The Courier recalled the conversation as he headed for an industrial zone about forty miles from Calais where he was due to meet up with several members of his team. He rarely got involved in the hands-on work since his most important role was to negotiate safe passage, but recent violent encounters with rivals meant he had to show his face or risk the morale of his team.

He was at the wheel of a large white van with French number plates through an area dominated by ugly warehouses built to house businesses that valued practicality over appearance. His destination was a secluded area, where his team should have been waiting inside one of the more dilapidated warehouses.

But, to his mounting alarm, he couldn't make contact with them - and that never happened unless there was a problem. He pulled over to call his back-up team.

They were already heading his way since they, too, had lost contact with the other team.

A short while later two cars pulled up. He briefly conferred with his people and then led the way to a quiet spot just short of their target.

Carefully checking there was no one around he jumped out of the van and watched as the back-up team grabbed Kalashnikov rifles they had stored in the boots of their cars. The weapons were quickly distributed among his five men and three women.

The plan was simple. There were only two entrances to the warehouse, front and back, so his teams would split, with him a fifth member to the frontal assault team. By now they knew something bad must have happened.

Fifteen minutes later, and on an agreed signal, they raced inside to find a macabre scene. The bodies of their four colleagues were lined up on the concrete floor, on their backs and with a single gunshot wound in the centre of their heads. There was no sign of anyone else.

He had just ordered his team to check the warehouse thoroughly when there was the deafening sound of gunfire. He saw two of his people thrown backwards by the impact of bullets. With no cover, he dived to the ground only to be hit in the shoulder, the force spinning him round before he reached the floor.

The noise was ear-splitting and he lay stunned, waiting for the pain to kick in. He tried to grab his rifle but the injury stopped him moving his hand more than a few inches. Just before everything went blank, he heard the sound of screaming but had no idea where it was coming from.

*

When he came to, several hours later, he was lying in a bed attached to a drip. He had a throbbing headache and his arm and shoulder were heavily bandaged. A man in a white coat walked in and he realised where he was: in a safehouse in the woods around the popular tourist spot of Le Touquet.

The modern five-bedroomed house was set back at the end of a long driveway and behind a thick screen of hedge which hid it from view. The man in the coat was a doctor who lived in the neighbouring property, and had treated his wounds while he was unconscious.

The man stood at the end of the bed and looked at him for a moment before smiling.

"If the lump on your head is anything to go by, *mon ami*, then you probably have an almighty headache and I wouldn't be surprised if you are slightly concussed. As to the wound on your arm, well, I suggest you pray to any God who listens to you.

"You were incredibly lucky. The bullet grazed the inside of your left arm; a few centimetres' difference and it would have either been your chest or into the shoulder itself. You might not have survived that. You lost two people in the shoot-out."

The Courier felt a sense of fury building, which rapidly turned to nausea. His hand trembled slightly as he reached for the glass of water at the side of his bed.

"Not too much to start with," cautioned the doctor. "I've got you on a drip, so no need to worry about dehydration." He was looking concerned, and the Courier became aware that he had started sweating profusely - the room felt hot and clammy - and for a moment he thought he would pass out again.

By sheer force of will he regained control and looked back at the doctor.

"What else do I need to know?"

"Your people say they have everything under control. As we speak, the bodies are being disposed of in a crematorium. The attacker had no ID on him, but they believe he is an Afghan, and they set fire to the warehouse."

He lay back in his bed, certain of one thing. Forget one last payday; get out now.

In the past he had suffered his share of setbacks - it was a dangerous business - but he had always felt the odds were stacked in his favour because he was the biggest shark in the pool. When rivals tried to get a piece of his action they knew they could expect serious retaliation, but his time at the top was now over.

He'd known a rethink was coming, and this had brought the timetable forward. Just as well that his recovery would mean he had plenty of time on his hands. His new plan would take longer to generate money but at least he would be alive at the end to enjoy it.

37

The doctor insisted he needed to stay in bed for another half a day. He'd hit his head hard; he was ordered to at least wait until his headaches had died down before moving around.

Nine times out of ten he'd have made a fuss but he knew the doctor was right. It felt like someone had embedded a hot knitting needle just above his right eye and, from time to time, was giving it a twist.

Half a day later and the pain had reduced from excruciating agony to irritating discomfort, but he amazed the medic by volunteering to stay where he was a little while longer. What he didn't mention was that being looked after round the clock actually left him with plenty of quality thinking time.

The following morning he was up and about, and he had a plan. He would strip everything back to basics and then let it be known that he was returning to the business of very special deliveries.

Priceless art of all types, rare jewellery, high denomination cash notes, the most prized antiquities: anything that was high value and hard for their owners to explain how it came to be in their possession, especially if it was featured on an official list of stolen riches.

This was a different sort of market. Much lower volumes, and the people needing the service tended to take a personal interest in how it was being handled. It was an oddity, but deliver a child to someone's home and they often pretended to ignore you; bring their stolen Picasso with you and you'd be invited to see which wall it would be hanging from.

The biggest issue was trust. The owners of a stolen masterpiece tended to deal only with people they had known for a long time and were generally unwilling to engage with third parties.

This was an area where the Courier was substantially in credit, having had many years of successfully moving items all over the world. He would have to explain his absence, but all he needed to say was that time out had allowed him to recharge his batteries and be back firing on all cylinders.

Talking of cylinders, he needed to arrange for a small fleet of transport vehicles, from cars to light trucks, to undergo specialist modification which would increase the variety and type of goods he could move.

Modern technology had improved the border defences between countries with hand-held detectors, supported by sniffer dogs, able to pick up the chemical scent of weapons, drugs, even money. The answer was to hide them in totally secure hidden compartments.

And to do it well meant going down the customised route. Making those took time, money and skill. The last two he could get his hands on quite quickly; the first? Well, there was no way of speeding that up, but he could be ready in weeks. He had enough money stashed away to cover that.

While he was waiting he could set up a small and discreet delivery company that had a base in the UK and one in North America. A handful of liveried vehicles and a basic website would be all the cover he needed.

Best of all, it was simplicity itself to buy meaningless-sounding awards for "excellent customer service" and it would look like the company was established and trustworthy. Job done.

Within a week the physical side of his operation was well underway, and he was already sending vehicles backwards and forwards between France and the UK. He wanted these runs to become as familiar to the guards as a cup of tea.

On its own, this tactic would to be enough to reduce suspicion, but taken with all the other measures it would create a degree of credibility that might just help tip the balance and prevent his vehicles being singled out.

Equally importantly it provided valuable intel, since all his drivers were trained to spot the techniques being used to protect crossing points. Most of these would be for entry into the UK, but he knew plenty of business would be coming from the East so he would want as much background on these borders as possible.

He wondered how long he might have to wait for work. Sometimes he could go from nothing to multiple clients, as if they had silently communed and decided they wanted their stolen art moved to new locations. There was one wealthy client who had amassed a huge collection of stolen treasures and he moved them with him when he drifted between his different homes in London, Miami and a vast estate in Chile.

The Courier would have loved that work, but the owner had found two groups he liked, and they did it all. Their competitive nature meant they were always at the top of their game, which is just what the client intended, and there was no way either group wanted to walk away from such lucrative work.

In many ways the whole concept was ludicrous and cost vast amounts of money that could easily be better spent, but why go to the trouble of owning something beautiful if you couldn't look at it in whichever home you happened to be in?

The Courier took his time deciding who to approach. He didn't want to create waves, so that eliminated some of the more excitable brokers, and eventually his choice narrowed down to two people.

At first it had been his intention to make simultaneous approaches. The first was a formidable French woman who tended to specialise in antiquities. She had amassed a vast collection, much of it looted from Iraq, which had helped her establish a spider's web of relations throughout Europe and the Middle East.

From her office in Paris she was responsible for moving some hugely valuable pieces around, all done without attracting even the tiniest hint of suspicion. Her success owed a great deal to the cover provided by operating a totally legitimate company that moved legal artworks all over the world.

She was always on the lookout for people to help transport her specialised items and had put a great deal of work the Courier's way in the past. The pair got on well and had even enjoyed a brief relationship, which had ended amicably.

But as tempting as it was to see her again, he knew he would receive less money because he would be working on her behalf, and she would want her cut for helping him out in the first place.

He decided to go for his second option. Sir Valentine Topper was a man with an eclectic range of contacts. He could always go for the French woman in a couple of months, but he reasoned that Sir Valentine was the man who would be able to put the most lucrative deals his way.

38

Hooley called a time out; he needed to clear his head. Something was nagging at him but, to his irritation, he couldn't pin it down even though he sensed it was important. That meant yet another coffee run was underway, which also meant more doughnuts for Roper.

He divided up the purchases and then sat back at his own desk. He'd gone for a stronger coffee than normal because he reckoned his brain needed the caffeine hit but was finding it very hard going. He'd only added an extra shot but it tasted a lot stronger than that.

He was going to have to do something. Glancing casually at Roper he noted he seemed to be occupied. His right hand sneaked into a drawer and his secret cache of sugar packets. He'd just got his fingertips on a bag when Roper spoke.

"You know sugar is bad for you; that last blood test suggested you might be heading for the first stages of diabetes, so you need to cut it out."

He froze with his hand in the drawer. He suddenly knew how Winnie the Pooh must have felt when caught with the honey jar.

"How did you know I was going for sugar?"

"Because you keep your supplies in the left-hand drawer. It's pretty much the only time you go for that one and, given that you just pulled a face after taking a sip of your drink, it didn't take that much working out."

Chagrined, the DCI withdrew his hand and braved another bitter mouthful, trying to convince himself that if he gave it enough time his taste buds would adapt to the strong flavour - but he still grimaced as he swallowed.

The coffee did have one benefit: the overpowering taste had cleared his head. He suspected it could probably clear drains as well.

"I know you love this cloak-and-dagger stuff but there is one question I have. Are we getting sucked into spy work that would be better off being carried out by intelligence professionals? I would hate it if we missed some key detail that even the most junior MI5 person would pick up."

"Well, I'm not sure you can make a distinction between a criminal investigation and an intelligence one. Surely, if you are plotting an explosion then it follows you are engaged in criminal activity, whatever the reason you might claim to be doing it."

Hooley was ready for the response since he knew Roper was very strong on the "crime is a crime" line.

"Yes, and I do appreciate that argument, but I think you agree with me: the thing about any form of detective work is that you would hope to be able to prevent things happening, as well as working out what happened after the event.

"So, if we are dealing with Russian spies, then surely any investigation should be led by the intelligence people? I know Bill Nuffield and his people are looking into it, but we don't have any idea of what they are doing and at the moment it feels like we are taking the lead. I'm worried that we are trying to do this with one hand tied behind our back."

Roper had been staring at him intently and now he jumped up.

"I think you might be right."

"I am." He always liked it when Roper appeared to credit him with brain power he wasn't entirely sure he possessed, although working alongside someone with his ability to make intuitive leaps was enough to make anyone doubt their abilities.

"So what's going through your mind?"

"I want to rethink our approach. If I am right that this is a rogue operation, then the chances are they won't be able to move things around so easily as if they were an official outfit.

"That means they need to consider how they bring everything into this country. Years ago all the KGB needed was diplomatic cover, but our people won't have access to anything like that.

"That will make things tricky for most of the bomb components, the electronics and suchlike, but it's going to be nearly impossible to bring in radioactive material. If they get caught, it won't just be us who will want to punish them; it could be their own side too.

"So, if we know they need to get assistance, that means a smuggling gang - but not one of your usual gang of baddies. You wouldn't want some South London heavy in charge of a load of plutonium.

"That means they will need to find the more rarefied gangs - the ones involved in moving the most difficult cargoes. Now, I bet there can't be many of those people around. I think it might be just a small handful and they won't advertise. Either you will be in the know or not at all.

"It's been said for a long time that some of the richest Russians in London use smuggling services to avoid the authorities when they want to move assets around. One way or another, it is Russians behind this."

Hooley nodded thoughtfully.

"OK. I can see now where you're coming from. Let me ask you in a different way - and I am going to come across a bit George Smiley here." Seeing Roper arch an eyebrow he stopped and thought for a moment. "You know I sometimes like to call you Sherlock? Well, George Smiley is the equivalent in the world of fictional spymasters.

"Anyway, the point is, I do have a question. What if there is a double bluff going on and this is all official and they can use diplomatic cover? Doesn't that put it back to MI5?"

Roper barely paused. "We can cover that easily. If we tell Bill Nuffield we are looking at this as criminal activity, then he and his team can focus on the intelligence side. That should make for a very efficient use of resources."

Hooley liked the response. "Good answer, and I think your idea sounds a very good approach all round. I would add one thing: we make sure that Nuffield provides us with daily updates on what his team are doing. That way you can be on top of their investigation and make sure we're not both missing something important that neither of us is dealing with."

A thought struck him.

"Talking of dealing with things, I've got some more news on my idea about forming an Odd Bods group. After talking to you I put some feelers out to a couple of my more sensible mates and asked them if they had anyone who might fit the profile.

"It turns out there is someone in the training section who is running the computer system, but my mate reckons she's being wasted there. He does know an expert when he sees one and he reckons she's great.

"She has a real flair for digging out details and doesn't need any motivating. You just point her at a task and she gets on with it. Her problem up to now is that she hardly ever says a word.

"People find that a bit unnerving. It's not they don't like her, it's just that no one can ever have a conversation with her. Even asking her if she'd like a cup of tea just gets a grunt. She only communicates by email, or even, and this is bizarre, prints out messages which she leaves on people's desks.

"They've tried to find a proper role for her because it's obvious she is clever, but they just don't know what to make of her. My mate says we would be doing her and ourselves a favour if we could take her on board."

Roper had listened closely.

"I get like that when I don't know people very well. It's like my brain empties out. The big change for me was working with you because you don't mind people being quiet. Julie says it's because you are a 'miserable old git' but I think she was joking. At least she said she was."

He didn't know it but Hooley was pursing his lips.

"She said that, did she?"

"Yes, a couple of days ago. She was looking for you and said to me 'I've been looking everywhere for the miserable old git.'"

Hooley narrowed his eyes. Sometimes it was hard to tell if Roper was trying to wind him up. "It's nice to know when your superiors are singing your praises. Look, what do you think? Shall I fix up for us to meet her? There's no rush, but if we can start lining people up then why not?"

"I think that would be good. And could you do something else? I need to know if you have any informants who know the big players in the smuggling business."

39

Roper had launched into a bizarre monologue the moment he met Hooley's contact.

"Blimey, me old china plate. I know we've been talking on the dog and bone but it's good to meet, even if it is a bit Mork and Mindy out here. Let's go and spend a bit of bees and honey because I'm Hank Marvin at the moment."

Hooley stared at him open-mouthed.

"What did you just say?"

"Cockney rhyming slang, 'innit?'"

The other man started laughing. From the neck up, he looked like a vicar from casting central, with a wide, innocent expression and protruding front teeth. From the neck down, his powerful shoulders and barrel chest said Boston Strangler.

He said. "I'm not sure many people would call it that. You don't really need to use the whole phrase, so you'd just say 'china' not 'china plate.'"

Before Roper could respond, Hooley chipped in again.

"I think I'm right in translating what you just said as - 'Hello, mate. We've been talking on the phone but it's good to meet, even if it is a bit windy out here. Let's go and spend some money because I'm starving at the moment'?"

He rolled his eyes before carrying on. "First of all, you only have to use the first word in the phrase. It barely makes sense."

Roper looked crestfallen.

"When you said he'd done some bird lime, sorry jail time, I thought it would make him feel at ease. I wanted to show that I was on the same level."

This last made Hooley's contact burst out laughing.

"You're the most comical Cockney I've ever met," he said, holding out his hand. "The name's Pete and it's a pleasure to meet you." He was quite a bit shorter than Roper and had to look up to meet his eyes.

"Given that you're about six inches taller than me, I think sitting down is the only way we will be on the same level. There's a nice cafe around the corner - I know the bloke who runs it - so we can talk in there. And, if you are starving, he does one of the best bacon sandwiches in London."

The meeting was taking place in Penge, a busy suburb of South London. Hooley had insisted they travel by train, claiming it would be much faster than coming by car. Roper had some slight association with the area, having briefly attended a private school in the nearby and considerably posher Dulwich, but he had never had the time to venture out of the immediate area of the school, so he was absorbing the surroundings.

It struck him that the DCI had been right about heavy traffic; the high street seemed to be gridlocked with buses, builder's vans and cars, plus the odd brave cyclist weaving in out of the vehicles. Pedestrians were everywhere.

They followed Pete away from the railway station and walked slightly downhill on the left-hand side of the road, passing fast food restaurants and greengrocers, until they reached a cafe. They walked inside, and Pete led them to a quiet table at the rear.

The owner came over to shake hands and take their order. He was short and thin, wearing a pristine white apron, and sporting a dark beard. His bright eyes seemed to sum them up instantly. His expression never altered as Roper asked for three bacon sandwiches for himself.

"Three?" asked Hooley.

"It's because of that man sitting by the door."

"What?" he shared a quizzical look with Pete.

"Didn't you notice? He had just picked up his bacon sandwich as we came in. It looked brilliant, you could tell the bacon was nice and crispy and it was on proper white bread with butter and tomato sauce."

"I thought you were a wholemeal-only bloke?"

"Not with bacon sandwiches. My grandmother taught me that you don't want bread that's got too strong a flavour. The point is, the sandwiches here are much better than we can get near the office so, since I am hungry, I thought I might as well go for it."

Hooley had to admit there was a certain logic to this and even Pete, who had only just met Roper, was looking approving.

"I still think three is a lot. You've told me off for ordering just one bacon sandwich."

"That's because you're fat."

For the second time Pete burst out laughing as he patted Hooley on the shoulder. "I'd give up while you still can," he said, wiping tears from his eyes. "You told me he was different, but you never mentioned he was going to be such a laugh."

Fortunately, the food started arriving and they settled into eating. It was as good as Pete had suggested and Roper had surmised from looking at his fellow customers. Despite having three times as much as the other two, the young detective still managed to eat all of his before they had finished.

"Very nice indeed," said the DCI, wiping his hands on a paper serviette. "If you're ready Pete, are you happy to get down to business?"

The man nodded so Hooley talked for the next few minutes, apologising for leaving out most of the key details but stressing how important it was and how short of leads they were.

As he had spoken Pete had become more and more sombre, until his features had gone quite dark. Hooley had never seen him react this way before so was concerned by his response.

"Your face is telling me that you might be having a problem with helping us with this."

Pete puffed out his cheeks and, if anything, looked even more mournful.

"I don't know, Brian. I really don't. I used to dabble in a bit of smuggling myself, years ago. In those days it was mostly beer, spirits and fags. Back then you didn't see much wine either - that only started in the mid-80s when everyone started going mad for Chablis and champagne.

"We used to sell a lot of it round here, off the back of vans and a few shops that would keep stuff in the back and flog it to punters they knew. Even the local filth, present company not included of course, turned a blind eye in return for a carton of smokes here and there.

"The blokes who brought it in were a tough lot but nothing nasty. They weren't angels, believe me I'm not one of those who pines for the 'good old days', but at least there were no guns.

"Nowadays it's a totally different story. Most of the smuggling routes have been taken over by total bastards, if you pardon my French. They cut their teeth on people trafficking mostly and you really don't want to mess with people like that. They're the sort that will kill you just for looking at them.

"But it can be even worse than that. If they think people are talking about them they come after you. I just don't think I can take the risk."

Hooley knew he was speaking from the heart.

"I can tell you are genuinely worried about this. The only thing I can say is that I wouldn't be asking if it wasn't serious, but you must do what is right by you."

Pete stood up. "All this talk of smuggled fags is making me want one. Hang on here for a few minutes while I go and have a smoke and think if there is anything I can do for you. I'm not promising, mind you, but if I can I will."

In the end he was gone for almost half an hour and Hooley was just preparing to give up when he reappeared.

"Sorry about that, but it turned into a three-smoke problem. Two to think about it and one more to check through what I was thinking." He paused to take a breath. "I do have something for you, but I'm going to admit I'm not sure how useful it will be.

"The bloke I am going to tell you about is a bit of a throwback. He has some sort of code that he sticks to, or at least that's what I've been told. I wasn't trying to con you when I said I've been out of the game for a while.

"There was a bloke about ten years back who had a reputation for being able to move anything. It was even said he was transporting kids around London by hiding them in suitcases, so you can tell what sort of fella he was.

"I never had a proper name for him and he was known by a sort of made-up name. I think he was called the Butler, or the Concierge, something like that. The idea was to make it sound like he offered a high class personal delivery service, or so I was told.

"But he was obviously tough enough to survive against the psychos who are running the business now - so if you could find him, I bet he would be a great place to start whatever it is you are looking for."

The DCI knew he had been lucky to get this much. He paid the bill and, after saying goodbye, he and Roper headed back to the railway station where they could catch a direct service back to Victoria.

"What did you make of him, Jonathan?"

"I thought he was telling the truth about how worried he was. There were no indications he was lying. Even I thought he looked scared."

"I couldn't agree more. I think we were lucky to get anything. When we get back, we can try chasing down the names he gave us."

"I Googled those two names while we were still in the cafe and nothing came up."

"I didn't notice that, you must have been very quick."

"You weren't supposed to see. I've been practising using the keyboard without looking at it and just using my thumb to type out the letters."

"I've seen you do some amazing things, I must admit, but that sounds impossible if you ask me. I can't even type on those little phone screens when I am looking straight at them in good light. Yet you're telling me you can do it without even looking. I mean - how?"

"It really isn't that hard once you get your mind into the right space. Anyone can memorise the keyboard, and then you just have to learn to judge the spacing so that you can spell out your words. I just made it something I really wanted to do and took it from there."

The DCI raised his eyebrows. "There's loads of things I tell myself should happen, but it doesn't seem to work."

If Roper had taken his comments in, it didn't show in his response.

"When we get back I can do some proper checking on the intelligence databases and have a look at some of the message boards on the dark web. They'll probably be encrypted, but the name may be there.

"I'm not that confident though. People know that even the dark web can be searched by the security services, so most of them are using impossible-to-access messaging services. So it is a long shot, but we have to try.

"The one hope is that he appears on something from about ten years ago, before all the new stuff came in. A few people have been caught that way because they didn't realise that a digital footprint can hang around for a long time."

40

Back at Victoria, Hooley was ringing round his contacts to see if anyone had heard of a smuggler called the Butler or the Concierge. He was not having the easiest of times.

"You must be joking, right. The Butler? Really? That sounds like something out of a Batman movie. Are you sure you haven't been inhaling again?"

The man talking worked in the immigration services and he and Hooley had never really got on; there was something about their personalities that made them rub up against each other. The DCI thought his man, James, was enjoying himself too much.

"Listen, mate," he said, trying to inject a note of passive aggression into the 'mate', "I know this does sound a bit daft, but this is a serious issue. Trust me, I wouldn't be willing to put myself up for having the Michael taken if it wasn't important."

He could almost feel the sneer coming down the line.

"I suppose this is all too far above my pay grade for you to tell me what it's about. Well, if I can think of anything, Detective Chief Inspector, I'll get back to you, but I wouldn't hold your breath if I were you.

"And if you don't mind me saying, and no offence," Hooley gritted his teeth; anyone who said that was about to say something unpleasant. "Ever since you adopted that mongrel Roper you've been coming up with a lot of funny stuff."

He sat back and made himself breathe slowly. He was experiencing some mixed emotions. On the one hand he could imagine punching James right on his stupid nose. But another part of him was dismayed that someone holding down such a high-powered job could be such a moron.

An hour later and he was still seething when his mobile beeped. Another old colleague, John Swinton, was on the end of the line. Swinton had retired from his customs position a few years back.

While work had brought him to London, he had retired to his beloved county of Yorkshire. He had been known to revel in that region's reputation for blunt speaking and the DCI feared he might be in for another bout of being called a fool.

To his pleasant surprise that didn't prove to be the case.

"I've been out on my allotment this morning, looking after my rhubarb. There's not many people I'd stop doing that for but you're one of them."

"Still living the Yorkshire dream then. Don't tell me, you've just made a cup of tea that's so strong you can stand the spoon up in it."

Years 'down South' had softened the accent but you could still hear it in the reply. "Aye, lad. There's one good thing about retiring: at least I got back to making a proper cuppa that you can actually taste."

Hooley smiled at this. He could recall once being offered a mug of tea that was so strong it had stained his teeth, or at least that's what he liked to claim.

"Well I'm sorry to interrupt your allotment duties. To be honest I wasn't sure you would get back to me, so it it's good to hear your voice."

"And you, Brian. Anyway, I don't have a lot for you, but I'll let you be the judge of whether it's important or not.

"A few years back, must have been around 2009 - and I can get that checked if it's important - our investigation team picked up that there was someone around who was making a lot of money out of people trafficking, especially kids. We didn't have a name, but we spoke to a few faces and nothing came back.

"I think we all assumed it was something of nothing, then about a year later we had one of those odd moments. We picked up a really nasty piece of work with a couple of women hidden in the back of his van.

"They were close to death when we found them and for a while it was touch and go if they would make it or not. He couldn't have cared less, and I remember wishing we could still 'accidentally' drop people down the stairs.

"Anyway, I digress. It eventually dawned on our little Herbert that he was in a bit of bother, especially when we explained we were going for a charge of attempted murder. I'm not sure the lawyers would have gone along with it, but the look on his face was priceless.

"Within minutes he started babbling about how he had information we would be interested in and came out with this story about a bloke who was using vans that he was disguising as some of the well-known delivery companies.

"No one even looks twice at those since they're everywhere. Our bloke insisted this man was the biggest operator in the market. We pushed him for more details but he didn't have much, just said the man was very clever, very careful and was making a lot of money.

"We decided this fitted with our earlier tip-off so put a bit more into it, but we got nothing. We thought that, if this bloke was out there, he's pulled out of the business, possibly after learning we were sniffing around.

"But it all stuck with me because there was something about it that suggested it was true. I couldn't help thinking that someone really ruthless, operating a sort of door-to-door delivery service for young kids, might well exist.

"Like I said, I hope you don't think this is the ramblings of an old man, but I hope it does help."

Hooley replied. "That could be very helpful; at least it's another clue, however small. Thanks for telling me. I think you're right - it does seem to fit with what we have, so it's good to be on the right lines.

"I'm only guessing, but if you operated in the way we do, then there wouldn't be much in the files about something like that."

"I have to admit that you are right there. It never does any good to actually admit you poured resources into what turned out to be a waste of time. The bean counters seem to take a special delight in holding your feet to the fire over that.

"You don't need to thank me, by the way, but you can show your appreciation in another way. I've got to come down there for a few days next month. If you're around you can buy me a pint."

Promising he would, Hooley ended the call and relayed the information to Roper. He listened carefully and then appeared to stare into the middle distance, which Hooley knew meant he was using his Rainbow Spectrum.

Moments later he blinked and spoke. "I think your contact is quite right: this does fit. It sounds like he might be the sort of man who would be involved in our problem. Whoever it is, he is going to be resourceful and clever, and this man clearly is.

"I haven't picked up anything yet but dark web searches can take a while. I've got everything set up so we have a good chance of finding it. We just have to be patient and hope we still have time."

"That sounds worrying; what's bothering you?"

"It's because I have been thinking it would take ages to get everything sorted out for moving what's needed and I said the plutonium was outside the UK. I've been wondering if I'm wrong and it's been here all the time.

"But then I'm not sure. If it was here why would they need to involve a load of rich Russians?"

41

Arkady Sokolov was addicted to the Ritz hotel in London and stayed there whenever he visited. Where some saw an over-the-top display of wealth, he saw glamour and the sort of effortless style that the British were remarkably good at.

He had flown in last night having prepared for the meeting with Georgi Yebedev by reading the files. They'd originally been put together by the KGB and now maintained by the FSB. Yebedev would have been alarmed by the amount of information his country of birth had on him.

In truth, Sokolov wasn't too bothered about most of the details he had read. He had really wanted to know two things: did Yebedev actually have the money he claimed to? It was surprising how many claimed oligarch status they didn't deserve. He had passed that test easily.

The second issue was whether he was currently an operational asset for his country or was one of those who might be termed as "reservists", ready to be used at any stage but currently non-active.

To Sokolov's mind, it was an important distinction. If he was current there would be too much FSB activity around him, possibly surveillance or phone taps and internet monitoring. That could prove disastrous. Again, Yebedev had passed.

The Russian fixer carefully studied himself in the ornate full-length mirror. He had inherited his physique, attention to detail and brains from his mother. From his father he had inherited a powerful love of opulence, which is why he loved the Ritz so much.

It always amazed him that the Brits could be so good at this sort of thing, along with running the sneakiest and most ruthless of intelligence services. He often speculated that the two ran side by side, since he suspected the dazzle of the glitz distracted you from what they were really up to.

He smoothed down his jacket and left the room; there was little chance he would fall into any traps, regardless of how cunning a plan was drawn up by MI5, since his mother had also drummed into him that he should never judge by appearance alone.

Her lessons were heartfelt since she constantly claimed that her husband had never turned out to be the man she thought he would be, claiming "not all that glitters is gold". Over the years he had come to prefer the English idiom "never judge a book by its cover". It was a lesson that had served him well over the years, and it had enabled him to successfully extract the genuine from the fakes.

Everything he had read about Yebedev suggested the man could be trusted, but he would make his final judgement on that once they'd had lunch in the dining room, having arranged to first meet in the Rivoli bar.

He walked in and was pleased to find his man already there, a glass of sparkling water in front of him. They shook hands and he also ordered water from the waiter who had silently appeared.

"A long time ago I'd have ordered vodka, lots of it. But I discovered I had inherited my father's weakness for drink."

Although neither man cared for alcohol, he liked to study people's reactions as he told the story; it was surprising how many would react in a sly way as they filed the information away, clearly hoping to use it as leverage later.

He was pleased to see Yebedev react with a small shrug. "You are very sensible. Too many of our countrymen have been trapped by the bogus allure of vodka. I always find alcohol makes me even more unintelligent than normal."

"I suspect you are being modest, but then that is better than being loud and showing off. I can't stand people like that."

He stopped talking as the waiter brought his drink and then said: "You bear a remarkable resemblance to Uncle Joe." He used the Russian nickname for Stalin which was a mix of mockery and respect.

"You are not the first person to say that - and I was even born in the same town, Gori in Georgia. For a while my father was convinced we had to be related but could find nothing. So, unless my great-grandfather had a very secret relationship with his great-grandmother, it is just one of those things.

"I have to admit I do get some odd reactions. In Russia people ask me if they can have their picture taken with me. It seems there are a few out there who still think he was a great leader; very strange. Having said that, there are those who cross the street to avoid me."

"What about here? Do people react in the same way?"

"Not really. I get the odd quizzical look, but most people ignore me. Many years ago I even tried the moustache but got far too much attention so I shaved it off."

The pair finished their drinks and made for the restaurant, where they were shown to the corner table Sokolov had requested. He felt it gave him the best view of everyone else including the immaculately-turned-out waiters pushing trolleys with dishes covered in silver cloches.

A huge party of twenty young Chinese women was being given the full treatment as their table was surrounded by waiting staff who simultaneously lifted the cloches to reveal the dish. As a spectacle it was pure West End theatre.

Sokolov had barely glanced at his menu, placing it straight down and seemingly having already made his choice.

Yebedev looked up from his study and said, "I am thinking of just ordering a main course. I prefer not to eat too much at lunch-time, if that is alright."

"Perfect. I am going to have the turbot with the champagne and caviar sauce. Indulgent, but not madly so, and I get to have a tamed version of alcohol, something that appeals to my sense of humour.

"I would suggest we keep business separate for now and just enjoy these beautiful surroundings while we get to know each other a little better."

By the end of the meal Sokolov was confident he could do business with this man and after he had signed for the bill, he suggested they head to his suite where they could be guaranteed privacy.

When they arrived at the room Sokolov surprised him by knocking on the door.

"One of my guards is inside. I never leave a hotel room empty; too many people can get access and we did a big sweep for bugs this morning. You can never be too careful."

As he spoke the door was opened by a very large and smartly dressed man wearing a black suit, white shirt and black tie. He looked like what he was: a top of the range bodyguard with chiseled cheekbones.

The man nodded respectfully and stepped back to allow them inside to a small sitting room. There was a door on the right, which Yebedev assumed led off to a bedroom. While he had eaten at the hotel many times, he had never actually spent the night there.

The guard left to wait outside, and the two men sat down on facing armchairs. Sokolov said, "Sir Valentine has told me what you are looking for, but I always prefer to hear it directly - it ensures there can be no misunderstandings later."

Yebedev talked for a little over ten minutes. He left out no details, including the role he would be playing, although he did not explain how he came to be involved. When he finished Sokolov spent a long few seconds staring at a point on the floor between his polished black shoes.

"It will not be easy, and we will return to that shortly. But first I need to know something. Why are you doing this? Why is someone like you involved?"

He had been expecting this question and knew he was going to have to answer it.

"I think it is because they want someone they have a hold over, and there is no way I can turn them down without risking everything I have built over the last few years. I have built a new life here in England and that would be over.

"If people here knew the truth about my wealth they would disown me. Of course, they suspect, but that is different to actually knowing. The people who approached me, the scientist, made it clear they would come after me.

"I can't risk that possibility; it wouldn't just be money. I was worried about the safety of my wife and family. You only have to look at what has happened to other people called traitors to know that.

"No one would protect me, not the British government, not even the Americans. There would be nowhere to run and hide. While I have no way of knowing if the threats are serious, I cannot take the slightest risk."

"You are right to take this seriously, and I have to tell you that even I cannot tell how close these people are to the Russian state. You know how things are there; it could be they are a part and also not a part. But I needed to know you truly recognised your dilemma."

"So, can you help me?" He didn't say it, but he secretly knew this was his only hope of meeting the demands placed on him.

Sokolov took his time again, this time standing up and gazing out of the bedroom window at the view over Green Park. It was still packed with office workers and tourists enjoying picnic lunches. Just occasionally he could see the appeal of a simpler life.

Eventually he turned back to look at Yebedev.

"It is good that you have been so honest with me, since if you had lied or tried to hold anything back I would have known and refused to do anything for you. As it is, I have decided that I should at least try to help - and the important word there is 'try'.

"I have never attempted to move a nuclear weapon, or even the component parts, so I will need to find out what is involved. Such knowledge will be very limited, so I will need a few weeks, but no more than that.

"I will find you once I have the answers to my questions. It may be that I have to pass the work on to another party but, even so, you still have to pay my fees. At the very least, I am going to have to form a partnership with someone and that will not come cheaply."

Yebedev had been leaning forward while he listened to the reply. He replied. "I will pay whatever it takes. I can afford to lose money; I cannot afford to lose my family."

42

Georgi Yebedev woke up inside a wooden shed. No, wait. Not a shed; it was the wooden shed that was supposed to represent the birthplace of Stalin. Somehow he was in the Georgian state museum dedicated to the life of the Soviet dictator.

He couldn't remember arriving, but he sensed he needed to get out fast before he was caught trespassing. Just then, loud alarms started sounding and he was thrown into a panic as he felt hands touching his body.

He woke, his heart pounding and covered in cold sweat, to find his wife shaking him by the shoulder. She looked cross.

"It's 4am and your mobile has just rung for the third time. Someone is desperate to get hold of you. I've been trying to wake you up, but you were sleeping like a dead man."

Her words made an involuntary shiver run through his body and she looked at him strangely, muttered something about seeing the doctor, and then threw herself back down on her side of the bed, her body language showing she did not wish to be disturbed again.

He lay there in the dark for a while, panting and trying to get his heart rate back under control, then swung his feet over the side of the bed and checked his mobile. As she had said, he had three missed calls, each just a few minutes apart and from a private number. No messages had been left.

He staggered to the bathroom, careful to take the phone with him, and used the toilet. Splashed cold water over his face to little effect, and left the room to go and make himself a cup of tea. He wasn't worried about the caffeine stopping him getting back to sleep; he wanted something to settle his nerves.

He padded down the stairs and into the huge kitchen, a temple to eye-wateringly expensive equipment, including a complicated oven that neither he nor his wife had ever turned on, leaving that sort of task to the domestic staff.

One of the maids had left a tray on the side with everything needed for making the tea; all he had to do was put a bag in a mug and fill it from the tap that delivered a constant supply of boiling water. It was the only bit of the kitchen that really interested him.

While the tea was brewing he placed his hands palm down on the white marble, enjoying the cool sensation. It was so pleasant he bent and rested his forehead against it. He was more or less back in control, but it was yet another bad night - and he had experienced many of those since getting dragged into the nuclear plot.

Perhaps his wife was right, and he did need to see the doctor. Right now, he would have welcomed being given a large dose of tranquillisers, or something to combat those dreams. Despite being quite mundane, in the sense that nothing happened, they were very vivid and contained an air of menace that stayed with him after he woke up.

He was using a tea spoon to squeeze the bag against the side of the mug when his phone started ringing again. He grabbed it, pressed the device to his ear and said "hello" in a voice that caught slightly so that it sounded like he had said "hell."

The voice on the other end was calm and businesslike.

"My apologies for calling you, but an opportunity has arisen, and you need to meet someone in a few hours. I thought you would prefer to be fully awake, so I have been trying for the last thirty minutes."

He recognised the voice as belonging to Arkady Sokolov; he was speaking English with the faintest accent. Sokolov added. "I'm sending a car to pick you up at 5.30am."

The call ended. He glanced at the oven clock, he had a little over an hour, more than enough time to enjoy a cup of tea and then have a shower and shave. He wondered about having something to eat but realised it was far too early for food.

He was waiting in the hallway when the shiny black Mercedes S-Class pulled up outside the entrance of his London home. He walked down the steps and opened the rear door to clamber inside. Once the door was shut he was concealed by the impenetrable black vanity glass.

Sinking into the comfortable leather seat he looked at Sokolov who scowled.

"He wants to meet us at a service station on the M25, at Cobham."

Yebedev recalled that Cobham was also home of the training facilities for Chelsea football team. The Russian owner could be often found there.

"That's near Roman's big project."

"It's just a coincidence. He likes the service station because when you leave there are two exits, so you can travel in either direction on the M25. It's all said to be very convenient." His expression suggested he didn't think there was anything convenient about it.

"Who are we meeting?"

"I'm afraid I'm not at liberty to tell you that. If the man likes the sound of your project, he will introduce himself at that stage. If he doesn't, then we need to find someone else."

They'd already crossed the river into south London and were on the outskirts of Wandsworth where they would pick up the A3 road. Despite the early hour, traffic heading into London was already snarled up through the one-way system.

Going against the rush hour meant they made swift progress and it seemed like no time before they were turning into the service area, which was huge. They drove to the most deserted point they could and stopped next to a large white van, indistinguishable from the dozen or more he'd noticed on the drive over here.

Nothing happened for at least five minutes although Yebedev took his lead from his companion who sat in long-suffering silence. The side door of the van opened, indicating they should get in.

The vehicle had two seating benches along each side. As the two Russians climbed in, the door slammed behind them and a light came on for illumination.

Facing them was a man in a dark blue boiler suit, the kind of thing worn by workmen anywhere. But he could have been wearing a diamond encrusted suit of gold for all Yebedev would have cared.

He had been instantly drawn to the man's eyes. They were the coldest he had ever seen, containing not a flicker of humanity. But there was unmistakable intelligence at play. This man radiated power and Yebedev had to force himself to break eye contact as he sat down on the bench, shuffling up so that his compatriot could also sit. All the time, the man never took his eyes off him.

"I want to hear your version of the task."

It was an order, plain and simple, and he didn't delay, repeating the story as he had just two days earlier in the Ritz. He was glad that he had held nothing back then because he was certain that he would have been caught out: and possibly met his doom in the back of this van.

When he finished the man glanced briefly at Sokolov and then spoke to Yebedev.

"I will help you. My fee will be five million pounds. Half now and half on completion. There will also be a bonus of five million payable immediately after we have finished."

Yebedev didn't hesitate; there was something about this man that suggested he wouldn't negotiate.

"I accept. I will make the arrangements to pay you the first instalment the moment I get back home."

The man suddenly leaned forward, taking him by surprise. He shrank back before he realised the man was holding out his hand, on his face the faintest hint of a smile.

He reached out and took the proffered hand, expecting his to be crushed, but in fact he was surprised at how gentle it was.

"You may call me the Courier. I have one rule: I make all the rules. Sokolov will be the point of contact and you must agree any additional fees with him."

He reached into a bag on the bench next to him and pulled out an ordinary looking mobile.

"This can only be used once, and only if there is a life-or-death emergency. The number you need is pre-programmed." He handed it to Yebedev. "Remember, this can never be used twice."

There was a scraping noise behind him and suddenly the van was filled with daylight as the driver had opened the door. Without a word the two Russians clambered out and watched the van pull away.

Yebedev said: "I don't know about you, but I could do with using the facilities before we head back into London."

43

Brian Hooley had been frowning at his screen for such a long time that even Roper noticed something was amiss.

"Have I said something wrong?" The question was genuine since he was aware that on occasions he could be direct to the point that even the DCI could become deeply irritated.

His comment seemed to snap the older man out of introspection and he stretched out his arms to try and ease a knot of tension that was building in his back, a problem that wasn't helped by the way he often sat slumped awkwardly in front of his computer.

"Sorry, Jonathan. It's nothing you've done - it's just Bill Nuffield. I've sent him three messages now and he's not getting back to me, not even to say he's busy at the moment and will get in touch as soon as he can.

"I've been thinking it's important we talk to him after our discussion about focusing the investigation between ourselves and his team. Things like that can get horribly difficult so I didn't want it to go wrong because we hadn't spoken to each other."

He picked up a pen and tapped it on his desk, the rapid-fire movement seeming to mirror his frustration.

"I hate it when people do this. One minute they are all over you and offering to help, the next you can't even get them to respond. I really hope that he's not trying to prove something here, like he's in charge and holds all the aces. If he is playing that game, then he will come to regret it."

Now it was Roper's turn to frown.

"Do you think it might be because he's got something which he can't tell us about?"

Hooley thought he followed that, but decided to wait for more.

"He could be worried he will give himself away if he talks to us."

"I don't think he will be worried about us gleaning something from his behaviour. At the risk of sounding like you, his counter-training is probably better than our training. He's not going to fall into that trap.

"For some reason he's messing about. I suppose I have to give him the benefit of the doubt and respect his right to do what he needs, but he should at least remain in touch, even if it's only at arm's length. I've sent him yet another request - if I still hear nothing by the end of the day tomorrow I may have to get Julie Mayweather to lean on him.

"I hate going over people's heads but if we don't all play by the same rules then it will go wrong and given the stakes we're playing for, I'm not prepared to take the risk for much longer. It works both ways because people will ask why I left it so long."

Hooley knew that he was partly looking for a justification for his actions. Getting Mayweather involved would help the situation, but it would also open him to accusations that he'd gone running to his boss at the first sign of trouble.

Everything about this was making him cross. He hated it when things became bogged down and was cross with Nuffield because, as a long-serving officer, he should have been very aware of the potential for trouble. And not talking always led to trouble.

He decided to go for a walk and clear his head. It was a gloomy day, with a light drizzle that felt like it could easily become heavy rain. The weather matched his mood and he stamped off grumpily, not sure where he was heading but just wanting to walk.

After about five minutes it dawned on him that he had made a schoolboy error. He had pushed what was at stake to the back of his mind, but all this did was let the tension build up; that's why he was getting cross at distractions.

Not exactly feeling better, but at least refocused, he turned on his heels and headed straight back to the office. Stopping at the cafe to pick up coffee, he hustled in and automatically checked his email.

Sitting at the top of a list that seemed to be mainly HR-style exhortations to work harder was one from Nuffield. For some reason he couldn't decide whether that made him feel crosser or better, a reaction that brought a wry smile as he realised he was being contrary.

He opened the message "Brian, as you Brits might say, a million apologies for not getting in touch. I hope that what I have got for you will take your mind off my disappearing act. Can you guys make it here this afternoon?"

Hooley read it again and fired off a response. "We'll be there at 2.30pm."

He rubbed his hands together in anticipation of finally having something new to get his teeth into, and turned to Roper to tell him that Nuffield had finally got in touch and was promising developments on the hunt.

*

The Century House security team were back to type and seemed a little too keen on their work.

He gave himself a mental slap. He really was going to have to calm down. It felt like any little thing was tipping him over the edge and he needed to rein himself in before he became a liability.

His mood improved when he saw Nuffield. At least he hadn't sent one of his minions. His authority saw them moved through, and they ended up in yet another room. The building was so large he could imagine people being lost forever.

As they pushed through the door Hooley saw a functional metal desk with drawers either side, a telephone, computer screen and keyboard. There was no printer, and the closest to a personal item was a ubiquitous framed photograph of Queen Elizabeth II. It was hanging lopsidedly, a bit like this case, he thought.

Those thoughts vanished when he saw that the room dog-legged round to the right, opening up to reveal a large conference table with eight chairs around it. One of those was occupied by a man wearing what Hooley thought of as the standard issue "spook suit", an inexpensive dark grey off-the-peg number. But what interested him was the pile of photographs he had in front of him: he could make out the top one, a picture of Georgi Yebedev walking down some steps.

Nuffield motioned his guests to get comfortable.

"We've had some progress with our surveillance teams. Before I show you the pictures let me talk you through what has been going on. I know you have Yebedev under observation in London, but we were pursuing another angle when we got this."

He nodded at his assistant who pushed the top picture towards the two detectives.

"This was taken by us, early yesterday morning." He nodded again, and a photo of a gleaming black Mercedes was slid across. "This car, which we were following, picked him up and took him to a rendezvous.

"That car was carrying a very well-connected Russian fixer called Arkady Sokolov. You can't see from these pictures, but he was sitting in the back. He's an interesting character, as nothing major comes out of Moscow without him having some sort of involvement.

"Fortunately, he's a man of habit and always stays at the Ritz, so when he flew into London we put a team on him. They were following him when they caught Yebedev being picked up. There is more to show you."

Another nod and three more pictures were slid across. The first showed the Mercedes alongside the van; someone who may have been Yebedev was climbing in with someone behind him.

A second picture, taken moments before the door was shut, showed the outline of a heavily-built man, but his features were unclear. The third photo showed the two clambering back out of the van.

Nuffield said. "These were taken at a service station on the M25 at Cobham. We believe the middle picture may show the man they met, but we can't be sure and even with our lenses we couldn't get a clearer shot - something to do with the dark interior, or so I'm told."

He stopped talking and looked at the two detectives. They were engrossed in the pictures, but it was Roper who first voiced what was in their minds.

"Do you think this could be the man we are looking for?"

Hooley held up a finger to stop him saying more.

"We need to give Bill the background first."

He carefully explained the meeting with his contact, and the suggestion that there was one "super smuggler" who was the person many turned to when the work was especially demanding.

"My man was a bit vague about it and quite honestly wasn't that keen on talking at all, but he told us this man was once famous for delivering trafficked children inside suitcases and taking them to addresses all over London. He had a big reputation in those sorts of circles apparently.

"Obviously we don't have any real details about him, or a description of what he looks like, but we were told that he made a point that he offered a personal delivery service for the wealthiest contacts. My contact reckons he was known as something like the Butler."

He nodded at Roper, who started talking immediately.

"What we do know is that this man is said to be highly organised, which is certainly something suggested by this meeting. But I think there is something more important than that.

"He is a big player in the smuggling world and yet we never once became aware of him until we were told about him by Brian's man. He is said to be clever and cautious. He sounds like the sort of man who summons people to come to him, not the other way around. Everything done on his terms or not at all. At least that's the way I read it."

"That's a very interesting analysis," said Nuffield. "It sounds highly plausible from the way you're telling it. We'll keep an open mind, but I think we need to start building our first scenario. This guy, the Butler or whatever - I just hope he's not the Joker - is being lined up to bring in the bomb equipment.

"My only reservation is: why aren't they bringing this stuff in using diplomatic cover? That would be the easiest."

"Jonathan has a theory about that which has convinced me." Hooley turned to Roper. "You're back on stage."

Fifteen minutes later and Nuffield was nodding respectfully.

"I think you may be right. And as you say, we watch the diplomatic side anyway, but the real action is going to be elsewhere. Actually, that all sounds like the kind of double bluff you Brits, and the Russians, are pretty good at."

44

There was nothing ironic about Tommy Dougherty's nickname of "Big Tommy." He was a giant of a man: six feet, seven inches tall and weighing in at twenty-three stones, or three hundred and twenty-two pounds in his socks.

A few brave souls even referred to him as "Mad Tommy", although rarely to his face. He'd earned that one early on in his career as a prawn fisherman based in the Port of Peterhead in the north-east of Scotland.

Taking his trawler Jenny, named after his wife, out for only his third fishing trip as a skipper, he ignored a storm warning in pursuit of a big catch. He was one hundred miles out to sea when the weather turned, leaving him no place to go. He'd wrapped his giant hands around the wheel and howled his defiance against the fifty-foot waves that came smashing down on his seventy-foot boat.

Amazingly, he and his four-crew survived and the legend was born, although years later he confided he had been so terrified and so convinced they were about to die that all he could do was shout at the top of his voice.

He never ignored a storm warning again, something that seriously pleased his crew, and they had all survived for more than twenty years in one of the most dangerous industries in which you could work.

Today he was returning to his home port with the hold barely half-full of the prized prawns, most of which were snapped up by Spanish buyers before they were landed - the skippers radioed ahead with details of what they had and when they would be landing.

The sun was beating down as he slowly headed for the quayside and he was pleased with the look of his boat. His wife said it was his one true love, and there was some truth in that. Six years ago, he had upgraded his engines to the latest environmentally-friendly ones. While his power output had dropped from 500kw to 400kw, his annual fuel bill had dropped by fifty thousand pounds.

He'd invested some of that money on paintwork and the Jenny now gleamed in a dark blue livery that was a match for the jerseys worn by the Scottish rugby team: his tribute as a proud and passionate Scot.

They'd been at sea for ten days and his phone had been pinging for a while with incoming messages that loaded as they came back in range of the telephone signal. With the boat tied up and his crew supervising unloading, he checked to see who had called him.

As always, his wife had sent him a welcome home text and that was mirrored by ones from his two boys, neither of whom intended to work in the fishing industry. And then, right at the end, one that made his heart turn over.

There were no words, just a yellow sun emoji. He scrolled down and sure enough there were two more, three in total. That meant they had come from the same person. The Courier was back after an absence of years.

The signal meant he needed to be ready to move within three weeks. More information would follow over the next few days, so it seemed he couldn't have timed his return from the North Sea better.

He'd made a decent living from the prawn business, but it was the work he'd done for the Courier that had made him a wealthy man and made sure his family was well taken care of. It was why his sons were soon heading to America to study degrees in law and medicine respectively.

He didn't do many jobs for the man, but he was a good payer and had never reneged on his promises. He looked at his crew through the cockpit glass and smiled as he anticipated their pleasure at the news. They too had shared in the bounty over the years.

*

Astrid Olsen wiped her greasy hands on her blue boiler suit as she stood up from examining the engine of the dilapidated twenty-foot inshore boat tied up at Stavanger, Norway. While the thick cotton outfit did nothing for her figure, it could do nothing to hide the fact that she looked like a Norse goddess - albeit one with a smudge of oil on her forehead.

She was almost six feet tall, with blonde hair and blue eyes, and her passion was fixing boat engines. It was said that, thanks to her, the hulls of many a fishing boat had worn out long before their propulsion units were ready for the breakers' yard.

As she went to get back to work her phone pinged with an incoming message. She looked and saw it was a yellow sun emoji. She didn't realise it but, as she waited, she was holding her breath, so it was fortunate that the next two emoji arrived within twenty seconds.

She'd started to wonder if she would ever hear from him again and was thinking she probably wouldn't. She wondered what had brought him out of wherever he'd been, but then she shrugged.

The whole point was that she didn't need to know. Olsen just needed to be ready to move. Within the next forty-eight hours the marine engineer would receive the means by which she could establish communication for what needed to be done.

Like "Big Tommy", she smiled at the thought of the money that would be heading her way. It had allowed her to remain as a small, independent engineering company at a time when so many were merging to try and save costs.

Olsen was in such a good mood she allowed her two apprentices to go home early, a rare treat as she was normally a stickler for timekeeping, frowning at lateness and normally refusing requests to leave before the time was due.

After tidying up her workshop - it was always immaculate - and making sure everything was in its right place, just as her father had taught her, she headed out. A hot bath and then a lovely dinner, cooked by her husband, awaited. The extra money had allowed him to stay home and pursue his passion as a writer and he loved cooking almost as much as putting words together, so they all benefitted from the extra cash, even if she needed to go on a run every morning.

Olsen arrived at work early the next day. She'd slept well, but had woken before dawn and her busy mind wouldn't let her get back to sleep - so she had slipped from the bed, enjoyed a coffee in the kitchen and then left to get on with the day's tasks.

Twenty minutes after arriving she heard the deep throb of a motorbike and went in to her office just as the rider, clad from head to toe in black leather and wearing a black helmet with a black visor that hid his face, walked in with an envelope.

She knew the drill and had her passport in her pocket, which she now handed over to the man who studied it carefully before handing it back along with the envelope. The rider turned and walked out. Seconds later she heard the noise of his bike receding into the distance.

Ripping open the envelope she saw that it contained a sheet of paper with five numbers on. Olsen memorised them, and then burned the piece of paper. Over the next few days she would receive two more envelopes with the rest of the numbers.

The left-hand drawer of the office desk was locked and had been for almost ten years, but she needed to open it now to check the contents. Olsen kept the small key on her main keyring and now she opened the drawer. Inside were the pre-paid phones she had bought a decade ago.

Happy that all appeared well, Olsen relocked the drawer. Tonight, she would be taking three of the phones home to charge them up. Her apprentices were about to get another lucky break by being sent home early.

When she had the whole number, it would allow her to phone a similar pre-paid device being held by the Courier. The instructions were to wait twenty-four hours from the exact time of the third delivery, and then Olsen would get her instructions and be told about her payment.

She knew that the Courier could have achieved better security using an encrypted app, but she also knew that he liked to do things in a slightly old-fashioned way, and who was she to argue with methods that obviously worked?

*

An hour later, and almost four hundred miles away across the North Sea, another black-clad motorcyclist had arrived at Big Tommy's modern five-bedroom house on the outskirts of Peterhead.

He was fast asleep, catching up after ten days of snatching a few hours here and there, but his wife was forewarned. She produced both their passports and the rider nodded once as he accepted her identity and handed over the envelope.

As she went into the kitchen to make a fresh cup of tea, nearly 600 miles away in London the Courier was going over his plans yet again. He had received text messages from the riders to say the packages had been delivered so he knew the network he needed was activated.

He tried not to have favourites, but he thought the two he was using for this job were probably the pick of his team. They were the first people he had thought of when this job had come to him, and he was confident they would not let him down.

There was also a third team getting ready to move. They had more specialised skills, since their job was to retrieve the stash of weaponised plutonium and ensure it was ready for transportation. If they left a trail of radiation behind them then the whole plan would crumble like a pack of cards. Now he had to wait for the location of the stash, although he had been given a general idea, in a rural spot in central France - so that he could make proper calculations of the necessary travelling time.

It had been agreed that, once the plutonium arrived in London, the bomb assembly should begin straight away. It would be a dirty bomb, meaning relatively less destruction to allow for more radiation. He certainly had no intention of being anywhere near the capital in just a few weeks from now.

The rest of the equipment, along with the technicians needed, was being brought in by Sokolov, with Yebedev having already arranged accommodation and a work space over to the west of London.

They wanted the prevailing winds to spread radiation over as wide a range as possible, and it was hoped that the money-making machine that was the City of London would get a massive and unwelcome dusting.

As the Courier understood it, detonation would depend on whether a ransom demand was met. He assumed that, faced with catastrophe, the government would pay up, but he had no way of knowing.

But there was one thing that was totally certain. There would be a massive manhunt for the people behind the plan and, while he had been giving a lot of attention to delivering his part of the bargain, he was starting to think about his own survival.

During his years of success, he had remained out of sight and below the radar. He doubted he would be able to do that much longer, but that's why he sweated the details. He needed to vanish without a trace.

45

"We're aiming to do the switch in ten days from now, so you will need to be in Stavanger on Monday week. I will have had the package delivered by then and I'm hoping to have it sitting around for as short a time as possible."

Judging by the quality of the line, Big Tommy thought it sounded as though the Courier was out of the country. There was a slight delay, which meant they had tripped over each other speaking. They'd resolved that by leaving a long pause when they each finished.

"From what you are saying so far, I'm getting the impression that this is pretty portable."

That pause; then, unusually for the Courier, a short laugh.

"If it's you doing the lifting, it will be child's play. I haven't actually seen it yet, but I am told the package is the size of a large suitcase and weighs in at about fifty pounds - so quite a bit for ordinary mortals, nothing to you."

"That's good to know, and I will do it myself; the other lads are no slouches, but it wouldn't do to drop it in the harbour."

This time the silence at the end of the line carried on for quite a while.

"It would be a disaster if that happened."

"No worries - that's why I said I would carry it myself. By the way, you haven't said what is in the package. I am assuming this is one of those need to know occasions."

"It is for the best that I am not telling you, and very much in your interest that your name never becomes associated with it. I can assure you will be quite safe while it is in your possession. For the remainder of this operation this is the last time we shall speak. As we were talking I arranged the first payment to you and the second will come when the job is done.

"I am adding one new thing. I don't anticipate any problems, but it would be foolish not to have a plan. In the event that things go out of control you will receive a single yellow emoji. If that happens you are to abort and make no attempt to contact me.

"You will still be paid, but I will have judged there were too many risks to see the job through. Now, quickly go through the plan for the last time and then we can both go about our business."

"I will be close to the Norwegian coastline the Friday after next. I will report an ongoing mechanical problem and request I be allowed to dock for work to be carried out by Astrid Olsen. I will explain I know her from previous work.

"From Olsen I will pick up the package and return to Peterhead, aiming to arrive on the Tuesday morning. I won't report in my catch and say I have already sold it to a private buyer. Once docked in Scotland, the package will be in the third load to be taken out of the hold.

"Two men dressed in working gear will approach and say they are there to collect the load for a Mr. Taylor. They will take the package and my role is done."

*

The clock started ticking even faster than the Courier had expected, and it very nearly caused disaster. The details of where the plutonium was buried came in via Moscow on the same day he had spoken to Big Tommy and Olsen.

It turned out his team was only thirty miles from the location, in the grounds of an abandoned farm outside Limoges. It was an amazing coincidence that gave him slight pause for thought, as though things were lining up too smoothly; but he put the idea aside.

The pick-up team assured him they could reach the location, retrieve the package and be gone while it was still daylight. As it turned out they had overestimated their ability, and the Courier had allowed himself to become distracted and didn't challenge them.

It took them far longer to find the package than they had anticipated, and it was fully dark by the time they pulled it from the ground, having had to dig out five big holes before they got what they were looking for.

They had just put all the equipment away when they saw headlights in the far distance. They started getting closer and it was soon obvious it was a vehicle approaching along the farm track. To their horror a police car pulled up and two officers got out.

The gendarmes had been alerted by a local man who was out foraging and had spied the pick-up team frantically digging away in the yard of the abandoned farm. Armed with a vivid imagination, he had deduced it was bank robbers returning to pick up their loot and had phoned the police emergency number.

The duty inspector had almost let it go without taking action but then changed his mind and sent a patrol car. Now the two officers were challenging the four men standing in the yard to put their hands up. The pick-up team were frozen in the harsh glare of the spotlights on the police car.

Unfortunately for the officers, a fifth man was just out of sight, having gone to relieve himself before they set off on the long drive north. He had sneaked unobserved to the back of the van, where he now produced a Kalashnikov rifle.

Taking a deep breath, he stepped out and started firing. He was ex-Special Forces, so seconds later both young officers fell dead to the ground. There was no time for hanging around and the pick-up team piled into their van and set off.

Had the police reacted sharply they might have intercepted the van, but it was forty-five minutes before a back-up car was sent and another thirty minutes lost before the alarm was raised, which was more than enough time for the pick-up team to be safely on their way. Because of the darkness, there was more delay in identifying the tyre tracks that proved they were looking for a van.

In London the Courier had received the news apparently calmly, but his misgivings instantly returned as he learned of the narrow escape. However, cancelling the operation would now be hugely problematic, as they no longer had the option of returning the plutonium to its original hiding place.

For better or worse, the delivery was on its way to Stavanger and, depending on road conditions and how many breaks they took, it would be there sometime in the next twenty-four to thirty-six hours.

He thought hard. He had a safe-house in Belgium; he would get the team to rest up there for five days. Otherwise the package would be spending too long in one place in Stavanger. It meant more changes on the hoof, but he felt there was little choice.

The Courier even revisited the overall scheme and considered bringing in the plutonium via an English Channel crossing, but he stuck to his plans. There was too much security and technology that way; it increased the risks.

He briefly thought about informing Olsen of the changes he had made but decided against it. The way this was going he might have to make more changes and he didn't want her thinking the plan was unravelling. That might worry her and risk her making a mistake.

Forcing himself into a positive state of mind, he reasoned that, although there had been a very narrow escape, the package was on its way and if there were no more problems it would be in London in twelve days' time. After that it wasn't his problem; once the delivery was confirmed he would be booking a flight to Mexico.

*

Three days after the murder of the two gendarmes, a French news agency received a call from a man who claimed to have alerted the police to what was going on at the farmhouse. He was put on to a reporter and, clearly excited at talking to a journalist, launched into a garbled account of what he had seen.

The reporter was only half-listening. Having to talk to "crazy people" came with the territory and she was inclined to lump this in with all the other examples she had heard over the years. She was about to butt in and wish him a polite but firm goodbye when he said something that jolted her out of her boredom.

"I'm terribly sorry, but could you repeat that last bit? There was a funny noise on the line and I only half heard you. I thought you said something about space suits."

The excitement on the other end of the line hit fever pitch.

"That is what I said. Remember I was a long way away, and even with my binoculars I couldn't see it clearly, but there seemed to be two men in spacesuits."

The reporter could see the beginning of a plan. "Could I just double check all your details again - you know, your name and telephone number; and do you have a picture of yourself you could email over?"

Half an hour later she was looking at a very clear photo of her star witness. To her relief he looked, with an open and honest face, like the sort of man who could be trusted even if he was saying something outlandish.

She approached her editor. He'd recently been muttering about the need to generate more "clickbait" news stories. She had just the thing for him.

One of the first people to see the story was the Courier. He valued information, so had set up a search alert for "Limoges" and "murder". When his laptop alerted him he had something, he read the story and then picked up the phone.

46

Thanks to the wonder that is the Internet, the story had morphed from a relatively sedate, if eye catching, "Witness claims to have seen spacemen at scene of shooting" to the rather more arresting "Aliens slay cops".

Unsurprisingly, the latter was the version that was being aired on social media and inevitably being picked up by newspapers all over the world. It was rapidly turning into a global "silly season" story and an account mocking the claim appeared in the print edition of the London Evening Standard.

Which is where it was spotted by Roper. He was so gripped by the headline he stared at it for almost five minutes, becoming so still that Hooley couldn't help noticing and wondering what had sent his colleague into a trance-like state.

He suddenly snapped back to life, his hands reaching for his keyboard as his eyes opened to stare at his computer screen. He spent a short while staring intently at the information he'd called up and finally spoke. What he said sent a jolt up Hooley's spine.

"I think the bomb is on its way to London - or it may even have arrived."

"What?" The DCI shouted, as the shock brought him to his feet. There was a world of difference between examining something as a possibility to being told it was now a reality.

Roper held up his copy of the Standard. "This story here is the clue. They're treating it as "fake news", but looking at other versions online you can see it started out in a more considered way. I've found what looks like the original version and that quotes an eyewitness saying he saw men in spacesuits digging in the ground in an isolated spot in France.

"That's become translated to him talking about space aliens - but what if he actually saw men in radiation suits? From my research I already know that it is highly likely the KGB hid stuff all over Europe. What if this was where they buried some plutonium and then forgot about it, at least in an official sense?

"This could be exactly the kind of thing that a rogue team might be capable of doing. They could have come into possession of the details and removed any trace from the records. This stuff could have been there since the start of the 1960s, just waiting for the right time, or opportunity, to be retrieved.

"I've been running these new details through my Rainbow Spectrum and it comes up as being highly likely. We can dismiss the idea that it is space aliens, but they would have been cautious about retrieving the plutonium.

"The chances are that it would be well contained and not giving off any radiation, but why take any chances until you were sure? That's exactly what I would have done, and from a distance those protective suits do look a bit like spacesuits, so an ordinary member of the public could have been confused.

"There is one thing we have to check, and that is with the French. My Rainbow Spectrum gives me a less than five per cent chance that this might have been something the French were doing - a small figure, but we would need to double-check it.

"I don't get the sense that it will turn out to be the French - I mean why would they kill their own police officers? - but there is the slightest chance that something did go badly wrong, so it has to be considered. Will you be able to do that?"

Hooley was still standing up, clenching his fists so hard his nails were digging into his palms.

"When did all this happen?"

"Five days ago."

Hooley sat down as the implication hit him.

"So that's why you're saying this could have arrived days ago. I need to speak to Julie Mayweather, and Bill Nuffield, and we need to start thinking about picking up those two Russians, Sokolov and Yebedev."

Roper started urgently tapping at his keyboard.

"Thinking about all this has made me forget that surveillance report that came in early this morning. Our team say there was no sighting of Yebedev last night. They said they can't be totally sure without checking, but they don't think he's at home.

"He's stayed away before - one night he just caught a private jet to the South of France for dinner - so they weren't too bothered. We need to find out if he's surfaced. It's midday now so that should be plenty of time for him to get back from a night away."

Hooley put the call in and a few minutes later he received a call on his mobile. He went ashen as he listened and then put the phone down.

"No sign of him and no sign of his wife. The children are away at school, so we'll have to check there, but is it just me or is all this confirming what you think?"

Roper was looking as serious as he'd ever seen him. "There's no way Yebedev is going to stay in London if there might be a nuclear explosion. He'd want to be well away from the danger area."

For the next hour the news was bad. Yebedev and his family had disappeared yesterday morning, the children being taken out of school with the claim that a grandmother was dying.

Meanwhile Sokolov had suddenly left the Ritz, cancelling the remainder of his stay, something he had never done before, and the duty manager reported that he had seemed "unusually" anxious to leave.

"I've thought of another reason why this might be bad news," said Roper. "It looks like they both suddenly received a warning after this spaceman story first appeared from an agency in France. That means someone was looking out for news and immediately tipped off our pair that the police would come looking for them."

47

There was a lot to like about the top floor of the ten-storey building located between Regents Park and the British Museum. It was in one of the nicest parts of London, with the park home to London Zoo, but also close to the restaurants, shops and cafes of the fashionable Fitzrovia.

But it wasn't for those reasons that Yebedev had been delighted to discover the entire top floor of four two-bedroomed flats was available on a twelve-month lease. It fitted perfectly with the instructions he had been given.

Access was available through a lift in the underground car park, making it easier to reduce sightings of any coming and goings. It was also the right amount of space for accommodating the team that had arrived over the past few weeks.

But its biggest advantage was its location to the west of London. That meant the prevailing winds would take the radiation eastwards, passing over some of the most densely populated parts of London.

While the explosive power of the bomb would be, relatively, fairly small, it was intended to funnel radiation straight up, the higher the better in terms of increasing the potential footprint.

The team that had assembled in London had flown in from all over the world. It was nominally led by a couple of Russians supported by a North Korean, an Iraqi, and a German who was the expert in electronics for such devices.

They had been arriving over several weeks and were all in place almost two weeks before the plutonium would arrive. Not that this bothered them; they were well paid and well used to hanging around after being rushed into position.

Everyone except the Korean spoke reasonable English but he had worked in Moscow so had a decent grasp of Russian, allowing the two Russians to translate anything that was causing confusion. Not that anything did - they all knew their jobs.

Within ten days, the bomb was assembled and waiting for its deadly heart. Once that was in place they could set remote timers and detonate. Now that this first phase was completed, they did finally pause to reflect on the enormity of what was being planned. But not for long, as they all convinced themselves it would never get that far. Surely the British government would pay up rather than face such a catastrophe.

The bulk of the work completed, most of the team, with the exception of the Russians, would be leaving tomorrow; they decided to go out for dinner, voting for a highly rated Lebanese restaurant that was close to where they were based.

To help get in the mood, a couple of bottles of vodka had been produced and the Korean and the German had really got into the swing of things, downing a series of shots before they went out and insisting on stopping at a pub for a couple more before dinner.

The Korean seemed to be in an exceptionally jolly mood, although no one could understand what he was saying. His speech had thickened with alcohol and even his Russian translators were struggling to follow what he was saying.

The man was so jolly that his companions started to wonder if this was going to end in tears, but he remained in an upbeat mood and his humour was so infectious that everyone was smiling even though they had no idea what he was talking about.

After arriving at the restaurant, he had something to eat and calmed down enough for the Russians to start understanding what he was saying.

"He wants everyone to know that it has been a pleasure to work with such a team of professionals and, while he expects we will never see each other again, he wishes everyone all the very best."

On the way back to their flats the German fell into conversation with the Iraqi.

"Do you think they will go ahead with the plan, or will they pull back at the last minute?"

The Iraqi considered the question for a while, and they walked past a Middle-Eastern cafe with people sitting outside smoking from hookahs.

"I certainly hope not," he said. "I've never been to London before, so I hadn't realised what an interesting place it is. After this job I can consider retiring and I think I could fit in around here. Might have to stay away for a while, but it would be a shame if something did happen."

The German nodded and pointed at a couple of seats that had become available.

"I hope you're right about that, but shall we enjoy it while we can?"

48

Hooley tried the phone again, but it went straight to answer, just like the time before and the time before that. Roper always answered his phone - there was no way he could ignore an incoming call - and now he had missed three in a row.

His worry was being magnified by his guilt, since he was wishing he had trusted his instincts when he had seen his colleague this morning. It wasn't that he had sat down without saying anything - that was par for the course - but the biggest sign that something was wrong was that he hadn't turned up with coffee and muffins.

Although he was dressed in his trademark skinny black suit it had looked slightly too large for him, as though he had somehow shrunk in size. Every time someone had come into the office Roper had ducked his head, displaying an awkwardness he had not shown since he had been suspended a few years ago.

He tried to concentrate on a memo that had just been hand-delivered, something urgent from HR, but his heart really wasn't in it. He glanced at the clock again. Roper had been gone for two hours now and wasn't taking any calls. He needed to do something.

For a few moments he imagined putting out a general alert, and then dismissed the idea as he knew he would never be able to explain to Roper why it had been necessary to take action that could be said to make him look like a criminal.

He pressed his fingers into his temples; he could feel the first trace of a tension headache building, and he knew that not taking some sort of direct action was the underlying cause. He needed to get out of the office.

Decision made his spirits lifted at the prospect of doing something. He was going back "on the beat", because he knew he was going to have start walking if he wanted to track his younger colleague down.

It was a daunting prospect, because how are you supposed to find someone in a city the size of London and a population of millions? At least he could eliminate the most crowded spots, and he hoped that Roper had taken himself for a walk and found a spot where he could sit without being bothered. He had one big advantage: Roper was a man of habit.

He calculated that Roper would have made for one of the many Royal Parks that dot the city; all he had to do was decide which one. On a hunch, he decided Roper would have headed east, drawn towards where he lived on the south side of the River Thames close to Tower Bridge, so that made Green Park a firm favourite since it was on one of the routes the young detective took when he walked home.

Before he set out he checked Roper's favourite cafe. The place was buzzing and the owner smiled when he saw him, but he hadn't seen Jonathan in a few days. His anxiety was growing and he could almost feel time pressing down. He hailed a black cab and was dropped off at the Buckingham Palace end of the park.

He knew that Roper came down here to enjoy watching startled visitors being ambushed by greedy pelicans. A couple of the birds had mastered the art of stalking up behind people enjoying eating outside and grabbing food straight out of their hands.

Thirty minutes later, he was feeling hot and bothered and wondering if he was in the right place. Suddenly thirsty, he bought a bottle of water and tried to push mounting doubts out of his mind.

London was a dauntingly large place and after fifteen minutes of furious thinking, he still couldn't come up with a better idea of where to look.

He was about to give up searching and go straight to Roper's apartment when two men walked past. They were both white, middle-aged, and wearing immaculate pinstriped suits with polished shoes, white shirts and what may have been some sort of club tie.

He had crossed the park and was now close to the Whitehall end, making him think they were civil servants, but then something else came to mind. They could be lawyers, since they weren't too far away from the ancient Inns of Court at the Temple area near Fleet Street.

Last summer Roper had insisted they take a picnic lunch in the Temple Gardens, insisting it was an area where you could feel the flow of history since legal chambers had been there since about 1300. Roper was particularly keen on the detail that the then-King, Edward II, met a gruesome end thanks to a red-hot poker. Hooley had not shared his enthusiasm but had ended up losing his appetite.

Ignoring the fact that his feet were aching, he hustled into the Temple area. To his extraordinary relief he spotted Roper sitting alone on a wall. He was quite still and had his head bent, staring at the ground.

Hooley walked up and tried to make himself sound as relaxed as possible.

"Well, you're a sight for sore eyes. I think I've done enough walking for one day. Mind if I sit down and join you?" The last word came out a bit squeaky from the enforced note of good cheer.

Roper didn't look up. "How did you find me? I turned my phone tracker off, so it can't be that." His voice was flat, and he looked very tired.

"I may not have your Rainbow Spectrum to fall back on, but I am a detective - so when you stopped answering my calls I decided to get out and do a bit of detecting."

"I know. You must have remembered me saying how much I liked it here; we're in a very busy part of the city yet this is an oasis of calm."

"Is that why you've come down here - because you need a bit of peace and quiet? Now I've turned up and spoiled it, but I was worried about you, especially when you didn't answer the phone. That really isn't like you."

"I had it turned off. If I'd let it ring I would have had to answer it and I didn't want to answer the phone to anyone."

"Do you want to talk to me about what's going on?"

"No. Actually I don't mean "no" I don't want to talk to you, I mean "no" I don't know what to talk about… or I don't know where to start might be better."

"So, are you saying you're confused about something?"

Roper was still looking at the ground between his feet. "It might be that, I suppose. I'm not sure."

Hooley took his time answering. It was one of the advantages of talking to Roper that he didn't mind long silences. He decided on the best way to approach this.

"Are you OK to just listen for a moment? I've got an idea about what is going on and the best way to explain it might be for me to talk about myself."

Roper didn't react at all and the DCI decided he might as well take this as a positive.

"This case is getting to me, especially the idea that someone might be insane enough to detonate a nuclear bomb. I've been having trouble getting to sleep at night and then when I do I have really vivid dreams that don't make any sense.

"Last night I dreamt I went to bed at home and then woke up in a ramshackle river hut on the Mississippi near New Orleans. I've never been there and wouldn't know what a river hut looks like, but in my dreams, I did.

"It was such a vivid dream that I even ended up sort of sleepwalking as I tried to find a way out. It was only when I turned the bedroom light on that I knew where I was. It was horrible, and I was covered in sweat, so much so I needed to take a shower.

"After that I was able to get back to sleep quite quickly, thank goodness, and I didn't have any more dreams - at least not that I remember - but that one I certainly did, and in fact do. That's the worst that's been happening, but there is other stuff too.

"At lunch-time yesterday it was my turn to get the food and when I got out of the building there was a party of schoolchildren. I kept thinking about them caught up in this and felt very strange for a while. I had to sit down and get my breath back.

"So, what I'm saying is this. I've been a policeman for a very long time and this is the worst that I have felt, so maybe you are feeling some of the same pressure I am, and that would be no surprise. And not talking about it is something we all do, so it's not just you."

Roper finally looked up.

"I keep thinking: what if I make a mistake and we can't find the bomb? Everyone thinks the Rainbow Spectrum will sort all the answers but even I don't think it works like that. I haven't felt like this since I was at school and couldn't make friends.

"I feel like people are looking at me all the time. Everywhere we go people say things like they have heard all about me. Well, what if that is all wrong? Or I have been lucky up to now, and I have used up all my luck and will never be able to do anything again?"

The normally pale Roper had gone sheet-white while he was talking.

"This morning I didn't even want anything to eat and I can never remember that happening before, but I just don't feel hungry. I haven't had any breakfast or any lunch so far. Last night I was in my flat and started to feel dizzy and the room sort of went around.

"But the worst thing is that my memory is not as good as it was. Normally I only have to read something once to memorise it, but I can't concentrate… and the other thing is, I can't find my Rainbow Spectrum."

49

Hooley had been so shocked by Roper saying he couldn't access the Rainbow Spectrum he hadn't known what to do or how to respond. He needed to get Julie Mayweather involved.

Making Roper promise to stay where he was, he had walked a short distance away and called her on her direct line. She answered quickly and listened calmly as he talked, relaying to her what Roper had been saying.

"Right, I'm dropping everything and coming to you. Do you think you can get him to his flat? I think the security of being at home might help."

The suggestion triggered a thought. He said: "I'm sure I can manage that and, when I get him home, perhaps I can suggest he does some of his flapping."

He was referring to the unique method Roper used to send himself into a light trance. He did it by listening to the sound produced when he gently wafted sheets of A4 printer paper held in either hand - and it had to be A4-sized. The exercise always helped him slow his racing thoughts and allowed him to take time out when he felt pressure mounting.

In the smallest bedroom instead of a bed it had a black leather reclining chair with a matching footstool. It was handmade, and had cost him more than four thousand pounds, but he had willingly paid the money as he loved the shape, finding it perfect for his relaxation exercise. It was one of the few objects he had ever expressed much interest in. Everything else he bought was for its functionality.

Mayweather said that she should be there within the hour, adding: "We need him on this case. It sounds to me as though he is having a crisis. We have to hope we can get him back on track.

"We are up against the clock. In fact, if Jonathan is right about the bomb being here already, I fear we may be entering the final countdown. We may need our shrink so I'll call and put her on standby."

"I presume you're talking about Dr. Beth?" said the DCI. Eighteen months ago, an American psychologist, Dr. Beth Shapiro, had been signed up by Mayweather to come and take a look at their team.

Mayweather ended the call. One of the things Hooley appreciated about his boss was that she listened to what was going on and was quick to react if she needed to. You knew that, whatever happened, she always had your back.

He sat next to Roper; "Right then, you are getting the Royal visit. Julie wants to come and see you, and says it would be best if we met at your place. She won't be there for another hour, so I suggest we crack on - and maybe you practice a bit of your flapping."

The younger man visibly brightened.

"That's a great idea. You're happy to wait until I finish?"

"Oh, don't worry about me. I presume you have beer in the fridge, so a nice cold lager and watching that view will do me just as much good as an hour's flapping session will have for you."

He saw Roper was about to respond and held up his hand to delay him. "I know you're going to say your way is healthier, and you would be right. But my way tastes better."

Roper was so enthusiastic that he didn't even argue when the DCI suggested a cab and, twenty minutes later, he had already placed himself in a light trance. Hooley was determinedly taking small sips of beer: one was the limit. They weren't out of the woods yet and clear heads would be needed.

Roper's place was immaculate, displaying little evidence that anyone actually lived there. It could have been dressed as a show home to encourage prospective buyers: even the television was a basic model, not the big beast you might have expected to find in such an expensive penthouse.

He sat on the settee. It looked like one you would buy from a Scandinavian furniture catalogue. It was comfortable and he gazed out of the window at the panoramic view. What the flat did have was great soundproofing, and it was only the buzzing of his phone that woke him up forty minutes later.

It was Mayweather, to say she was minutes away. He sat up, rubbed his eyes, and then got to his feet. He needed to stretch his back - the settee didn't make a great bed. There was still no sign of Roper, so he rang down to the duty guard to let him know he should allow access to Julie Mayweather.

He had just ended the call when Roper almost gave him a heart attack by silently walking up behind him and tapping him on the shoulder.

"Bloody hell, Jonathan, you're as light on your feet as Mayweather. I thought she was the only one who could creep up on me like that."

Roper looked puzzled. "I didn't creep, I was walking, and I just wanted to let you know I had finished and was ready for the next phase."

Before the DCI could respond there was a knock at the front door. Their boss had arrived, and Roper let her in.

Many years ago, his grandmother, who brought him up after the death of his parents, had drummed into him the need to show visitors hospitality. The Deputy Commissioner had to refuse a long list of drinks and snacks while still standing in the doorway.

She said, "Honestly, Jonathan, I don't want anything to eat or drink, but if I could come in and sit down, we have work to do."

She knew her man well and had pitched the request just right, as he stopped doing an imitation of a waiter and showed her inside. Even though she had been here before, she was still impressed by how much space he had in such a prime location.

"I bet you can rattle around in here on your own. Anyway, why don't we all sit down and get started? You choose where you are most comfortable, and Brian and I will fit in around you."

Roper took the single armchair and waited as the pair sat on the settee that was at right angles, with Mayweather sitting closest to him. She said, "Brian has told me what you've been saying, but can you run through it again?"

Some people claim that the way to tell someone is lying is to get them to tell you a story over and over again, saying that if it is repeated exactly then it must be made-up because they are sticking to a script.

They hadn't met Roper. His memory meant he knew exactly what he had said and so he repeated it exactly. Hooley, who didn't have a script to check against delivery, was pretty confident there had been no deviations.

He finished speaking, so Mayweather jumped in.

"Brian and I will try and deal with each issue there, and I think we do have answers for you, but at any time you don't agree with something, just let us know. Before we start I'd just like to say that you look very well. Everything about you is neat and tidy and your body language is nice and loose."

This was the last thing the DCI had been expecting her to open with but then he recalled that she had called Dr. Beth. Perhaps the psychologist had suggested it. It certainly seemed to work.

"Now the first thing to tell you is that feeling stress about this is perfectly normal. I think Brian has already told you about what it's doing to him, and I am also having trouble sleeping. To be honest you wouldn't be human if you didn't feel this.

"We are trying to find some very dangerous people with an even more dangerous weapon." She stopped, and then added: "Did you see the way I avoided calling it an atomic bomb? It just goes to show the way your brain finds ways not to think about terrible things.

"But, as I was saying, the stress is very real and very present. The fact you are able to talk about the effect it is having on you is good. You shouldn't be keeping those thoughts to yourself. But Brian and I are just as bad.

"We've put so much effort into remaining calm that we've forgotten to acknowledge the problem, and that just makes things worse. But never mind; we are doing it now."

She looked across at him. "If you want to stop me at any point, get stuck in."

He responded with a firm shake of the head, so she carried on.

"The fact that so many people have heard about you is a great compliment. There are thousands of detectives out there, but very few have won your sort of recognition. But remember this. The people who do know about you and Brian also understand how hard it is to do your job.

"No-one is expecting you to get absolutely everything right. What their reaction does show is how pleased they are to have you on their side. I know these things are hard for you to understand, but it means they totally respect you on the basis of what has gone before. You have earned the right to be considered a top detective, and nothing can take that away.

"And that brings me on to the last point. You are in a team and it is a team where everyone has everyone else covered. It may turn out that your suspicions are wrong, but that's why other people are looking into different ideas. If your lines of inquiry don't pan out, others will. So that's a big thing. You are not alone anymore. You are part of a team."

Hooley could almost see waves of tension floating off Roper. "Of course. I've managed to forget all that, which isn't like me at all. I suppose that is the stress."

"That's exactly what pressure does to anyone. It knocks things out of shape and leaves you doubting yourself. But that's OK. Once you realise it is happening you can do something. You got this rolling when you spoke to Brian this afternoon."

"This is really helpful. I feel lighter in some way and my brain is coming back into focus."

Roper stood up and headed out of the room without a word, leaving the two police officers staring at the Roper-sized hole in the room.

He reappeared. "I'm sorry. I need to spend a bit more time in my flapping room. Brian, would you like a drink? I'm going to be about an hour, maybe less."

"I'd be delighted and, tell you what, let me show our boss out and then go on to that lovely little pub round the back here; you know the one, it's where we went last summer."

Roper disappeared again, and Hooley said, "I'm going to take that as a 'yes'."

They left the flat and headed for the lift, neither saying anything until they were outside. Mayweather's driver was waiting close by. She held up both hands to indicate she would be ten minutes.

"I think I'll join you for a quick one, although it might be a soft drink."

Hooley nodded. "I've had my beer for the day. Jonathan and I will be heading back to the office shortly. If you don't mind me saying so, that was brilliantly handled. I really didn't expect you to start with telling him how well he was looking."

Mayweather said. "You can thank Dr. Beth for that. She told me something she had been keeping back in case it was needed. She discovered that his bad experiences of being bullied at school left him feeling he must actually look different to attract attention.

"He told her that, when he went somewhere new, the bullies started on him straight away, so he convinced himself it was his appearance. She told me it was vital to send reassurance there is nothing wrong, that it didn't mean his problems were starting all over again. It was also her idea to remind him he is part of a team."

"Well, that was brilliant; and I think he may be back on track, but I will be keeping a close eye on him. We can't get away from the fact that he is probably the only one who can crack this problem. We need him back at his best."

50

He'd grasped the significance the first time around, but he wanted Roper to run it by him again. At the back of his mind he was hoping hearing it for a second time would make it sound less worrying.

"The information has come from an MI5 source: someone they regard as a low-level asset at the foot soldier level. Not a front-line operator. That's why the significance of this was missed first time round.

"In fairness the information came through in a complicated way. It is from someone known to the informant who was, in turn, passing on what a third person had told him, so it was hardly the most direct line of communication."

"I thought this was exactly the sort of thing the intelligence types liked? All murky and difficult to pin down," said Hooley. He waved his hand in the air. "Sorry. Stress brings out the grumpy old git in me."

Roper just carried on. "The third party reported that a mixed nationality group of men had been seen around the Regent's Park area. Normally he wouldn't have bothered about it, as it is that sort of area, but there was one thing that made them stick out.

"One night it appeared that they had gone out for dinner and one of the group appeared to have had quite a lot to drink. He was in very high spirits and talking loudly. He was saying how pleased he was at the way things had gone.

"The rest of the group were trying to keep him under control and at one point he started saying something and a big man, who appeared to be the leader, went up to him and whispered in his ear. After that he shut up."

"So, tell me again what he said that provoked the reaction?"

"He started talking about how the rest of them should be grateful that he had had so much recent experience. At that point the bigger man shut him up straight away."

"Not being a party pooper, but there isn't anything in that which sets off any alarms for me."

"I agree, but let me get to the end and explain why I think there is something here. This man was speaking Russian, but with a very thick accent. He was also said to be of East Asian appearance. The man who saw him says he was dressed very badly, like he'd stepped out of the 1970s and didn't have a lot of money. The rest of the group looked well-dressed in a contemporary way."

The bad feeling he'd had the first time round had grown. He almost voiced his fears but instead asked Roper to run through the timeline again.

"This happened in London four days ago. The MI5 informant is adamant about that since it was the same day as a big football game when his team were badly beaten by a Spanish side and the third party was complaining that the group had turned up at his pub just after the game finished.

"So, if we accept that as correct, then that is eight days after somebody shot those policemen in France - or to put it in another way, we are now twelve days past that point; so if this is connected then the plutonium is definitely here."

Hooley took a deep breath to try and slow his heart down. He was feeling hot and a little disoriented.

"I think I can see why you are making these links but talk me through it."

"Well, the fact that someone is speaking Russian makes you start thinking about connections to our case; obviously it might be a coincidence, but it could be more. What if the East Asian person was actually from North Korea?

"Everyone knows how hard the North Koreans have been working at developing nuclear weapons, so what if this man was on one of the development teams? Then you factor in that the Russians have always had links to North Korea, especially on the nuclear programme, so I've been asking myself if it's plausible that this man has been brought in because of his expertise. Even better, it is unlikely that any Western intelligence agency would be aware of him, so he could travel incognito."

"I don't want to be negative, but it sounds like there are an awful lot of assumptions in there. I'd be willing to guess that you have already run this through your Rainbow Spectrum; what did it come back with?"

"It's complicated, but it seems to make my idea that this is a rogue operation more likely, given all the different people involved - but it has identified that there must be someone who is currently at a very high level on the Russian side."

Hooley would have liked to put his head in his hands. He'd kept hoping this would all turn out to be a misunderstanding but Roper kept coming up with more reasons why it was likely to be true.

"What is your instinct saying we need to do next?"

"I think I may have something: a lead on where the bomb might be and it's because of this information that I think I can pinpoint it."

"That's fantastic, Jonathan: some good news at last."

Roper looked slightly embarrassed at his boss's enthusiastic response.

"I've been looking for property that Yebedev might have rented, or bought, over the last twelve months and that turned out to be a bigger task than I had thought.

"Not only does he use multiple company names, he has also been amazingly active - so I was swamped with information and none of it stood out. But my guess was that he would be looking for a building that's quite high."

"I'm not going to like the answer to this, but why high?"

"Because they will want to try and mimic the effects of an 'air-burst' detonation. With such a small device they will want radiation spread as far as possible, so the higher up you are the better. They can't drop a bomb, so a tall building is the obvious choice.

"But for some reason the only buildings he had directly acquired an interest in, at least as far as I could tell, were mostly outside London, so that didn't seem to fit at all. Then, yesterday, I got a new company name to check out.

"He called it the ALBE Corporation London, and this morning I discovered it was behind a leasing in West London called Park Buildings. Which reminded me that his two sons are called Alexander and Benedict, so taking the first two letters of each name gives you ALBE.

"I've looked deeper; it's a ten-storey apartment block and he has leased the entire top floor for twelve months. Now that would fit my theory about them wanting to be high up. At first, I was thinking that would mean being somewhere like Canary Wharf, but security there would be too tight.

"This might suit them better, because it is not going to be top of the list of places to check out, but it gives them plenty of space to create a bomb and provides them with on-site accommodation since they wouldn't want to draw attention with a lot of comings and going.

"There are two more things that make it more probable. The building is very close to where our Russian-speaking East Asian man was seen, and the second is something that has only just occurred to me. To make this a really big threat they would want the radiation carried on the wind.

"On the right day with wind direction in your favour, a detonation on top of this building could send a cloud drifting down through the centre of London and on into the City. I'm sure you could probably work it all out to see how big an area would be affected."

Hooley's mouth had gone dry, and he looked around for something to drink but there was nothing in view, so he made himself swallow hard and said:

"We're going to need the SAS, and we're going to need them now."

51

Tom Phillips seemed to materialise in the centre of the office; one second he wasn't there, the next he was. The SAS Major glowed with health, and he'd kept his head closely shaved. Hooley had never been able to tell his age, settling for a guess that put him between thirty or forty years old, but even then he allowed for another five years' leeway at the upper end.

As the DCI shook hands, he noted that the man was radiating that air of competence that made you feel there was nothing he couldn't take on. He was exactly the kind of guy you wanted at your side if you thought you might be going into battle. And that was something Hooley felt was looking inevitable.

Roper was also delighted to see him. He had formed an unlikely bond with the army officer when they had worked together to bring down a team of ex-Special Forces soldiers who were supplying victims to ruthless scientists conducting illegal medical experiments.

"Well, I might wish for happier circumstances, but it's great to see you both again. And if you don't mind me saying so, Brian, you look like you've lost quite a bit of weight since we last met. It's a good look and suits you."

"You can give the credit to Jonathan for that one. He keeps a close eye on me and makes sure to point out the healthier eating options. He doesn't win every time, especially when it comes to the pub, but I do listen."

Greetings over, the Major was quickly down to business.

"When I heard that the request had come in from you guys, I knew it was going to be interesting. I've got my tactical team preparing a bit of kit, but why don't you give me the heads up on what we are going to be doing?"

Hooley replied: "I'll let Jonathan do that, but first you need to know this operation has been escalated since we spoke a few hours ago, and the decision has been made to turn this briefing into a COBRA meeting. When you hear what we are up against, that will make sense."

"I'm under the impression that COBRA meetings are when the top brass are talking major threat to life scenarios. Like terrorist bombs."

"That's not always true; sometimes they can be very routine, but in this case the risk assessment couldn't be any higher. Jonathan, can you run us through it? Keep it as short as you can for now. The details can be gone through later, but the Major needs to know what bit he is going to be getting involved in."

Being literal-minded meant that Roper was very direct.

"There's an atomic bomb at the top of a building near Regent's Park and we need you and your team to go up there and get it."

To his credit, the Major didn't flinch, but his complexion darkened.

"Well, that was to the point. I think the phrase 'worst nightmare' springs to mind. I look forward to hearing some more details but from what you've said, and I am glad to report that I had already alerted my top drone team that they might be needed, so they're on the way.

"My senior operator was on a course down in Dorset, so I got a buddy in the Royal Marines to collect her in a helicopter. They only had a Chinook free, so it will be landing in Kensington Palace shortly. I'm told Harry and Megan are the most senior royal's about today, so they won't complain."

"That's great," said the DCI. "We've got all the plans for the building being pulled together and they will be at COBRA when we arrive. Julie Mayweather wanted to meet you as well, but she's had to go to Downing Street to brief the PM.

"We've got transport waiting outside. When we get there, the plan is for Julie to deliver the key briefing then we break up for the next phase, which will see you and your team get involved. The feeling is that we are almost out of time, so the pressure is on.

"The idea is that we will take action today, which means we have to get inside those flats and deal with what we find. Or, perhaps I should say, that's the part you will be doing. Once you've done that, a team of nuclear scientists will be following you inside and making things safe - we hope."

"Give me five minutes to brief my team. Have you set up a rendezvous point for Park Buildings, so they have somewhere to go? There's no point dragging them in for the whole COBRA meeting."

"Being sorted now. There are some fancy new Command and Control trucks being moved into position. I'll text you where they are setting up, which is about five hundred metres from the location."

"That sounds perfect. Can you let them know that I will have two officers who will need access to the trucks? I also have a large white van which has the drones. My people will alert your team when they arrive. Another question: have you got eyes on the building?"

"Only human ones at the moment. Our surveillance experts have arrived and are mapping any access points, but they are under strict instructions to do nothing until you arrive. Breaching that building will be entirely on your authority. Specialist police teams are heading for the site, but you will be the Officer Commanding."

"Good. I think this is the only sensible way forward given we are under such terrible time pressure. I've got one final request, and I hate to ask this, but I think we may need Jonathan there to make sure we don't miss anything."

He turned to Roper. "I'm asking you to put yourself in direct danger. I have no right to do that and you have every right to refuse. I wouldn't blame you if you wanted to stay back."

Roper didn't hesitate. "I want to be there."

52

COBRA was a fancy name for a less than fancy place. Normally it was heavily staffed by senior civil servants. Today it was full of people either standing up and shouting or sitting and shouting.

The reaction had followed Mayweather's briefing, and she was now waiting for everyone to calm down, so she could take questions. As well as military and police officials, senior figures from the emergency services were also present. The possibility of a nuclear attack had been discussed here in the past, but never in these terms.

It had been intended that Roper, Hooley and Major Phillips would be there, but at the last minute it was decided that Mayweather was more than capable of dealing with questions; the really important bit was getting to the bomb, and if Roper was going then the DCI was too.

The three men were just arriving on site. "Last chance to bail out," said the Major.

Before either man could reply, they pulled up behind what seemed at first glance to be super-sized mobile homes, with impenetrable blacked-out windows and sporting an array of satellite dishes.

Inside, the clever design allowed them to be packed with computing power and communication systems. Hooley guessed they would boast jamming systems to take down mobile phone networks. They were greeted by a tall young woman in battle fatigues who was in charge of one of the smoothest and quietest operations Hooley had ever seen. He felt like he had just stepped on to the set of a sci-fi movie, which, in a way, he had.

The woman, Captain Helen Bowers, obviously knew the Major well, as she first saluted and then warmly shook him by the hand. She started explaining progress so far.

"When you give us the go-ahead we can cut all power to the building, take out the landlines and Internet and scramble any mobile signals. We have also accessed the roof space and will be able to ensure they cannot receive any satellite signals.

"I have been informed that a top-level decision has been taken to make this operation a priority rather than trying to move people away. The view is that, with the time available, either this will work or people die anyway, so why start a panic?"

Before anyone could react to this apocalyptic comment, two more people appeared: a man and woman. They looked like brother and sister with cropped hair, brown eyes, broad shoulders and expressions of intense glee.

They made Hooley jump by simultaneously shouting "Sir!" as they saluted the Major and then looked at him expectantly.

"Have you got your toy to show us, Jenkins? I think Brian and Jonathan will be very interested."

The woman had been holding one hand behind her and now pulled it to the front to display an oblong-shaped device, about A4 size, with a tiny propeller mounted on each corner. Roper gazed at it in awe.

"Is that one of the new generation drones?"

Jenkins smiled in acknowledgement. "It's about the best we've got. Just enough fuel for twenty minutes' flight, so should be plenty in these sorts of urban conditions. I've got half a dozen more outside. One for each side of the building and two in reserve."

"How quickly can you get them in the air?" asked the Major.

"We'll be ready when you are, sir. Everything is warmed up and ready to go."

Major Phillips glanced at his phone to read a message that had just beeped to signal its arrival; then he looked at the Captain.

"My assault team is here so we're going to head into the building shortly. I've got eight units with me and the plan is to split them between the top floor and the roof."

He turned to Jenkins. "I want eyes on that top floor by the time we arrive there and at that point we cut all outside power and communication. That's it. That's the plan. So let's be careful, but let's be quick."

The Major departed, leaving Hooley and Roper in the Command and Control centre, and a few minutes later they were watching crystal-clear video feeds as the drones shot up the outside of the building. Arriving at the top floor, powerful cameras zoomed in. Two of the flats came back as totally empty, one had the curtains on one room partly closed, and one flat showed two men sitting down playing some sort of video game.

Roper and Hooley were both staring at the curtained room.

"Can we get any closer to see in there?" they said at the same time.

The Captain muttered into a throat mic, and moments later the window grew larger and larger until, in one corner, it was clear there was something electronic there. The screen on the far end, which had been showing the two men, suddenly filled with smoke.

The Major's voice came over the airwaves. "We just fired a flashbang into the flat - it's the last thing you expect ten floors up."

Moments later the screens filled with black-clad members of the Major's team. Seconds after that it was all over, and the two detectives were soon following on the heels of the bomb experts piling into the building.

With the power still off they were using the stairs, and by the second floor Hooley was waving Roper ahead. "You get up there and carry on. I'll be fine coming up slowly." He watched enviously as Roper bounded away up the stairs.

Panting heavily the DCI finally arrived at the top floor. He was too busy catching his breath to notice how quiet everything seemed. He walked in to see what was going on and could immediately tell by the collective body language that all was not well.

One of the SAS troopers directed him to the Major and Roper. He walked in to find the detective gazing out of the window and the SAS man looking serious and troubled.

"What's the problem?"

"There's no bomb here, just preparations for a bomb. And if you believe the two jokers we picked up, there never were any plans to build one.

"They insist they were paid to do exactly this and no more. They claim the only intention was to check out our responses and ability to pick up such a threat, but they were never going to do anything.

"It's impossible to know how much of what they say is true; they may even believe it themselves, acting like 'useful idiots' if you like. But there is no bomb here and they certainly aren't acting like people who have been thwarted at the last moment. They are far too relaxed about it."

At that moment Roper walked over. He looked troubled.

"This has to be a set-up. I've been thinking back, and they provided just enough information to make me start thinking there was going to be a bomb here. The North Korean man speaking Russian was obviously part of it. They knew I would make the mistake I did."

"Don't take this on yourself, Jonathan. All you did was come up with an honest appraisal of what you thought was happening. The question I have is: why go to all this trouble? Is that worrying anyone else?"

An hour later they were heartily wishing they had never asked the question.

53

The message had arrived after they got back to the Victoria offices. The two detectives had slumped at their desks, morosely sipping coffee, while the Major paced restlessly. Then Hooley's phone had chirped.

As he answered the caller started speaking. He spoke clearly with no hint of an accent. His words were short and to the point.

"There is a bomb and we will set it off. If you want to avoid a disaster the price is allowing us to have sixty minutes unfettered, remote access to the system at GCHQ. You must reply within six hours. Use the email address you have just received. Do not make any attempt to trace it. We will know."

Hooley looked at the message. It was the same as the verbal one he had just listened to. He handed it to the Major who, with Roper looking over his shoulder, spoke it out loud.

Roper was the first to react. "That's actually quite clever of them. They could find out a lot of valuable information in that time and make a small fortune out of it, and we would never know what they had taken."

Both the DCI and SAS officer spent the next fifteen minutes on the phone, and at that point Julie Mayweather appeared.

"Let's decamp to my office. We've got more room there."

They followed her out, with Roper bringing up behind, apparently deep in thought. As the other three sat down he said, "Can I say something?"

The Deputy Commissioner made a 'you have the floor' gesture, to which she had to add "go ahead" before he would start talking.

"We need to try and check some things with the Russians if that is possible. I would especially like to know if the scientist, Maria Vasilev is around - and do they know where Arkady Sokolov is?"

"Actually, I was going to raise that just now," said Mayweather. "Bill Nuffield has been on that since we found out that Yebedev and Sokolov had dropped off the radar. Don't ask me how but given the high stakes here, he's reached out to the FSB.

"He's got some sort of personal contact there, I don't know who or how, but there is a degree of trust. Something about keeping lines of communication open. He says his contact was genuinely surprised and frightened at hearing about nuclear bombs.

"I was told that our people are inclined to believe this. The FSB insist they can find no trace of the pair and Nuffield says that this all goes to support Roper's theory that we are dealing with a rogue team."

"Is he totally convinced that there is no official Russian connection to all this?"

"That's what he told me. He didn't seem to have any doubts."

Mayweather's office was big enough to offer the scope for pacing around, which Roper did now. He was moving slowly, and it was clear to all three that he was deep in thought. Hooley held up two fingers to suggest they give him couple of minutes. The other two nodded approval.

In fact, it was less than a minute before Roper spoke. "All along there has been something bothering me. I couldn't help thinking the plan was a bit obvious, and how were they going to make enough money out of it?

"Holding an entire country to ransom means you would be on the run for the rest of your life, so why was their plan so simple? Money was never going to be the answer - it's too difficult to move the sort of amount we would be talking about.

"Then they could have tried to transfer it electronically but that would have been traced, no matter how many accounts it was moved through. With the entire world looking it would never stay hidden.

"And I don't think I am showing off when I say that it was a very clever ruse to have sent me off in the wrong direction - although I was right to say the bomb was on its way - but I think there is another player here. I think the bomb was meant to be in that building but this new player changed the plan at the last moment.

"I don't mean the original idea to dig up the plutonium and get it to the UK. I think that someone else seized control at that stage and took over, and it must have been someone the original plotters made contact with.

"And I keep coming back to your contact telling us about this 'Concierge' character." I've been trying to place him in the Rainbow Spectrum and he doesn't fit. That usually means that it's an important thing that I don't know enough about."

Major Phillips had jumped to his feet.

"Might your Concierge be known by a different name and would he be connected with people trafficking, drugs and that sort of thing?"

"What's making you say that?" said Hooley.

"There's a bit of legend about a Brit who did brilliantly serving in the French Foreign Legion. He was promoted to the rank of Colonel when he was just 25 years old.

"That sort of thing is unheard of, but they really rated him and were grooming him for senior command. Then, to everyone's shock, he stepped away before his contract came up. Just upped and left without a word.

"He'd decided to go into business for himself and, using the contacts he'd made and the reputation he'd built, he wasn't short of money and men to build his own team. Everyone expected him to go down the mercenary route, but he had other ideas.

"He went into the smuggling business and I heard about him a few years ago because a couple of wannabe SAS types decamped to work for him.

"In very short order they made a lot of money, so it was said, and then retired. It was claimed that this man – who was known as the Courier - was a brilliant strategist who seemed to love outwitting people almost as much as he did making money.

"I even heard a horrible rumour that he was transporting tiny kids around London inside those suitcases you can take on a plane as hand-baggage. I must say I thought it would take a special type of scum to do that."

Jonathan jumped in. "That ties in with what we were told about him. I think you must be right, this Courier is the man we want."

The Major went on. "The Courier dropped out of sight a few years back but then a member of my team, Trevor Robinson, suddenly left without a word. I was surprised and asked around because he was a sort of mate, not close exactly but enough for me to check nothing bad was going on.

"Brothers-in-arms and all that, I guess. Anyway, I didn't find out much at first but a couple of months later I bumped into someone I knew. A bit dodgy, if I'm honest, but I always had a soft spot for him.

"Turns out he not only knew I had been looking for Robinson, the meeting wasn't accidental. Robinson wanted me to know he was alright and to stop looking. It was obviously a bit of warning, but I can never resist a challenge.

"So, I persuaded my dodgy mate it would be in his best interests if he told me exactly what he knew and then I could leave things alone. He's a sharp lad and decided to spill the beans, or at least the bit he knew.

"He told me that Robinson was working for this Courier now and was set for life. But in his new job he definitely didn't want to be talking to serving officers in the SAS. So I left it there.

"There's one bit more. My dodgy mate can't resist bigging himself up and claimed he worked for this Courier from time to time. He said the man only worked with the best and my bloke has an almost supernatural ability to talk his way into anywhere: a very handy skill on occasions.

"We'd had a few beers and he produced a picture on his phone which he said showed the Courier. It was quite blurry and taken from the side so didn't show his full face. My bloke said it was the only known picture of him and he'd taken it because he couldn't resist the challenge.

"I suspect he was lucky to get away with his life, but the point is I might be able to recognise him if we have a picture of him."

Roper had been fiddling with his phone and surprised everyone by answering the question. "There's nothing on the Home Office data base of anyone called the Courier. I was checking while you were talking. We need Bill Nuffield to check the classified database - but I've got another idea about how we can find him."

54

They had all turned to look at Roper but when he continued speaking they realised they were going to have to wait. "I know we're running out of time, but I need to go for a walk, clear my mind and make sure I'm not jumping to the wrong conclusions."

He pointed at Hooley. "You come with me - but no talking."

The brusque order made Mayweather arch an eyebrow, and the Major suddenly took a keen interest in the carpet by his feet. As he got up to follow Roper, the DCI was sure that the SAS man's shoulders were shaking with suppressed laughter.

He supposed he could have made a fuss but knew there was no point and if Roper said he was onto something, that was all that mattered. He really didn't get that bothered about status anymore, far preferring to get results.

They walked out of the building and into the crowds - this was one of the areas of London that always seemed busy - and Roper led them towards Vauxhall Bridge and crossed the river to turn left on the Embankment. As they approached Lambeth Bridge he started to slow then picked up the pace again towards Westminster Bridge.

Here they re-crossed the Thames and then hung an immediate left along Millbank and the return leg to the office. It was a warm day and they passed a young couple sitting on a bench. Hooley noticed enviously that they were drinking take-away coffee.

He'd have loved to have stopped for a drink but there was no chance since Roper was clearly on autopilot. This was one of his regular walks and familiarity allowed him to switch off while he was thinking.

Hooley wasn't a gambling man, that addiction had nearly ruined his father - but he might have considered a very small wager that Roper was thinking about his Rainbow Spectrum.

The biggest clue was the speed at which they were walking. Normally Roper was the man who put the "brisk" into "a brisk walk", but it was as though the brain power he was siphoning off for this bout of problem-solving was slowing him down.

Not that Hooley was complaining. This pace was perfect for him; it got his heart going but didn't leave him hot and sweaty. Many were the times he had been forced to wait outside the office in order for his heart to slow back down to normal.

As they arrived back at Victoria, Hooley could sense Roper was coming back into the normal world.

"Have you had enough time to think about everything?"

"Yes."

"Do you want to go straight back, or do we have time to pick up coffee?"

Roper didn't bother answering, but two minutes later they were in a short queue. Hooley ordered for them all, including a bag of muffins, most of which would be finished off by Roper and the Major. Supplies in hand, they headed back out.

"Before we get in, can I ask if you are alright with the way things are panning out? You must have been disappointed that the bomb wasn't where we expected, yet you seem to have taken it very well. You're not upset and thinking you made a mistake?"

"I'm fine. I did make a mistake, but it was an honest one, and after Julie spoke to me things were different. I hadn't realised I was part of a team, so that made a big difference because now I know other people are there working away.

"It's a bit like going to watch Chelsea play football. We've got a really good player at the moment who is scoring loads of goals, but he can't do it on his own. Other people have to help make the space and pass the ball to him."

Hooley burst out laughing. "That's brilliant, Jonathan - that makes you the star striker for the Special Investigations Unit."

He was still smiling as they walked back into the building and into Mayweather's office. She was working through some paperwork - Armageddon might be around the corner but forms still needed to be filled in - but looked up expectantly as they walked in. Roper distributed the food and drinks as the DCI went off to fetch the Major.

As usual Jonathan bolted down his hot coffee, his mouth and throat seemingly impervious to heat, but unusually he didn't touch the muffins because he was so keen to get going. The Major showed no such inhibitions as he wolfed his portion.

Hooley was wondering who would win an eating competition between the pair when Roper started talking.

"Sorry to delay, everyone, but I wanted to be sure about what I was doing this time and that walk has settled it. We need to find this man, the Courier, because I have no doubt he is now running this whole thing.

"I think they must have approached him for help getting the plutonium here and he's taken over. He probably realised that he was better than the people he was dealing with so decided to grab his opportunity. Once they told him where the plutonium was they lost their biggest bargaining chip.

"Which means we now have to find this man, and I believe we should invest some effort into checking CCTV in and around the Ritz during those periods when Sokolov was staying. He seemed to use it as his office, so he will have wanted people to meet him there.

"As soon as Major Phillips said he had seen a picture of the Courier, it all started to make sense with my Rainbow Spectrum. Suddenly I could see where this man might fit in. Going out for a walk just now has convinced me it is the right approach.

"With the Major's help we should be able to identify a picture of him. I know we still won't have a name, but at least it is something that we can send out to police officers patrolling the streets, and we have London's network of cameras to fall back on."

Mayweather looked energised. "We need to get on this as soon as we can, then. I suggest that Jonathan, Brian and the Major head for the Ritz and set up a base there. This is a national security matter, so I can get a warrant very fast to get them to hand over footage.

"I know the head of security there, he's ex-Met. He was telling me they keep digital footage going back several years.

"I'm sure he can provide you with an office, and then we can have teams working on all the different cameras in the area. Now, before we get moving, is there anything else you want to add, Jonathan?"

"It's Saturday tomorrow and I think that is when he might be planning to strike, and I think he will be aiming for somewhere in the central part of London. Imagine the headlines around the world with all the tourists who would be caught up in it.

"I do have another idea. This started out as a discussion about a suitcase bomb, so they were thinking about making it portable. The best way to move something like that around would be in a van, especially in London. They could get really close to a target and just park up."

"We discussed exactly that in one of our gaming scenarios," said the Major. "I was told a bomb would be pretty heavy, so you would need a vehicle to transport it and white vans in London would be an obvious disguise."

"I think I may have nightmares tonight - that's if I can get any sleep," said Hooley. "Shall we get going? I don't know about you guys, but I feel the need to do something rather than just sitting around.

"I've only ever walked past the Ritz in the past, so in any other circumstance I would be looking forward to it; but right now I'm not sure I could enjoy one of their afternoon teas."

"Surely you could manage a small plate of cucumber sandwiches, those ones with the crusts cut off?" said the Major. "Oh, and a plate of those fancy little cakes?" he added, warming to his theme.

"What about you, Jonathan? I bet you could manage something."

"Actually, I haven't had anything to eat since yesterday. I don't feel at all hungry."

Hooley's mouth fell open. "I guess there's a first time for everything."

55

Len Davies, a former Superintendent at Scotland Yard, met them in the lobby of the hotel. He was about five-ten, but he had a ramrod-straight posture that meant he looked taller.

Davies, who was dressed in a dark grey business suit with a crisp white shirt and plain blue tie, also had a very discreet ear mic that Roper assumed kept him in touch with his security staff. The former policeman was friendly and efficient, quickly leading them through to security control.

They were shown into the main room which had a bank of screens running feeds from the different cameras that the hotel employed. Even with the four of them inside, there was plenty of seating for all.

Davies waved his arm around to take in the equipment. "We have cameras covering the outside areas of the hotel and also the public areas, including the lifts and corridors. Obviously, we don't have anything from inside any of the rooms. We also have cameras outside the building, so that leaves a lot of footage for you to look at.

"Julie Mayweather has already spoken to me and explained how important this is. I've now spoken to my bosses and it has been agreed that you can proceed immediately. We know the warrant will come through and this is too urgent to delay."

"I understand you keep your material for some time," said Hooley.

"We have records going back two years that you can access from any of the terminals in here and then we have material copied on to DVD that go back another five years. A bit over the top, but better safe than sorry.

"I have one of my technical people on standby. Once you let me know what you are looking for, he can help you retrieve the relevant information. The cameras we use are very good, recording in high definition. The first thing I did when I got here was upgrade the system to the best you can get on the civilian market, and I make sure we install upgrades.

"All those years as a copper being forced to look at rubbish quality CCTV pictures made me determined that we weren't going to have the same problems. It's even in colour."

"You're a man after my own heart," said Hooley as he turned to look at Roper. "Right, Jonathan, this is your show. You lead the way."

"We need to go back over the last twelve months and it needs to be the same dates that you had a Russian guest staying called Arkady Sokolov. He may have been here quite a few times and we need the footage for those periods."

The ex-policeman stood even straighter when he heard the name, his eyebrows raising.

"I know Mr. Sokolov personally. Trust me when I say I know appearances can be deceptive, but he is one of the most charming guests we have staying here. He always says how much he loves the hotel and he is always a generous tipper and polite to the staff.

"Not everyone with money is like that, I can assure you. As you say, he comes here quite a lot and always books a two-room suite, preferably a corner suite. Although come to think of it, he left early last time - most unusual."

"And I doubt you have seen him since," said Hooley.

"No, that's right, and I would have remembered if he had been back. As I said earlier, you will have a lot of footage to look through, but I assume you are looking for people who visited him while he was staying with us?"

"Once a cop, always a cop," said the DCI.

Davies made an "of course" gesture with his hands. "I don't want to tell you how to do your job, but it might be worth starting with the corridor footage from the rooms he stayed in. Your man might be on that, so it could save time."

He clapped his hands. "Time's moving on, so let me talk to reception and get the dates he stayed with us and my technical man will be right with you to sort you out. I'll also get some tea and coffee sent here. Any problems, just get reception to page me; I'll be right with you."

Within an hour they were underway. The Major had been assigned the task of checking the corridor footage and they were hopeful he would get a quick hit. Roper was starting with cameras in reception and Hooley was looking at external footage.

The man they were looking for, according to the Major's description, was "a biggish man, probably a bit more than six feet, and solid-looking like a boxer, with powerful shoulders. It's the best I can do for you. If I tried to add anything else, it would be just my imagination adding things."

On several occasions the Major was called over to check on a potential suspect only to shake his head, and there was a moment when both Hooley and Roper shouted "Yebedev!" almost simultaneously as the individual feeds they were studying captured him walking in from outside and up to reception.

Roper said. "There must be every chance the Courier turned up at that time, or just after it."

The Major looked thoughtful and went back to his own viewing screen and after ten minutes checking he found what he was looking for, or rather, he didn't find it.

"Jonathan can you come and look at this for me?"

As Roper sat down the SAS man rewound the clip he was looking at. He pointed at the date and timestamp in the top right corner.

"Right there. This jumps twenty-four hours. September nineteenth is missing."

The DCI immediately paged Davies, and ten minutes later all four men were crowding around the chair that the technician was sitting in. He confirmed the day was missing and then made checks on the system.

"There's a note that says the corridor camera went down on that day. It was checked out and nothing found, so it was put down to a system glitch and footage was rolled on. If the Major hadn't picked up the date stamp we wouldn't have known."

Davies said. "Now this is a surprise because we have never had an individual camera go down before, at least not without some obvious reason."

He looked at his technician who nodded in agreement. "This stuff is solid. I don't recall ever having problems with it."

Roper jumped up with excitement. "I think this is going to be the date that the Courier was here. Somehow, he put the corridor camera out of action. I bet he came straight in with a bit of a disguise, a hat and sunglasses maybe, so Brian and I missed him arriving.

"But when he got up to the room level he wanted to make doubly sure he wasn't spotted. Very clever of him and more proof that he is a very careful planner. I think we need to concentrate on the external footage, and maybe expand beyond the main entrance."

Two hours later, it was Hooley who made the breakthrough.

"There," he shouted, jumping to his feet and pointing at his monitor. "I think I've got him." He'd been looking at a feed which showed people approaching the main entrance from Green Park.

With Roper and the Major standing behind him, he rewound the footage and hit play. Tourists and office workers swam into view and then a man appeared, stooping as he put a hat on.

The SAS man pounded him on the back, making his eyes water.

"Well done, Brian, that's the man I saw on the camera phone. There's no doubt in my mind that we have him."

The technician was rushed back and, before long, he had isolated the perfect image and printed off several copies, as well as downloading an attachment for Hooley to fire off to Mayweather.

Roper studied the portrait. The camera had caught their man apparently looking at something a few feet ahead of him. He was squinting slightly as if trying to focus on whatever it was. Roper always got the feeling that pictures could capture what people were really like. This one was making him shudder.

He tried to imagine he was looking at someone who was evil but could detect nothing like that. It was Brian Hooley who helped him sum it up. "He's a determined-looking bloke, isn't he?"

56

There had been a short and intense debate about whether to issue the picture to the media. The 'no' side were fearful it would stop the Courier from negotiating and increase the risk of him going ahead with his plan to detonate the bomb.

However, the argument was swinging towards those who wanted to get his picture published - the politicians said the public would never forgive them if they discovered the image had been withheld - when Roper was asked for his view.

"I say no. If we publish his picture he has nothing to lose and sets off the bomb. At least this way we can talk."

That would probably have swung it anyway, but then Hooley received another message.

"I want access to the GCHQ system at noon today or else the bomb is set off."

It was 7am on Saturday. Hooley, Roper and the Major were at a mobile police command centre on Whitehall. Roper had just returned from a long walk, this time on his own, when the message had pinged its way on to the DCI's mobile.

He showed it to Roper and said. "What do you think about the evacuation plans, Jonathan? The view is that, since we haven't come up with a solution, we stop all the trains coming into London and put up road blocks to stop traffic from a radius of five miles out."

Roper took his time. "We have to stop people coming in. I don't think he is going to try for a really big explosion, but it will be somewhere high-profile, like a tourist target in the centre: anywhere from Big Ben, to Buckingham Palace and Trafalgar Square, and maybe all that area around Waterloo. It would be easy to hide a vehicle around there."

"Hard to argue against your analysis, Jonathan," said Hooley. He was looking tired after a restless night and starting work at 5am. "What about you, Tom - any thoughts?"

"I wish I had, but I'm willing to go with Jonathan on this. We need to do something."

"Are the rest of your drones here in London now, Tom?" Roper looked hopeful.

"I take it you mean the longer-range ones. Yes, I got a message last night. Jenkins reported they are all here and in working order. What have you got in mind?"

"Could we have one up covering the central area? And do it now, while it's fairly quiet."

"Give me five minutes and we can be on the way."

The big drone was at a little over 1000 feet and had swept down the Victoria Embankment from the area of Lambeth Palace and towards the High Courts on the Strand, before heading back towards Westminster on a return sweep.

The cameras were of an astonishing quality and Roper was careful studying a slowed down feed, concentrating fiercely on the pictures slowly crossing his screen. He was studying every inch of the flight and had his face pressed close to the screen.

He didn't once look away and Hooley could not imagine how he was able to do it without inducing a massive headache. At various times Roper stopped the feed, carefully rewound it and then studied something that had caught his attention, before carrying on.

The drone completed its first sweep of the central area without finding anything. He turned to the drone controller.

"Can you take us back over the area around the London Eye?"

Jenkins soon had the drone hovering over the spot and somehow Roper was managing to stare even more intently at the feed. Both Hooley and the Major had to fight off excitement as they sensed he might be onto something.

Roper was oblivious to what was going on around him and had started tapping at a keyboard, calling up some information; he read it carefully and then turned back to the screen showing the drone footage.

"Look there: at that area close to the London Eye. That looks like workmen are digging on the pavement."

The two men could clearly see a large hole, an all-too-common sight for London.

"I've just checked, there is authorisation to be digging up the pavement at that spot - but it's at 7pm this evening, not 7am this morning. That's got to be the Courier and his team. He's probably hoping people will think the 7pm start time is a mistake and it is OK to be there."

Major Phillips didn't need any more convincing. As he dashed away he was shouting at his team leaders to access the footage.

Inside the police command vehicle, the live footage continued to roll. Hooley and Roper watched as a man backed out of the rear doors of a van parked up on the pavement. He was wearing high visibility gear and a white protective helmet.

As his foot reached the ground he reached up and adjusted his helmet then carried on walking away from the van and over to the hole which was being dug.

"That's him, that's the Courier." Roper was whispering as though frightened that if he shouted out the name the man they were hunting would hear and somehow escape.

Hooley couldn't decide. "Are you sure?"

Roper rewound the footage. "Watch as he reaches for his hat. He uses his left hand and he has a slightly odd quirk where his right shoulder dips down. That's exactly what happened when you found the footage of him outside the hotel."

Hooley whistled in amazement. "For a bloke who can't spot an emotion if it lands on his head, you have a good eye for detail."

At that moment the Major reappeared, and they showed him the footage and told him about Roper's conclusions.

"Well, that's a definite go in my opinion. Brian, do you want to talk to Julie, so she can get the top table to give us the green light? My lot are more than ready to go so I'm going to start moving into position. We don't want this bastard getting away."

Roper and Hooley followed him outside to watch the team of troopers set off. While the majority were in the black outfits and body armour he had come to expect, the DCI noted that this group was a more eclectic mix than he had seen in the past.

Over to one side a man and woman in running gear were being intently briefed and he watched as they jogged off in the direction of the London Eye. Following them was a particularly shabby looking man who could only be a beggar and then a young Chinese couple, clearly tourists with backpacks and cagoules wrapped around their waists.

The Major spotted him looking. "Urban warfare. I had no idea what we might be up against, so I asked for all available resources. Not all are our people, but they have trained with us and know what they are doing."

The entire team was now en-route; those in military gear would be staying well back, although a couple that looked like police officers would be getting quite close. The other pairs would be walking right up to, and past, the location of the terrorist gang. Their job was to glean any details they could.

As the Major watched his teams set off, he was being studied by Hooley. He could tell the officer wanted to be with them, but his job was to watch the feed from the drones and make sure his people had everything they needed.

"I think there may be some of that revolting coffee left in there," he said, gesturing at the mobile command centre. "Let's go and get some - it will take your mind off things. They know what they're doing, and the technical people are right behind them to make the bomb safe."

Back in front of the screens with the live feeds, they watched as first the 'joggers' went past and then the 'tourists' marched by with the 'beggar' lurching along behind, apparently the worse for wear from drink. He plonked himself down on a bench about fifty metres from the van.

A few minutes earlier they had watched the Courier clamber back inside the vehicle and, since then, nothing. Finally, they got the call to move in; it was the green light they wanted. But before they could move in the Courier climbed out. He was in normal clothing as he headed off towards Waterloo Bridge at a rapid pace.

"Where is he going?" said Hooley, asking the question they were all thinking.

The Major started speaking urgently into his mouthpiece as he warned that the Courier was on the move.

He was closing in on the steps leading up to the Bridge when the two "police officers" appeared.

They were talking to each other, apparently oblivious to the Courier who kept moving forwards. But as the "officers" drew level they suddenly charged. They were two of the Major's men and very fast. The Courier was almost faster.

One policeman went down clutching his throat, bleeding from a stab wound. But the second officer fired his Taser at point-blank range into the Courier's face. The man stopped still and then fell twitching to the floor as he was blasted with fifty thousand volts.

Meanwhile, the main hit squad had attacked the van, specially designed power cutters ripping the door open. Inside were two men, one of whom started to move his hand towards the bomb. He was dead a few milliseconds before his companion.

The bomb team came hurtling up and spent an anxious ten minutes examining the weapon. In that time the Major had looked at pictures and seen that one of the two men was his former soldier, Richardson.

"Not quite so made for life, now, are you?" he said, so quietly that Hooley and Roper missed it.

It was hours before they got away, and Hooley was looking forward to having a pint of bitter when his phone went off. It was DI Newlove.

"Brian. I just wanted to let you know that your man Roper came up with the goods. We finally found a fingerprint in that house. It was for a right villain called Harry James. Turns out he's moved onto people smuggling and we picked him up after he was spotted moving backwards and forwards between Folkestone and Calais.

"Funnily enough, he's not that keen on spending the rest of his life in prison so he's ready to name names. Says his boss is called the Courier. I was wondering if you could do me a favour? We can't find anything about him but you might have better records.

"Any chance you could have a look and tell me what you can find out?"

"I can tell you one thing straight off: it's a very small world."

57

"There's what we call an alphabet soup of people all lining up and demanding access."

Major Phillips had just come from the latest briefing session following the arrest of the Courier. "To name a few we have the BND, CIA, NSA, SIS, GCHQ, MOSSAD and the DGSI. Even the FSB have been demanding to be allowed in. If I started on the rest of the world we'd still be here tomorrow.

The Major had turned up at Victoria bearing gifts - coffee and muffins. Roper had pounced on them like he hadn't seen food for days.

Hooley passed him another muffin. "As you can see, he's recovered his appetite. He hasn't stopped eating, and I bet the lucky so-and-so doesn't put a single pound on."

Roper gulped down a mouthful. "Plenty of walking and a high metabolism."

"I need to do a bit more than walking if I eat like that. A ten-mile run with a pack would do it," said Major Phillips, with a wistful expression.

"I've only got to think about eating one and I put on weight," said an even more mournful Hooley.

It was the first time the three men had met since the Courier had been captured three days ago. Since then British security services had taken over and, it seemed, had been joined by the rest of the world's secret services.

While Hooley and Roper were now out of the loop, the Major had remained on the inside but had insisted he be allowed to brief the pair on what was happening following the arrest.

"Let me start at the beginning with what he has told us so far. It turns out the Courier's real name is Nigel Cross and he's a forty-two-year-old who was born in Lewisham, South London, to a drug addict mother. He had a tough time of it. She nearly killed him before he was taken into care and was unlucky enough to find himself under the power of the worst type of abusers.

"At the age of fifteen he gave the first signs of what was to come when he made a bomb out of fertiliser and used it to kill both his abusers and destroy the block of flats they were living in. Amazingly, no-one else was hurt.

"He then disappears and a year later, despite his age, turned up in the French Foreign Legion, now calling himself Nigel Smith. They loved him, he was a great soldier, became fluent in French, and was offered a chance to become an officer before he was twenty years old.

"But he already had his eye on bigger things and left when his time was up. After that, he dropped off the radar for a while but reappeared five years on as the Courier, one of the most successful smugglers about.

"He was top of the game until he turned 30 and then dropped out of sight again. He won't tell us what he did next, but something brought him back into the smuggling game, where his previous reputation brought him into contact with Yebedev, Sokolov and Vasilev.

"We're now at the point where he is offering to give up those three, and lots of others that he says we don't know about yet but played a key role. He also confirms your theory, Jonathan: that once they pulled him in, he simply took over. It was his idea to sell the dummy in west London, and also to ask for access to GCHQ secrets.

"The other thing that's getting everyone going is his promise to reveal the location of more weapons that were buried in the ground all those years ago. The Germans have nearly had apoplexy because they've always believed there is stuff hidden away in the former East Germany.

"The French are demanding first dibs because of the plutonium found on their soil, and have joined forces with the Americans to demand exclusive access to him. We're refusing because if we release him to our 'allies' we know we'll never see him again.

"Just for good measure, the Israelis want in because he's hinting there is more plutonium out there and that's got people in the Middle East and North Korea interested. It's even being said that the new guy in the Philippines wants a piece of the action.

"So basically, he's given us, the British, a huge headache. We can't possibly do a deal with him because he threatened to nuke London, and everyone else is trying to persuade us to get over ourselves and close our eyes and think of England.

"It's at a big impasse which is how I've been able to get out for a while. He's promising to give us a taster of what's in store tomorrow morning, so when I left there was a big shouting match with the French and the Americans demanding to be allowed to sit in.

"My guess is that they will be allowed in, because when it comes to military action we're the 'three amigos' so I guess we won't be able to say no."

"And I thought catching him was difficult enough," said Hooley. "What have they got you doing in all this?"

Major Phillips looked embarrassed at having the spotlight shone on him. "Actually, I'm going to be one of the two interrogators who will be talking to him tomorrow morning. So far, these things have been short and sweet. He says what he wants then clams up while we think about it.

"I should be able to get back to you with an update. I heard that the Prime Minister personally intervened to make sure you were in the loop."

*

As he predicted, he was back the next day and his expression was grim. Roper stared at him and then said: "Sir Robert Rose."

"How could you possibly know that? I've only just found out and I was in the session."

"I'd suspected it for a while, and as soon as I saw your face I knew."

Hooley raised a hand in the air. "Er, could anyone tell this person what on Earth is going on?"

The Major produced a rueful smile. "I think Jonathan should tell you. He probably knows more than I do even though I was there, and he wasn't."

Roper was unfazed. "Sir Robert Rose is worried that the UK is losing its moral courage and is being undermined by a 'snowflake' generation that is too frightened to stand up and fight for the things that it believes in.

"He found a willing accomplice in Maria Vasilev, who felt that her own country had gone the same way. She believes that for all the aggressive words from her leaders, they are more interested in cyber warfare than real warfare.

"Between them, they came up with a plan to explode a nuclear bomb in the UK and make sure they left enough clues to make it look like a Russian state-sanctioned operation. Sir Robert probably believes that it would be worth a few lives to achieve his goal."

Both men were staring at him open mouthed. The Major recovered first. "You're spot-on about Sir Robert, but he hasn't mentioned anything about Maria Vasilev yet.

How did you work that out? You'd better tell me, then. I need to report in."

"It's quite obvious, really. They are both from the same generation and spent their entire lives involved in a battle with each other, and each other's people. They would have known about each other and probably even respected each other for their beliefs.

"Everyone forgets that the Cold War was pretty intense, and a lot of people were left fighting it long after it was supposed to have stopped. When we met Sir Robert there was something about him, and in my Rainbow Spectrum I could see the possibility that he might do something.

"Do you remember, during our interview, when he suddenly started talking about knowing who your enemy was? It stuck with me at the time, then I pushed it to the back of my mind. It's only in the last twenty-four hours that I realised that he said was a clue.

"Then it was obvious he would need an ally from the other side, as it were, and Vasilev was perfect. He would have known all about her and was aware she knew where the plutonium was buried, so she would have been the obvious choice."

The SAS man was on his feet. "Amazing, and, with that, I gotta get out of here, unless you have anything else you want to mention."

"Well I do have some ideas about where Sokolov and Yebedev might have gone to."

"You do? Where?"

"I think the first place they would have gone is Brazil, for cosmetic surgery, but by the time we find that location it will be too late. But I think I know where they will have headed next."

"What, you mean together? Or just starting from the same place?"

58

Roper and Hooley had finally got back into a routine. They were working on inquiries linked to the bomb case when security called Hooley to say that a woman named Susan Brooker was there for her interview. He went blank, and then remembered.

"Do you recall that a while back we talked about recruiting people to a new squad? Well, someone is downstairs. I'll be honest, I forgot she was coming. I can make an excuse if you like and rebook it, although I'd better go and explain in person."

"Actually, a break would be good right now. I think I may now be a world expert on places to hide away in South America." Hooley nodded and spoke into the phone.

"Give us five minutes and then bring her up, please."

He made a cursory effort to tidy up, then decided to go and fetch some water. He cleared a space in front of his desk and placed two cups within easy reach.

At that point the woman arrived. She was slim, about mid-20s, with short brown hair, was wearing jeans and a T-shirt and had her glasses perched on the top her head. She was standing in the doorway smiling nervously.

"Come in, come in. Sit down and make yourself comfortable."

She looked anxious but stepped inside, reached the chair and somehow got tangled up in it so that she fell forward, knocking the cups of water up in the air and straight over the DCI.

As he stood up, blinking water out of his eyes, he heard Roper say: "I like her."

Before he could reply Roper's phone went off. He stared at the number on display and frowned.

"Hello. Jonathan Roper here."

He listened intently, not moving at all. The person on the other end had quite a bit to say since he remained like that for the next couple of minutes. Then he ended the call.

"That was Sam. She's coming back early and is going to stay at my place."

"That will be nice for you. When's she coming?"

"She said she was at the airport now with the plane taking off in two hours. I wonder why she's coming back now? We weren't even due to talk for another two weeks. All she would say was that it is important and I was to be at the flat when she got there."

Hooley kept his face as neutral as he could. He had no idea what was going on, but in his experience nothing good came out of sudden changes in plans.

Three months later

Major Tom Phillips was queuing up at the British Airways first class check-in for the Terminal 5 direct flight to Santiago, Chile. He was travelling under the name Ian Henderson, a resident of Barnes in South London. It was an identity that would remain active for no more than six weeks.

The woman checking him on to the flight was in a talkative mood and, as she handed his boarding card and passport back, she said, "Enjoy the flight today. The plane is pretty empty so, unless there's a last-minute booking, you'll have first class to yourself."

He'd picked up a copy of the London Evening Standard as he came in and now he put it down on the check-in desk as he picked up the print-outs and placed them in the inside pockets of his immaculate blue blazer.

The woman glanced at the front-page headline. There was only one story, the murder in custody of the man known as the Courier, who was being held in Wandsworth Prison and had got into a fight with another prisoner.

"I don't think anyone will be sad to see the back of him. They should give whoever killed him a medal. Am I going mad, or was there a story linking him to that retired civil servant who died in a house fire last week? I remembered it mostly because of the pictures of the house before it burned down. Beautiful place, Grade II listed, I think."

The Major smiled at her as he began to turn away. He held up the paper. "I try not to follow the news if I can. It's either made-up or depressing."

She smiled back. She'd noticed he didn't have a wedding ring. He'd be a nice catch for someone. "Well do have a nice flight. Business or pleasure?"

"You might say it's going to be a bit of both."

THE END

Thank you for reading the third novel in the Jonathan Roper Investigates series.

I wanted to create a character who was a little bit different and I think Roper fits that bill. His autism and lack of social skills provide him with both insights and problems. My sense that Roper would be an interesting fit for the modern world was influenced by my autistic son. He is non-verbal but despite this it has been heart-warming to see him develop; partly down to the brilliant support of so many carers, but also because of his own determination. This determination is a trait he shares with Roper. It was always my intention that the Roper series should be regarded as series of "page turning thrillers", each one capable of being read alone. While it offers some small insights into the autistic world, I also wanted to show some of the unexpected side of autism. There can be humour there and I hope that my portrayal of the relationship between Roper and his long-suffering boss, Brian Hooley, demonstrates that.

I am a self-published author and would really be grateful if you could leave me a review on Amazon. The number of reviews a book accumulates on a daily basis has a direct impact on sales. So just leaving a review, no matter how short, helps make it possible for me to continue to do what I love… writing.

For more information on upcoming launches please either like me on my Facebook page: Jonathan Roper Investigates or join my VIP readers list at: www.michael-leese.com. You can also write to me at the following email address: hello@michael-leese.com – I always enjoy reading your comments and thoughts about Roper, Hooley and Mayweather, and do my best to respond to all correspondence.

Not read book 1 yet?
Here are the opening
chapters for

Going
Underground

Beckenham, Kent.

David Evans looked at the familiar face of his Personal Assistant, Sylvia Jones. It was the weekend and technically her day off, but he wasn't surprised she had come to work. He returned her smile, thinking again how lucky he was to have her.

"Sorry to interrupt you, Mr. Evans," she said. It would always be Mr. Evans, despite his gentle efforts to get her to call him David. They'd been together for more than twenty-five years. He was certain that if she ever left then part of his business would depart with her. He was a solicitor who had done well from the property boom.

He glanced down at his tie. He always wore a shirt and tie, even at the weekend. His wife teased him for being stuffy, but she liked the way it demonstrated a commitment to doing things in the traditional way. Today she had picked out a light blue shirt with blue-striped tie. She thought the combination suited his ruddy complexion, pale blue eyes and grey hair. Evans realised he had allowed his mind to wander, leaving his PA waiting for a reply.

"I said would you like a cup of tea?" she repeated. She wasn't irritated by his failure to speak. She knew he was possessed of an imagination that snatched him away from the real world. Like her boss she always made an effort to dress properly, as she liked to think of it. Today she was wearing her standard office outfit of a black skirt, loose fitting white blouse, which she used to try and disguise an ample bosom, dark stockings and dark loafer-style shoes that were solid and comfortable. Balanced on the tip of her nose were her new tortoiseshell glasses purchased after grudgingly accepting that she could no longer see her computer screen. Evans thought they suited her, but kept that to himself as he knew she hated them. Her make-up was minimal and her hair looked as though she had just come from the salon, which she had. She always had her hair done first thing on a Saturday.

Evans ran his hand through his own hair. It was a habit his wife said had got worse since it started falling out. She claimed he was constantly checking he still had some. He didn't know about that, but was happy to admit that he would love it if he could return to the thick brown mop he had taken for granted in his younger days.

He switched from thoughts of youth to the needs of today as he replied. "Tea would be delightful, but you really don't need to be here you know. How is your mum by the way?"

She seemed to shrink into herself for a moment, or was that his imagination? "She's been better for the last few days. It seems to go up and down. But she's well enough for me to leave her with one of our neighbours, at least for a couple of hours. It gives me the chance to get out of the house. It can get a bit claustrophobic. Anyway, I can always be back in 10 minutes."

He thought 'claustrophobic' was something of an understatement but knew better than to push the point. "You know best, of course, and I do understand how you can sometimes need a break from family life."

She backed out and he returned his attention to his computer. He was spending more time in the office at weekends so he could indulge in his hobby. He caught himself. This was his passion and it was increasingly dominating his thoughts. He'd always enjoyed his work as a solicitor. Over the years he had steadily built up his suburban practice. But it had all got a little predictable; so this provided the mental challenge he was looking for. He was at an age, sixty-two years, when he was considering retiring and this would more than adequately help him fill the time. He'd even started taking on the odd commission and had just completed an especially challenging task that had taken up many of his days off. Today he was reviewing his work. It was easy to make mistakes and he was a perfectionist.

Ten minutes later he was deep in his research again and this time he didn't even look-up as he heard his PA backing through his door holding a tray in her hands. The room could have come straight from a museum about 1950's England. Polished brown furniture dominated and he sat at an elegant high-backed Captain's Chair, finished with green leather, in front of a large desk. On the client's side were two comfortable chairs that were almost old enough to be classified as antiques. The carpet, an ancient Axminster that had probably done 30 years' service, was a light-brown with a thin green thread woven in for contrast. Against one wall was a row of gun-metal cabinets and on the wall above them was a picture of the Queen taken on her Silver Jubilee. It was only lacking a Bakelite radio tuned to the Home Service. The nod to the present day was his flat-screen monitor, printer, shredder and mobile phone. An iPhone, because his children had told him it was the best.

Jones turned carefully as she made it through the door then crossed to the desk where she placed her tray on the dark green leather top. She'd done this, hundreds, maybe thousands, of times before. The tray held tea made just the way he liked it; loose-leaf English Breakfast in a Brown Betty pot that had been carefully warmed before the tea leaves were covered in freshly boiled water, the brew left to stand for four minutes. Jones placed a strainer over the white, bone-china cup, with matching saucer, and poured out his drink; the milk went in afterwards, not before. She leaned across the desk to place the cup within easy reach of his right hand. On other days, there might have been a plate of biscuits but Evans had promised his wife that he would lose a few pounds.

So far, she had followed the routine exactly. Now she did something different. She lifted a white cloth to reveal a Smith & Wesson M66 Combat Magnum. It was loaded with .38 Special rounds, rather than the more normal .357 Magnum cartridges. It had been explained that this was probably one of the most straightforward guns to handle. It was said to combine effective stopping-power with simplicity of use. The choice of ammo was also supposed to help. Slightly less recoil. Marginal gains. She was told this was the way to go for the first-timer. The one thing they kept repeating was: just one shot, that's all you'll get. Don't expect to get a second. When it came to the real thing she would start to panic; everyone did. This would throw off her aim; making it unlikely she would hit the target twice. Now she picked up the gun - the safety was off and the first round chambered - and started to take aim. At that moment, something alerted Evans. Maybe her ragged breathing. He turned to see his PA standing there with a gun.

Flight, fight or freeze: the basic responses to fear. Evans froze. He was so astounded he didn't take in that she had adopted a text-book shooting position; knees lightly flexed; one foot placed slightly ahead of the other; taking her weight on the balls of her feet. But there were two things he couldn't miss. The gun was pointing at him and he could see her finger starting to exert pressure on the trigger.

1

London's traffic could be unbearable, even if you were experiencing it from the luxurious back seat of a Rolls-Royce Phantom. When it was slow going like this, Sir James Taylor enjoyed a game of his own devising: watching cyclists present the finger as they weaved past. While they couldn't see in through the rear privacy glass it was a reasonable assumption that a City fat-cat might be lurking inside. To win the game he had to guess how many fingers he would see on any given trip. Get it right and he would treat himself to a glass of champagne at home. Guess wrong and he would donate £500 to charity. So far, the champagne remained unopened and the cost was mounting. He didn't mind. If you could afford a car like this, it was the Mark 11 version and worth north of £400,000 with a few customised finishes; you could afford to pay your debts.

But in the last half-an-hour the car had managed to move forward about three feet and he had already lost. Not even the soothing tones of Vivaldi floating out of the hand-built stereo system could ease his mounting impatience as he stared at an unchanging view of Fleet Street from the Ludgate Hill end.

"Traffic seems particularly bad tonight, Adam," he said to his driver.

"Yes Sir," he replied, nodding at the Sat Nav screen. "This is telling me there's been a student demonstration in Westminster. They've managed to grid-lock the area so it's causing problems all over central London."

Sir James snorted. "What are they moaning about now? Someone asked them to hand in the annual essay?"

The driver's shoulders shook slightly as he suppressed a laugh. He always tried to remain the cool professional when he was working, but Sir James had a wickedly sly sense of humour. He glanced in his rear-view mirror and saw his boss undoing his seatbelt.

"Getting out Sir?"

"Yes. I can't stand any more of this. I need a bit of exercise so might as well walk home from here. It's a decent trot to Eaton Square and might help me shed a few pounds."

The driver thought that if Sir James lost any more weight he'd be positively skinny, but kept that idea to himself.

"You might as well call it a day. I won't need you again until tomorrow morning at the usual time."

With that he opened the door and stepped out to the pavement. There was a burst of sound from the street; pedestrians talking, laughing and cursing at the cyclists and vehicles. The noise was accompanied by the thick hot smell of engine fumes generated by so many idling engines. Then the tumult was shut out as the door closed with an almost imperceptible clunk. From his incredibly comfortable seat behind the wheel the driver watched his boss walk past the Punch Tavern and then disappear into the crowds near a sign pointing to St Bride's Church. He left it a few minutes to make sure he wasn't going to change his mind and then pulled off his peaked cap. With a bit of luck someone might even think the car belonged to him. Now all he had to do was work out how he was going to get out of this traffic jam and back to the secure underground car park at Canary Wharf, where his own Nissan Micra was currently occupying a small corner of the Rolls' parking place.

2

The thick file thumped down on his desk, making Chief Inspector Brian Hooley jump. Once again, his boss Deputy Assistant Commissioner Julie Mayweather, had surprised him.

"As light on your feet as ever, Ma'am," he said.

A hint of a smile touched her brown eyes but her expression was dead-pan.

"Sir James Taylor," she said, nodding at the file.

He felt a sudden spike of interest. He gestured at the pile of documents. "The billionaire that's been missing for a few weeks now?"

"Six, actually, and not any more; he's been found, or some of him has."

Responding to her deputy's raised eyebrow she added. "They found a torso a couple of weeks back. The head, hands and feet had been cut off. Made it bloody difficult to ID him, but they managed yesterday.

"Everything you need to know is in there, come and see me once you've gone through it."

With that she turned on her heel and left his office as silently as she had entered, her size six feet seeming to glide over the carpeting. Hooley turned to his left to close the document he'd been studying on his computer. Then he started on the material in front of him. He was pleased it was a physical copy, being of an age where paper won over screen every single time.

An hour later and he had a clear picture in his mind. On the basis of what he had just read Sir James was a man who gave capitalism a good name. He'd started out as a trader and then rapidly set up his own hedge fund, making billions for himself and his investors through specialising in what were described as ethical investments; the sort where some attempt was made to share profits around and not deal with despots. Five years ago, his wife had died after a short but brutal battle with breast cancer. He took two months off to mourn her death and then announced he was quitting the financial world. Instead he was going to use his fortune to help others.

He created a charity in his wife's name, The Miriam Foundation, and set about giving his money away. Since he had so much, it was going to take a long time. Unsurprisingly breast cancer charities were among the early beneficiaries, but he also donated large sums to children's causes. He and his wife had never been able to have their own, despite their dearest wish. He was especially generous to scientists and doctors involved in new techniques to aid conception. A year ago, his work was rewarded with a knighthood. It was an obvious high point, but also reminded him of how much he missed his wife and how proud she would have been to come to Buckingham Palace to see the Queen tap his shoulders with the sword.

Then six weeks ago he had vanished. He was last seen at a board meeting at the Foundation HQ in Canary Wharf. Those present said he had been in an ebullient mood, identifying some new recipients for donations and paying attention to various reports. The meeting had wrapped up shortly before 5pm. Sir James had declined a drink saying he was heading home and looking forward to eating a shepherd's pie prepared by his house keeper, by all accounts an excellent cook. She had made it that morning and left it in the fridge for when he got home.

She was the one who had first raised the alarm. The following morning, she arrived for work at 7am as usual.

Checking the fridge, she noted that the food was untouched. She went upstairs and realised he had not used the bed in the suite of rooms that made up his bedroom on the second floor. She looked outside to see that the driver was already there with the Rolls-Royce. He told her that he had assumed Sir James was inside as he had last seen him getting out of the car in Fleet Street the previous evening. He had taken to walking a lot since his wife died, partly because it kept him fit, but also because it helped fill in the time rather than being alone.

For the next few hours the woman had waited anxiously for news - Sir James was normally the most predictable of people - then decided to check with the Foundation. This sparked off a chain of phone calls, all of which revealed the same thing: no one could get hold of him. Just before 1pm an increasingly anxious PA had called the police. For the first couple of hours it had been treated as a routine missing person's report, but over the next 48 hours it was rapidly bumped up in importance, eventually landing in the lap of a Superintendent John Williams. Hooley had worked with the man and knew he was a good officer; and so it proved. His team did everything by the book, including an appeal which generated press coverage around the world. It's not every day that a billionaire goes missing.

But as the days went on the mystery deepened. The last person to see him alive was the driver, who found his world turned upside down as police examined every aspect of his life. An equally sharp light was turned on the housekeeper, his PA and the foundation board. This also revealed nothing. It was as though he had disappeared from the face of the earth. Every possibility was considered and given that he had got out of a car near the River Thames, CCTV footage covering Blackfriars Bridge was checked, and re-checked in case he had jumped. The river police were put on high alert, but no body was found.

The only slight oddity which had emerged was that Sir James had created his own DNA profile. It was not something he had ever discussed with colleagues, but it was assumed he had done it because he could and might have been thinking about needing specialised treatment at some stage in the future. Whatever the reason, it was this that eventually led to the identification of his body.

Four weeks into the search, in an apparently unrelated incident, the torso of a man had been found in the cellar of a disused warehouse in East London. By then Supt. Williams had issued an instruction that any unidentified body should have its DNA taken and the details passed immediately to his squad. In this case there had been a slight delay because the mortuary where the body ended-up was understaffed and over-worked. But yesterday the news had come in that the partial remains were those of the missing billionaire.

As he finished reading Brian Hooley sighed and sat back in his chair. His eyes felt gritty and he rubbed at them to try and get some relief. A thirty-year veteran of the Met he knew when trouble was heading his way, and it was clear what this was going to be. He picked up one of the pictures that were included in the notes. Holding it in his right hand he was struck that even in a photograph Sir James radiated a powerful aura. He was clearly a man used to taking centre stage and he looked the part. His perfectly cut salt and pepper hair and silver rimmed glasses complimented his pink-cheeked complexion. He thought it highly likely that the suit Sir James was wearing cost more than he earned in a month. He carefully replaced the photo in the file and made his way to his boss's office.

3

Hooley was surprised his backside wasn't imprinted on the faux-leather seat of the right-hand chair of the pair placed in front of Mayweather's desk. He'd spent enough time sitting there over the years. His boss watched as he settled in and then absent-mindedly took off her reading glasses as she leaned forward. She was wearing her usual outfit of formal white blouse, a black tie and her light-weight dress uniform.

"What do you think?" she said, placing her small hands on the desk.

He noted she looked fit and focussed and it reminded him that he'd let things slip a little since his wife had thrown him out. Maybe he should start walking up the stairs again. It was five floors to the incident room, near Victoria Station, so that would help. And maybe stick to white wine rather than pints of lager.

He brought himself back to the moment. They'd worked together long enough not to rush each other. Both operated best when they had time to think.

"Between us," he shrugged. "I think this may turn out to be a hospital pass. The investigation so far looks first rate; the chances of us finding something new are pretty slim. I fear we might end up looking like hapless plods."

He scratched the tip of his nose. "For public consumption; the identification of the body is the perfect moment for a new team to take over, review the excellent work already done and make significant progress in resolving what has proved to be a frustrating case."

This time there was more than the hint of a smile in her eyes as she nodded her appreciation of his comments.

"I think you should write down that 'perfect moment' stuff and send it to the press people. It might help them spin this into a success story."

Mayweather steepled her hands under her chin as she shook her head slightly.

"The trouble is it's our hospital pass. Once the ID came in about the body, Sir James' friends were able to get to the PM. He called the Home Secretary to ask what was going on; the Home Secretary called the Commissioner to put the squeeze on, whom in turn passed responsibility to his Chief of Staff. Then I got the call. To be fair to Hugh Robertson, even though he was steaming, he only shouted at me briefly and then apologised and admitted he was being ridiculous. But it is our case. If I remember correctly the actual phrase used was 'You're the Special Investigation Unit - so do something special and find out what's happened.'"

Despite his opening remarks Hooley understood this was always going to be the case and was already thinking about what they would need to do which probably meant doing everything all over again, if he was any judge. At least now they had a body and a location to work with.

"We need to treat this as a new case so we can start re-interviewing everyone, beginning with the chauffeur and housekeeper. Let's see if anything has shaken loose since they were last spoken to." He was gently clicking his fingers as he counted off the tasks. "I think I might go and talk to the guy who found the body again. I'm not saying he did it, but what was he up to in there? That warehouse was, as far as he knew, empty. All he was supposed to do was check the locks but said he could smell something so got his hands on the keys and went back".

"William's team says it is a solid old structure and the body was in a deep cellar at the very back. Our man must have an acute sense of smell to have picked something up from outside and through a locked door. I wouldn't be at all surprised if he was looking for a little out of the way place to store items that have fallen off the back of a lorry".

"The reports say it took twenty minutes before he stopped throwing up enough to complete the 999 call. They've got call records of him trying three times and breaking off to be sick. That'll teach him to go around opening body bags he stumbles over in dark cellars in the East End."

That thought clearly pleased him as he grinned before adding. "It's got to be worth putting the squeeze on him to see if anything pops. If we get all that going and put DS Toni Barton on drawing up a detailed case plan, at least we'll be covering all the bases. But my concern is that we will have very slim pickings to choose from."

Mayweather put her glasses back on then carefully pushed them down her nose. She had a habit of looking over the top of the frames and making eye contact while she was thinking.

"You're right about that and in fact the warehouse is an oddity, the way ownership is hidden behind layers of off-shore companies. Maybe it's somebody waiting to cash in on property prices, but I don't like it when things are secret."

She paused and gave him another of those over the top of the glasses looks before adding. "What's your take on his head, hands and feet being missing?"

Hooley took a breath. It was one of the issues that most troubled him. "It's certainly slowed things down from the point of view of identifying him. I suppose it's lucky he had his DNA sampled, or whatever they call it. The initial report says the cuts were very clean and precise. I might be persuaded to speculate that this indicates a very high level of care was taken; which might suggest this was a professional killing, rather than a crime of passion, or spur of the moment.

"I also wonder if we will ever find the other bits of the body. One of my mates has been looking into a horrible idea. He was investigating a whisper that some undertakers turn a blind eye to the odd bit of extra baggage in a coffin, especially for a cremation. He didn't get anywhere with it, but, in the world we live in, who knows? It's a sort of 'here are the remains of Tom, Dick and Harry.'"

Mayweather suppressed a shudder. She wasn't an especially religious woman but she had long-ago learned that respect for the dead was vital. Police officers often deployed black humour to help keep the awful things at bay, but in any murder, you were looking at a human being with all the relationships that entailed.

She looked out through her office door and across to the large incident room, her gaze drawn to the digital wall clock that showed it was past 7pm; they needed to wrap up for the day. They were going to have a lot to do tomorrow.

"Anything else of immediate interest, Brian?"

This time he took a deep breath.

"I think we should get Roper back in."

His remark led to her taking her glasses off. She held his gaze for several seconds.

"Are you sure? I can still vividly remember what happened last time. That was almost a disaster."

"I know, and I'm not defending him for that. But he has paid a price and learned some very tough lessons."

Mayweather still looked doubtful.

Before she could say anymore he jumped in. "You don't need to decide tonight. Let's talk again tomorrow once things are underway. Maybe I can go and see how he is. If I have any doubts I will tell you straight away."

He looked away for a moment and she wondered if he was apprehensive. Was he more concerned about bringing

Roper back than he was letting on? She knew that he felt a sense of unfinished business there and hoped that wasn't his main motivation.

Hooley made his way out, turning in the doorway for a final plea. "I really think we might need his help."

Made in the USA
Lexington, KY
30 December 2018